Shadowstone Academy

Book 2: Rise of the Watchers

Barbara Hartzler

BOOKS BY BARBARA HARTZLER

THE MONTROSE PARANORMAL ACADEMY SERIES

Montrose Paranormal Academy Book 1:The Nexis Secret

Montrose Paranormal Academy Book 2: Crossing Nexis

Montrose Paranormal Academy Book 3: The European Conspiracy

Montrose Paranormal Academy Book 4: The Seer's Army

Montrose Paranormal Academy Book 5: The Last Ruby

Montrose Paranormal Academy Book 5.5: The Secondborn Seer

Montrose Paranormal Academy: The Complete Series Box Set

THE SHADOWSTONE ACADEMY SERIES

Shadowstone Academy, Book 1: Broken Trinity

Shadowstone Academy, Book 2: Rise of the Watchers

Shadowstone Academy, Book 3: Sacred Stone Squad

Shadowstone Academy, Book 4: The Final Stand

Shadowstone Academy Boxset: The Complete Series

THE GENESIS ACADEMY SERIES

Genesis Academy, Book 1: The Seer's Legacy

Genesis Academy, Book 2: Oracle Unlocked

Genesis Academy, Book 3: Oracle Rising

Genesis Academy, Book 4: The Last Amethyst

FREE Prequel Offer

Want to read the prequel for FREE?

Read all about how James was banished from Montrose Paranormal
Academy ... and when Lucy's visions really started.
Join my mailing list at www.barbarahartzler.com to download your exclusive free copy of Montrose Paranormal Academy, Book 0: The Nexis
Awakening today!

For Rachel, who believed in this book even when I didn't

CHAPTER ONE

PAIGE

Fluffy white clouds floated lazily past my window as the plane hurtled through the sky at five hundred miles per hour. Air whooshed in my ears, making them pop.

I stretched in my seat, reaching up to touch the cabin ceiling overhead. We were only two hours into a seven-hour flight, and my eyelids were already starting to droop.

Eric's hand landed on my leg, his warmth sending tingles up my spine. "Why don't you lay back and relax? It's going to be a long flight. And we've got plenty of time."

His smile deepened until a dimple appeared on the apple of his cheek. I had no idea he even had a dimple, and it was adorable. Sparks danced up my arms, making my insides melt just a little.

"You're right." I grinned back at him. "Maybe I will take a little nap."

I pressed the button on my armrest and reclined my seat back as far as it would go, three measly inches.

Leaning into my neck pillow, I closed my eyes. Normally, I couldn't sleep on planes or even road trips, for that matter. Travel always gave me a buzz of excitement—so much to see and do.

But less than a week ago, I'd been kidnapped by my almost-boyfriend's roommate and dragged into some underground lair on campus so he could extract my powers for some nefarious purpose.

So yeah, I was totally fried. Now that I finally had some downtime, my overworked brain was ready to wind down, and my body ached all over.

We still had over five hours until we reached New York. I couldn't wait to see my family again for fall break. But right now, I needed to get my beauty sleep.

The muted blackness behind my eyelids, coupled with the rocking plane motion, soothed my pounding headache. With a sigh, I finally let myself fall into dreamland.

Until the black behind my eyes shifted into watery shades of gray.

Blurry shapes danced across my field of vision, slowly coming into focus.

Charcoal-tinged skyscrapers towered overhead, glinting silver in the light drizzle that fell from the dusky clouds. My boots tromped through puddles on a gray sidewalk.

Ten feet ahead, a built guy in a black trench coat raced out from an alleyway. But he wasn't alone. Five other guys sprinted out behind him, with black masks covering their mouths and noses.

I held my breath as they squared off with us like a military squadron. That's when I realized I wasn't alone on the streets of New York. Eric, Lucy, and Will all fanned out around me.

"What should we do?" I hissed to Lucy, calling up a ball of energy in my hand.

"Shields up." Her eyes flicked to the glowing pink sphere of electricity in my palm.

Instantly, we were enveloped in a lavender protection bubble, followed by a blue invisibility orb that expanded around it.

My sad little pink bubble sputtered to life, eventually spreading around Eric and me.

"Thanks for the assist." Eric tipped his chin at me, then looked to my sister and Will. "You guys come in pretty handy in a fight."

"Quiet," Will bit out, glaring daggers of steel at us. "It's not over yet. Be ready to shoot." He nodded to Lucy and me.

I shifted my power to my hands, but my pink bubble burst as my sad little secondborn Seer power crackled back to my palms.

Of course, Lucy's bubble remained strong, even as her hands pooled with purplish-blue lightning.

Would I ever get the hang of these stupid powers?

Then the burly baddies whipped out their sapphire necklaces, and my heart sank. None of our powers would work on them until we zapped those sacred stone pieces away from them.

Lucy leaned in and whispered in my ear. "I'll go for the leader. You go for his right-hand man. Then we'll work our way back."

I nodded, not trusting myself to speak and shift my focus again. I had a job to do.

My hands trembled, and my pulse raced as the leader lunged forward.

"Argh!" Lucy let out a battle cry and raised one hand, zapping the guy with her electricity.

She poured her juice into the chain around his neck. In seconds, the link snapped, sending the sapphire clattering to the pavement.

Then she turned up the wattage and zinged him in the chest, leaving him a jiggling mess on the ground.

My target blinked as his friend hit the ground but didn't hesitate another second.

I raised both hands out in front of me in a defensive stance. Jerking back, I shot my powers into the thin piece of metal around his neck.

With a snarl, he reached out and grabbed my wrist. "You're coming with me, *spare*." He spat out the word like it was detestable.

I writhed in his iron grip, but he yanked on my arm, almost wrenching it out of its socket.

"Paige!" Eric yelled and lunged for me, only to be blocked by another goon.

The whole squad advanced on my friends.

As I thrashed and kicked at my attacker, my heart hammered against my ribcage, and my power churned in my gut.

"No!" I screamed.

I opened the floodgates inside me and let all of my power loose.

The necklace snapped off my attacker's neck and flew into the side of the nearest building.

Electricity jolted from my arm, where the goon's hand crushed my wrist bones. His body started to jiggle uncontrollably. Then his eyes went wide.

Finally, his knees buckled and his fingers went slack as he slammed into the pavement.

But I was too late. Lucy had already taken out one more goon, but that still left Eric and Will defenseless against four big meatheads.

Each of our boys fought two guys at once—and they were losing.

One of the goons knocked Eric out, and his partner hoisted him over his shoulder like a sack of potatoes.

"Eric!" I screamed and sloshed through the puddles to reach him.

Two other guys had strong-armed Will and were dragging him down the alley, right toward a waiting black van.

We took off after them, but they were almost a block ahead of us.

As Lucy and I rounded the corner into the alley, we watched the van door slide open.

Will's head snapped around at the sound. He fought and kicked to get himself free, but one of the goons pulled out a taser.

The scene in front of my eyes seemed to flash forward at hyper speed as Will was jolted, then went limp. Our attackers tossed him into the van, then Eric next.

"No!" Lucy screamed, tears running down her face as we raced after them.

But the van took off, tires squealing as they peeled out down the alley. Leaving only the smell of burned rubber in their wake.

My whole body shook as I reached for my sister.

She wrapped her arms around me and sobbed into my shoulder.

Then the scene faded into a mess of blurry shapes as the blackness took over once again.

I jerked awake with a gasp.

"No!" My voice croaked out a strangled whimper as I inhaled a breath of stale, recycled air.

Something crusty bit into the sides of my mouth as I jolted up-right, blinking and rubbing my eyes.

My pulse thundered in my ears as the realization hit me.

I was still on the plane. It was all a dream.

Or a premonition.

"Did you just have a vision?" Eric cocked his chiseled chin at me, his blue-green eyes narrowing.

"God, I hope so." I collapsed back against the seat, forcing my eyes to stay open.

I didn't want what I just saw to be true. Maybe if I didn't close my eyes again, the whole thing would never happen.

PAIGE

A male voice crackled through the overhead speakers. "This is your captain speaking. We are about to make our descent into New York. Flight attendants, please make the cabin reading for landing."

The message repeated in four other languages, the foreign phrases buzzing through my ears.

I rubbed my crusty eyes and struggled to reorient myself.

Sucking in a few deep breaths, I squeezed Eric's hand and adjusted my seat upright.

The whole vision was just a premonition of a possible future. Eric and Will wouldn't be dragged away to who-knows-where if only I could wrap my mind around how to fix everything I just saw.

But my head was swimming, and I could only gape at Eric.

Except he stared back at me with the same wide-eyed stare that must be plastered across my face.

"Did you see something, too?" I leaned in closer, waving my hand in front of his eyes.

He flinched and shook himself. "I saw something. I think it was the same thing you saw. Except I wasn't asleep. I was wide awake, and then my vision suddenly went black."

"Weird." I tilted my head, studying him closer. Right now, he looked about as wide-eyed as he did after our first, and only, kiss.

Why couldn't my powers come with zero side effects?

Voices murmured behind us, and I peered through the seat at Lucy and Will. They were whispering to themselves, eyes darting toward me every five seconds.

"But we can't let them trace us back to headquarters." Will's words got cut off by the whirring of jet engines.

Lucy's eyes went wide, and I leaned in closer. "James will think of something."

Why were they looking at me like I was crazy? Or did something even crazier just happen?

Then it clicked. "Did all four of us just have the same vision?" I glanced at Eric, jerking my head toward the Chosen Ones behind us.

Eric whirled around to look at Lucy and Will, just as a flight attendant waltzed by.

"Please put your seats in their upright positions." A skinny guy with a crisp haircut and even crisper gray uniform scowled at both of us.

We bobbed our heads and kept our mouths shut.

As soon as Mr. Crisp scurried out of earshot, Lucy and Will both leaned forward. Eric and I craned our necks to peer at them through the small opening between the seats.

"If we all just saw the same vision, then I'm guessing Paige's powers are growing." My sister's eyes widened as they landed on me. "Or this has something to do with the fact that we're all wearing sacred stone pieces."

"Either way," Will's gaze darted from me to Lucy, "if it's truly a premonition, then we only have two hours to stop what we just saw."

"You mean the two of us getting kidnapped? Yeah, let's make sure that doesn't happen." Eric's voice cracked, and his knuckles went white as he gripped the armrest between us.

"I better send out the word before we get too close to the airport and the plane loses WiFi." Will leaned back in his seat, pulling out his phone and texting furiously.

Lucy reached over the seat and patted my head. "Don't worry. We'll contact James and get a team to back us up. He'll know what to do."

Then she was gone, pulling out her phone to text our brother.

But I couldn't move. My limbs were frozen in this strange, twisting pose as I watched my sister and future brother-in-law try to prevent one of my visions from coming true.

"What are we going to do?" A memory of that awful premonition flashed in my mind, and I turned to Eric. "I can't let you get taken."

He shuddered, his scruffy chin jutting out. "That's the scariest part of this whole thing. I can't believe I just watched myself get kidnapped."

"Not helping." Lucy's face was suddenly in the seat opening, her gaze bouncing from Eric to me.

"Right, sorry." Eric shook himself, his lips curling into a wide, unnatural smile. "Once we land, we'll find the Guardian reinforcements that always linger around the airport. It'll be okay. You'll see."

A lead weight settled in my stomach, pinning me to the seat as the wheels touched down and the plane landed with a jolt.

Air roared just outside my window as the brakes kicked in to slow the plane's crazy speed.

My ears popped, and suddenly Eric's words sank in. "Reinforcements? What kind of reinforcements?"

He leaned in and whispered in my still-ringing ear. "The Guardians have a security detail at every major airport. Especially all the New York airports, with the Sector 1 HQ nearby."

"Oh. That's good." I blinked at him.

Would these so-called reinforcements be enough to stop the Watchers from kidnapping our boys? I swallowed down the bubble of bile that rose in the back of my throat. Obviously, I had my doubts.

The plane taxied into its slot and finally came to a full stop. Everyone jumped out of their seats, stretching and groaning after the long trans-Atlantic flight.

Murmurs erupted around us, and my thoughts brain fog suddenly cleared. Tingles trilled up my spine as the realization hit me.

I yanked on Eric's arm and pulled him closer. "If the Guardians have people at the airport, wouldn't the Watchers have spies too?" I shivered at the thought of those black-clad goons waiting for us at the gate.

His lips twitched. "Probably. But just the fact that you had that premonition changed everything. We'll be watching for them now. And getting help of our own."

I wrapped my arms around his waist and squeezed him tight. "I just don't want what I saw to come true," I mumbled into his rumpled sweater.

"It won't." He squeezed me back, one hand smoothing down my hair. "We'll make sure of it, okay?"

I nodded, gulping back the hot tears that beat against my eye sockets.

We gathered our carry-on luggage and blended into the crowd of people filing off the plane, up the jetway, and out into the airport.

Since this was an international flight, we were all herded toward customs. Eric stayed by my side as Lucy and Will split off into a second line, probably hoping we could all exit customs at the same time.

I held my breath and handed the agent my passport, but he just stamped it and said, "Welcome home," with a strange glint in his eye.

Eric was right behind me, and we met up with Lucy and Will in record time.

I reached out and hugged my sister. "Way to grease the wheels a little bit."

She arched her eyebrows at me. "Don't worry about a thing. We've got it all covered."

For once, I hoped she was right.

The minute we exited the gate toward the parking area, we were greeted with a blast of loud music.

Bagpipe music.

CHAPTER TWO

Paige

Blaring strains of off-key bagpipe music blasted through the terminal. And for some weird reason, there was a smile on my sister's face.

Lucy walked up to the bagpiper, clapping at his performance.

The music faded with a screech, and the guy cocked his head at her. Almost like he knew her.

"Good to see you again, lass." The fluffy gray whiskers of his mustache lifted into a smile. "I have a wee present for you."

In a flash, he unhooked a pouch hanging from his blue and green kilt. The plaid pattern looked eerily similar to my Shadowstone Academy uniform.

Before I could blink, he handed the leather pouch to my sister, and she slipped it into her purse.

"Thanks, Steve." She grinned at the funny-looking guy in a beret and knee socks covering up part of his hairy legs.

He winked at her, like actually winked, and leaned in close. "I'd avoid baggage claim if I were you. Air is the only way to travel." Then his eyes flicked to a sign overhead. "I also advise disguises."

Without another word, he sauntered away, putting his pipe to his lips and belting out a lively jig.

A crowd gathered around him, oblivious to the confused teenagers milling around the terminal.

We all stared at each other, blinking like crazy.

"Could that guy be any more cryptic?" Eric turned his slack-jawed expression on me.

Passengers rushed by our little group, but still I shivered at the cool airport air and pulled out my bright pink scarf.

"At least the last line rhymed, sort of." I tightened the scarf around my neck.

Lucy lifted her chin to stare at the sign Steve had not-so-subtly pointed out. Then she elbowed Will.

He jerked his head up, then his eyes widened. "That's it. The Air-Train. Let's go now before they find us."

"What?" I stared at him, then actually took three seconds to read the sign. Sure enough, there was a big green sign overhead that said AirTrain with an arrow pointing to an exit. "Of course."

"But—" Eric started to protest.

"No time to explain. We've got to go." I grabbed his hand and raced after Lucy and Will. We all jog-walked as fast as we could without looking too suspicious toward the AirTrain terminal.

Luckily, running wasn't abnormal in an airport.

Eric snapped his fingers. "Duh. He meant the AirTrain and not the airplane we just flew to get here." He smacked his forehead with his free hand. "That took me way too long."

I chuckled under my breath as we slipped into the AirTrain terminal and followed the crowd to the platform waiting area.

A sign overhead read *Next train, two minutes.* Then the numbers switched to one minute. I tapped my toe against the shiny concrete floor. One minute was an eternity when you were trying to escape a spy. Or ten. Who knew how many Watcher spies were lurking at the airport today, just waiting for four teenagers who were anything but normal?

The train whooshed into the station, the door opened, and the crowd pushed us into the train. Eric found a row of benches that faced each other, and the four of us plopped down with a thud.

I glanced out the window to take in the city skyline, and my heart stopped.

Four burly black-clad thugs in ski caps and black covid masks raced into the station.

"Uh, guys." I tapped the window as my heartbeat thudded in my ears.

Everyone glanced out the window, and a collective gasp echoed in triplicate around me.

"We only have two minutes until they jump the next train and are right behind us." Will turned to Lucy, eyeing her purse. "Time to see what Steve gave us."

"Oh, right." Lucy shook herself, pulled her purse into her lap, and dug around inside. She pulled out a worn black leather pouch with a tassel and a snap clasp. Unsnapping the flap, she pulled out four oblong objects. "One for each of us, I guess."

She handed them out.

"Great. Does this mean we're going to have to tase people?" Eric held the black rectangular weapon in front of him, examining it from every angle. Then he slipped it in his pocket.

"I guess so." Will bobbed his head slowly. "And we only have ten to fifteen minutes to figure out what our next move is."

Lucy cleared her throat. "I think I have an idea of what Steve's plan was, or the Guardians' plan. Or whoever." She reached into the pouch again and pulled out four subway tickets.

Will's head swiveled unnaturally toward the map on the wall. "There are only two subway stations at the end of the line. Both go into Manhattan, but Jamaica Station gets us closer to HQ."

"Okay, but does that mean we should take Jamaica station or Howard Station, to throw them off?" Lucy's eyebrows shot up.

Suddenly the bagpiper's words played back through my head. "Who says we can't do both?"

Eric shifted in his seat to look at me. "What do you mean?"

My lips lifted into a grin. "Remember the bagpiper, uh Steve, said, 'I advise disguises'? Maybe we can rig up some makeshift disguises and give our clothes to homeless people or something to throw them off the trail."

Will tugged on my pink scarf. "Are you really ready to give your cashmere scarf away?"

A lump rose in my throat, but I shoved it back. "Anything to stop my premonition from coming true."

My words hung in the air as we all stared at each other.

Will nodded, his Adam's apple bobbing. "Thank you for that."

Crackling static blared from the speaker overhead as a robotic voice declared, "Next stop Howard Station, Jamaica Station. End of the line."

Everyone left on the AirTrain rose to their feet. My limbs shook like autumn leaves, but somehow I managed to stand up.

The second the doors opened, a phantom clock started ticking down in my head.

Tick, tock. Tick, tock.

Two minutes and counting.

The press of exiting passengers pushed us forward. Then we were off to the races.

Eric grabbed my hand as Will grabbed Lucy and we split up, each duo veering off in opposite directions.

Will pulled Lucy toward a sidewalk bodega where he haggled with a guy over a pair of black beanies.

Eric stopped in front of a touristy kiosk and threw down some money for a black I Heart NY T-shirt and a matching headscarf.

I reared back, squinting down at the atrocities he thrust at me. "You can't be serious."

He cocked his head and tugged on the ends of my ombre hair. "You're too distinctive for your own good. You've gotta cover up that two-tone hairdo of yours."

"Excuse me for being distinctive." I scoffed at him, even as I slipped the t-shirt over my head.

His lips curved into a grin. "I never said it was a bad thing."

The way those sea-blue eyes circled my face sent butterflies dancing a jig in my stomach. But we didn't have time for flirting.

Smirking at him, I handed over the telltale pink scarf and twisted my travel-tangled locks into a tight bun at the nape of my neck. Then I wrapped my head with the surprisingly lightweight black scarf with red hearts all over it.

Wrestling free of his jacket, he donned a matching T-shirt over his long-sleeved black shirt.

But his plan worked. We blended right in with the other tourists.

My pulse jangled in my eardrums. Our two minutes were almost up.

"Let's go." He laced his fingers between mine and tugged me toward the Howard Station entrance.

A group of teenagers scurried past, crowding around the entrance. I grabbed my scarf from Eric and caressed my fingers over the soft material one last time. Then I looped the scarf around the closest girl's backpack, tying it tight as she slipped down the stairs toward the subway.

"Nice work," Eric hissed in my ear as we headed toward a skinny-looking homeless guy in a threadbare trench coat hunched over a trash can.

The late-October wind swirled around us, making the decision even more clear.

Eric thrust his finely-crafted leather coat at the guy. "Hey, man. Someone left this on the train. It's yours if you want it."

When the man glanced up, I could see he wasn't much older than us, except his cheekbones were sunken in with dirt streaks all over his face. The smell of dried urine and body odor permeated the air. The boy bobbed his head in thanks.

With a nod back, we took off. First, Eric veered toward Howard Station. Then when the homeless guy slipped into his coat, we suddenly shifted directions toward Jamaica Station. Keeping my eyes in front of me, I booked it down the stairs into the subway tunnel, swiping my pass like a pro.

We raced to the platform and boarded the first train to Herald Square. Harsh fluorescent lights streaked across the dirty floor of the subway car. The stench of stale air weighed heavy on me as we found seats in the back of the car.

"Do you think they made it?" I glanced at Eric.

He slipped one arm around my shoulder, and I huddled into his side. "I hope so," he murmured into my hair. Or headscarf, rather.

Across the aisle, I heard a Goth-looking girl whisper to her boyfriend, "At least she gave her pink scarf away."

I reared back, rubbing my eyes to take in the sight to my left. A girl in a black knit hat with black eyeliner ringed around her eyes, like a raccoon mask, smiled at me with her painted black lips. Lucy had teased her hair into the rattiest mess of tangles I'd ever seen.

"Sis, is that you?" I tamped back the urge to scream.

Her boyfriend, with the spiked-up blond hair and the matching black-ringed eyes, grinned at me. "You guys did good. I barely recognize you."

"Yeah, same here." I blinked and blinked, but it was still Lucy and Will sitting in the back of the subway with us. Just the goth version of my sister and future brother.

"This is nuts," Eric whispered in my ear.

Lucy must've used all of her black eyeliner to give herself and Will this all-too-real goth look.

But then she smiled, and I could see it all so clearly. "I don't know how you ever got her into those awful T-shirts. Let alone a matching headwrap."

"Tell me about it," Eric mumbled and rolled his eyes. "Let's just say it was a challenge."

"Understatement of the year," Will scoffed.

My hand flew to my chest. "He told me I was too distinctive. And he was right, for once."

All three of them burst out laughing, and I relaxed back into the hard plastic seat. The ticking in my head dissipated, replaced by the rocking of the subway car. We were almost home free. Now we just had to make it back to headquarters in these ridiculous disguises. Something that *wasn't* in my premonition, by the way.

"Next up, Herald Square." The subway operator announced the next stop over the loudspeaker.

We all rose to our feet, keeping a safe distance from each other, and filed off the car.

Gray daylight trickled down from above as we trudged up the dank stairs toward the street. Eric and I hung back a few paces so it wouldn't look like the four of us were together.

I glanced around at the tall buildings rising up toward the gray sky all around us. Then my stomach twisted into a thousand knots.

Tugging on Eric's sleeve, I leaned in. "This looks all too familiar."

"I know, but we didn't have on crazy disguises in your vision, right? Something's changed this time." Eric's lips twitched as if he tried to shoot me a reassuring smile and failed.

"Yeah, I guess." I shrugged one shoulder even as every muscle in my body tensed up, ready for battle.

Then the bottom dropped out.

Six burly guys in black popped out of the alley in front of us.

My throat went dry. It was happening all over again.

CHAPTER THREE

PAIGE

Every hair on the back of my neck stood up. Skyscrapers towered around me, a mix of charcoal-tinged concrete and silver glass. My heart beat a new rhythm in my chest.

This looked exactly like my vision.

Tears welled in my eye sockets.

Except one thing was different. This time, we were all in crazy costumes. Did that mean we really could change what happened in my premonitions?

No better time to find out.

The six military-looking dudes inched forward, muscles clenching in fight position. One snarled at us, and a matching growl erupted from all of them.

Lucy reached for her purse, and then it dawned on me. The tasers. More than one thing was different this time. We also had real weapons that couldn't be disarmed by the sacred sapphire pieces.

"Shields up." Lucy grabbed Will's hand, and he nodded at her.

Lucy's lavender protection bubble crackled to life, doming all four of us in its center.

Will's invisibility bubble arced on top of Lucy's dome, encasing us in effervescent blue light.

"Let's take the offensive this time. Get ready to shoot." Will pulled his taser from his pocket and held it high.

The horde of Watchers advanced, whipping out their sapphire necklaces just like I'd seen in my vision. In reality, their flaring nostrils and menacing scowls made it just a notch scarier.

"Same plan as before," Lucy called out from her spot in front of me.

I glanced at the gray sky overhead, mentally going through my vision again. Tingles zipped all over my body. We were really going to do this.

Pulling my own taser from my jacket pocket, I flicked the weapon on, feeling the hum of electricity at my fingertips. If only my secondborn Seer powers were this reliable. But at least my combat training at Shadowstone Academy included tasers.

The leader lunged forward, poking his snarling head through the bubble.

"Now!" Will yelled, pointing his taser and shooting. But not at the leader.

I blinked and glanced at Lucy, who aimed her taser at the leader and turned up the volume.

Then I remembered. I needed to get the right-hand guy. My arm outstretched with a mind of its own, aiming at the attacker who stepped forward to help his leader.

With a flick of a button, the prongs of the taser shot out, jolting him with electricity.

The big dude writhed around, the veins on his neck popping out as he grunted and twitched.

The leader had already collapsed to the sidewalk, one leg still jiggling.

Lucy snatched his sapphire with a triumphant grin. "Got it. Who's next?"

"Recharge!" Will shouted from somewhere on my left.

At last, my guy fell to the pavement, his weapon clattering to the ground beside him. Lucy reached out and snapped the chain off his neck, too, her eyes full of glee.

Will and Eric had disabled two other attackers, leaving only two more to contend with.

The remaining two Watchers glanced at each other, then leapt over their fallen comrades with a battle cry.

Lucy raised one hand and let out her own guttural scream, purple electricity flowing straight to one guy's neck.

Will did the same, only with his taser.

One, two. The remaining assailants clattered to the sidewalk. Lucy and Will wasted no time snatching up their sapphires.

My sister turned to me, eyebrows arched. "These will come in handy later."

Then she slipped the sapphires into her purse.

I gaped at her, stunned into silence by her quick thinking in a real-life battle. Would I ever learn to fight like that?

"This isn't over, Tiger." Will grabbed her hand and tugged her forward. "We still have that van to contend with."

"And who knows how many guys they've got in there." Eric shuddered beside me.

The worst part of the premonition flashed into my head, sending my pulsing boiling in my veins.

I'd never let them take Will and Eric. Gritting my teeth, I glanced down to check my taser. The green light blinked back at me.

Fully charged.

Every muscle in my body tensed, readying for the next fight. "Let's do this."

Eric's lips twitched in an upward motion as we both fell in line behind Will and Lucy.

Hugging the side of the closest building, we made our way to the telltale alley. A drumbeat pounded in my head with every step we got closer to the scene of the crime. Or a would-be kidnapping, in this case.

Will held up one fist, and we all halted instantly. Then he crouched to the pavement, squatting on the balls of his feet. Ever-so-slowly, he inched his head into the alley, peering around the opening.

The seconds ticked by, until at last, he pulled back. Easing up to standing, he turned to face us.

"There's at least one guy in the driver's seat, and nobody else hanging around." His eyebrows furrowed into a V. "If there are any other soldiers, the only place they could be is in the van."

Lucy whirled around to face me. "Think, Paige. Do you remember anyone coming out of the van?"

Out of the blue, emotion clogged my throat. I gasped as tears welled in my eye sockets. "I don't know. I can't remember."

The only thing I could picture right now was Eric and Will being hauled into this scary van. And it was all too much.

"Relax. Just breathe." Will took both my hands, his tone calm and soothing. "Maybe this will help."

He closed his eyes, and a shimmer of bluish light flooded from his fingertips into mine. My eyes drifted closed as snatches of the premonition played through my mind once again. Except this time, I was hovering overhead, not really a part of the action. More like a casual observer, a little bird floating in the sky.

The original fight scene played out below me—Lucy zapping one guy and me failing with mine as Lucy dispatched another goon.

Then it hit me. There were three guys on the ground and four fighting Will and Eric. Where had that extra guy come from?

"There's one more guy. Probably headed this way right now." My eyes snapped open.

A whoosh resounded from somewhere down the alley, followed by the crunch of heavy boots on gravel.

"Here he comes." Will held out his taser.

As the black-clad figure rushed into view, Will zapped him with electricity. He grunted and fell to the ground.

Another grunt and more footsteps reverberated down the alley.

"Get the driver," Lucy hissed at me, waving her taser like it was useless.

With a gulp, I stepped up as the driver raced toward us. Then I zapped him with my taser, pouring all the remaining juice the weapon had left.

The guy froze still as a statue, then slid down the side of the building, eyes blinking at me.

"Huh," I stared at my weapon. "The second round must not have as much juice."

"These must be two-shot tasers." Will slipped the weapon into his pocket, and Lucy and I did the same. "Eric, looks like you're the only one who has a shot left."

"Great. So what now?" Eric glanced around the sidewalk as a couple across the street gawked at us.

"We better get these guys off the street," Will said.

"And back to headquarters. I'll call it in." Lucy pulled out her phone and dialed James, no doubt.

"Let's make sure these guys don't go anywhere. I'm sure your brother will want them for questioning." Will glanced at Eric and motioned for him to follow. "Let's check the van."

Eric's eyes widened, and his knuckles went white around the taser, but he followed Will to the creepy black van.

Lucy turned to me. "Guardians will be here in five. With a cleanup crew."

I exhaled a breath, finally allowing myself to relax a bit. My shoulders ached from clenching my muscles.

Lucy took a few steps closer. "We're okay now, sis. We're gonna be okay."

I nodded, even as tears clouded my vision and stung my eyes. "It's hard to believe I actually stopped a premonition. At least one that was happening to me."

"I know, I know." She reached out and looped an arm around my waist. "You did good today. You listened to your instincts and didn't let fear paralyze you. That's all you can really do."

I jerked my head her way. "Is it always like this?"

She shook her head. "In the beginning, yes. But over time, it gets easier to trust your powers. Especially as they get stronger. You're doing great. Trust me."

"Oh. Okay." I blinked and wiped the salty water away.

Squealing tires screeched to a stop behind us as sirens blared and lights flashed red and blue around us.

I whirled around to find two white SUVs with POLICE labeled on the side clogging up the street.

"You called the police?" I squinted at my sister.

She shook her head once. "Not exactly."

Cosette and Sedrick popped out of the first van, dressed in police uniforms. They raced down the alley toward Will and Eric, followed by two more Guardians I sort of recognized.

Silver handcuffs glinted in the red and blue lights as four of the rogue Watchers were rounded up into the second van. Then the Guardian cops went back for the last four, shoving the mostly unconscious soldiers into Cosi and Sed's van.

Sedrick jogged around to the driver's side and flashed us his pearly grin. "Good work, you guys. Hopefully, one of these idiots will cough up something good."

Cosi leaned across the seat. "Why don't you take their van and meet us at HQ?"

"Good idea," Lucy nodded at Cosi.

As we took off down the alley to meet Will and Eric, Sed turned on the lights and sped off down the street. The other Guardians did the same.

"What just happened?" I turned to Lucy as we met up with the guys.

"Sometimes, you have to make a scene to avoid suspicion." She opened the side door and hopped in.

Eric stood frozen at my side, not moving an inch.

I leaned in and whispered in his ear. "I'll get in the back with Lucy. You go up front with Will."

"Good idea." He squeezed my hand and leaned in to kiss my temple.

Even in the middle of chaos, his kiss still did funny things to my insides.

I shot him a small smile. Then he squared his shoulders and opened the passenger door.

I climbed in the back and sat on a tack box beside my sister, swinging the door shut behind me.

Will hopped into the driver's seat and took off down the alley. "Hang on. We're only five minutes out."

Eric swiveled in his seat to look at me. "There's no way we could take down eight soldiers without someone in New York seeing."

"True that." Will clapped him on the shoulder, never taking his eyes off the road. "If we make it look like a crime scene, people will look the other way, assume the police are handling it, and go on their merry way."

"I hope you're right," I muttered as he pulled into an underground parking garage. "All I wanted was a nice visit with my family for fall break. When will this madness ever end?"

I stared at Lucy, studying her face.

Her shoulders rose and fell. "I'd hoped that the Watchers and the Guardians could come to some sort of peace. But the collapse of Nexis left a giant power vacuum. And certain people in the Watcher Corps are rushing to fill the void."

"Sherry Montrose." I gritted out the name under my breath.

Lucy nodded, eyes flicking to the back of Will's head. "She's gaining influence on the Watcher Council."

"She's been playing the long game. And we have yet to see the extent of her plan." Will spat out as he hopped out of the van.

I grimaced at Lucy. "Something I said."

She lifted one shoulder. "I'll tell you later."

With a nod, I climbed out of the evil Watcher van. We walked through the parking lot and up the stairs to headquarters in silence.

At least there weren't six muscled Watchers waiting for us this time.

Chapter Four

Paige

We stepped into the elevator of a boring, nondescript office building. Lucy pressed in the secret code of floor numbers, and the elevator plummeted several stories below ground.

With a ding, the elevator door popped open.

"Finally!" Sedrick jogged across the pristine white-tiled lobby of Guardian Headquarters, New York, to meet us. "What took you guys so long?"

Will clapped Sed on the shoulder, rolling his eyes. "It's been like fifteen minutes, man. Chill out."

A giant grin rippled across Sed's ebony face. "It should've taken five."

"Or could it be that you haven't seen us in a few months, and you actually missed us?" Lucy smirked at him.

Sedrick paused and put a finger to his chin. "Nah, that can't be it. Though it must be nice, living the high life in Europe. I bet you guys go skiing every day. That's messed up, you know?"

"We hardly have time for anything fun unless you count training in a frigid field or throwing my sister the sweet sixteen bash of the year." Lucy arched her eyebrows at him, waiting for a challenge.

He shrugged, a giant grin all over his face. "Sounds like the high life to me."

Lucy rolled her eyes. "Why don't you take us to your fearless leader?"

"If you insist." Sedrick's grin faded away. "He's not too happy about this whole thing, you know."

"Believe me, I know. He'd be a bad brother if he wasn't annoyed when his sisters get attacked on his turf." Lucy tried to shrug it off, but I knew it'd be a long conversation with James when we finally saw him.

Not the ideal way to start fall break. But with the help of my premonition and the bagpiper spy, we all managed to come out in one piece. A shudder skittered down my spine at the thought of the alternative.

Sometimes I didn't hate these secondborn Seer gifts I'd been given.

Sedrick led the way past the gaping receptionist and navigated us through the war room. Computers and screens flanked the far wall, all with maps or CCTV footage. Men and women in suits walked around yelling and chattering about the latest intel.

Sedrick opened the door to my brother's office. The sweet aroma of coffee filled the air, and I inhaled a deep breath.

The chaos outside melted away as Sedrick closed the door.

"Thought you might need a little pick me up after your terrible morning." Cosette stood at a coffee bar on the far side of the room, steaming milk and pulling espresso shots.

I skipped past the boardroom-style table and the lounge area, crossing the room to wrap her in a hug. "You're the best."

She laughed and pushed me away. "I'm guessing you want the first latte. Here you go."

"Thank you." I picked up the mug of coffee goodness and tipped it to my lips.

Just then, James burst into the room, almost making me spill my latte on my I Heart NY T-shirt—which wouldn't be the end of the world, actually. Lucky for my shirt, I pulled up in time, so only a little coffee dribbled down my chin. I quickly lapped it up.

"I'm so glad you're safe." James stomped over to Lucy and wrapped her in a hug. Then he headed for me. "I see you've found the essentials, sis. Welcome home."

He gave me a quick pat on the head, then marched straight to his gleaming mahogany desk. "Please have a seat. We have a lot to discuss."

We all piled into the office chairs in front of his desk.

My brother's chiseled, some would say, handsome face suddenly turned serious. "I was hoping to have a nice fall break with my sisters. But unfortunately, plans change."

Cosette went around handing everyone a latte, then sat one in front of James.

"Thanks, Cosi." His face lit up as he glanced at her, then he turned back to us. "Instead, it's time for your first situation report."

I glanced at Lucy, and she gave me the side-eye.

James snapped his fingers and sat up a little straighter. "The good news is that your run-in with the rogue Watcher soldiers has been contained. Sedrick, status update. Go." He took a sip of his latte and pointed at Sed.

I blinked and sat back in my seat. My goofy brother was suddenly all business. I guess the Nexis Ruby War changed him. Or he was finally getting used to his new position as captain of the New York Guardians.

Sedrick rose to his feet and stood at attention. "Sir, the eight suspects were subdued by our out-of-town guests," Sed gestured to the four of us. "Most have regained consciousness and are being interrogated as we speak. You will be updated the moment any credible intel has been substantiated."

"Thank you, Captain Rodriguez." James turned to Lucy and me. "Good job notifying us of your premonition with enough time to contact operatives. I trust Steve was of use to you?"

Lucy nodded at him, her lips pulling into a half-smile. "Yes. The tasers and train tickets were instrumental in our escape."

My jaw dropped. Everyone was talking so formally—almost military-like. Was it all part of the situation report protocol?

James steepled his fingers in front of his face. "I wish I could tell you guys that this was just an isolated skirmish with rogue Watchers. But I can't. We're starting to see a pattern emerge. Especially after the intel gleaned from the attack on Paige at Shadowstone Academy last week."

Eric reached out and grabbed my hand, lacing his fingers through mine. I turned to gauge his reaction. His Adam's apple bobbed as he swallowed hard, but he didn't say a word.

Interesting.

Will scooted his rolling chair closer, leaning in. "Does this pattern have anything to do with one Sherilyn Montrose climbing the ranks of the Watchers?"

James gave him the barest hint of a nod. Eric and I turned to stare at him, but the completely neutral expression on Lucy's face spoke volumes. She didn't seem the least bit surprised at this revelation.

Me on the other hand? I sank back into my chair, Eric's hand the only tether to keep me from rolling away.

That crazy lady had ordered an attack on me, using her son and other minions to spy on me all semester. And now she was rising through the ranks of the Watchers? Who else would she hurt on her path to power?

My mind flashed back to that awful night in the Watcher's underground lair. But I couldn't go there. Not now.

"Does this mean another war is about to break out?" I couldn't keep the squeak out of my voice on the word war.

I'd seen what Lucy, James, Will, and everyone else their age had gone through in the last war. It was hard to imagine that another war might be on the horizon so soon.

James cleared his throat. "So far, Sherry Montrose is denying the whole incident. She's even denying Rocco as her son."

"You can't be serious! He only kidnapped me and tried to transfer my powers into the sapphire on her orders." I scoffed at this, blood rushing to my cheeks. Images of Rocco bursting into my dorm room flashed through my mind, but I couldn't go there. Not right now. He was still out there somewhere, getting away with his crimes.

"I'm afraid so." James leaned his elbows on his desk. "She's making a play for the leader of the Watcher Council by attacking the validity of the Neutrality Committee. She's twisting the whole incident as Guardian propaganda and saying the attack at Shadowstone was a Guardian ploy to strip the Watchers of their power."

"Such an Emperor Palpatine move," Eric whispered under his breath.

"If only the Watchers had actually seen *Star Wars*, maybe we wouldn't be in this mess." James rested his chin on his hands. "Regardless, one thing is clear. Sherry has a plan to take over the Watchers. For now, our best play is to try to stop her. And come up with a plan for when we fail."

"What a cheery thought, bro." I sank by in my chair, letting them drone on about their plans.

I couldn't believe this was happening. I was almost too shocked to think straight. What could a group of teenagers do against such blatant manipulation?

I guess the sacred stone squad was all we had now.

Paige

I walked out of my brother's office feeling more dazed and confused than ever. Even Cosi's great latte hadn't helped me swallow the bitter news James delivered.

Sherry Montrose wanted my power for some key component in her evil plan. But she was a little too clever and crafty to reveal her cards just yet. I'd never expected her to deny her own son. Or come after me, instead of my sister. That little tidbit took this to a whole new level of creepy.

Felicia met us in the lobby, arms outstretched. "Baby brother. There you are."

She wrapped Eric in a bear hug and mussed his auburn hair.

He cringed but let her play her games. "Hey, sis. Can we get out of here?"

"Sure thing, guys. Follow me." Felicia led us back into that dreaded elevator.

The door opened to another underground level, and the five of us walked through the parking garage together, along with James and Cosi.

"We're this way." Felicia's gaze landed on a black luxury car off to our right as she glanced between Eric and me.

Eric pursed his lips together, then reached out and wrapped me in a hug. "I'll see you tomorrow for our training session, okay?" he whispered in my ear.

I nodded, squeezing him tight. He pressed a quick kiss to my cheek, then hurried after his sister, who was already walking away.

"C'mon, Paige. Don't be gross." Lucy yanked on my hand, pulling me toward a black SUV on the left that had all four doors open, plus the trunk. "It'll be a tight squeeze, but I'll volunteer you for the middle."

"Ugh," I rolled my eyes, trying not to glance back at Eric. "Don't you want to sit by your own boyfriend?"

Will tossed our purses in the back. "She has a point, gorgeous."

"Ha." I folded my arms across my chest. "After you, sis."

"Fine," she huffed, sliding across the leather back seat.

"Oh, no. You get to snuggle up next to your boyfriend. The tragedy." I slammed the door shut, staring at Felicia's car as it sped out of the parking garage.

I lifted my hand to wave, then thought better of it. A funny feeling hit me straight in the chest. Part of me already missed Eric, but this sinking feeling was about something more. I bit my lip. Felicia seemed light and happy, and Eric was as unreadable as ever. Would their father be at home to greet them? I shuddered at the thought. I hoped not.

At last, we hit daylight, and I couldn't tear my eyes away from the view out my window. James drove through the quiet business section of New York that housed headquarters into a more residential area on the west side of Central Park. Adorable little brownstones replaced the skyscrapers. James turned the SUV into an alley and pulled into a garage behind one of the homes.

He led the way up the stairs, through an enormous state-of-the-art kitchen with an eat-in breakfast nook, and into a family room with matching gray furniture and cream walls that screamed Mom.

"Mom, Dad. Are you home?" James called up the stairs.

My heart leapt for joy as the front door opened, and Dad trudged in, carrying two suitcases behind him. One of them was pink.

"Let me help you, sir." Will rushed to take our luggage of his hands.

"How did you get this?" Lucy raced up to her beloved pink suitcase.

Dad wiped his hands on his slacks and smiled. "Just delivered with a little help from the Guardian network, JFK division."

"Sweet." I couldn't wait another second and raced up to Dad for a hug. "Is this your new house? Nice digs."

"Yes, sweetheart. This is our new home." Dad gestured to the wall where a collection of perfectly-framed family photos of the five of us over the years hung on the wall leading up the stairs. "Your mom is out getting groceries for dinner tonight. Why don't you head up to your rooms and rest? I heard my girls had a busy morning."

"We did." We both said in unison, glancing at each other.

I busted out laughing and let Dad lead us up the stairs.

"This floor has three bedrooms and one bath, which, unfortunately, you'll all have to share." He looked pointedly at me. "Your Mom and I have the top floor to ourselves, with a master suite and an office."

"Oooh, the penthouse. Nice, Dad." I elbowed him in the ribs.

He grinned back at me. "Paige, you're in here. Lucy, you and Will have the middle bedroom."

"As usual," she muttered under her breath.

Dad arched his furry eyebrows at her. "You're lucky I don't make your *boyfriend* sleep on the couch."

"Dad." My sister's eyes went wide as she glanced at Will.

He glanced at me, and we both chuckled to ourselves.

Dad reached out and ruffled her hair. "And James has the back bedroom."

I clapped my hands together. "Sweet. That means I have the best view."

I rushed into my room and left my sister behind to argue with Dad about her boyfriend.

The view of the street and the park beckoned me into my new room. Mom had decorated the space in soft grays and pinks, much like my old bedroom, but in a sophisticated, New York way.

I flounced on the bed and wondered if I'd ever get up.

Dad rolled my silver suitcase into my room. "Looks like you're making yourself at home already."

I smiled up at him. "Sure, I miss our home in Indianapolis. But I've always been a New York girl at heart. This is a dream come true."

"Glad to hear that, honey." He reached out and ruffled my hair. "Dinner is at seven. Don't be late. You know your mother."

"Indeed, I do." I winked at him.

He shut the door behind him, and my eyes drifted closed. Before I knew it, my alarm was going off, saying six-thirty p.m. How had I slept so long? It must be jet lag.

I hurried into the bathroom, refreshed my makeup, and headed downstairs for dinner.

Mom made her specialty, lasagna.

Before I knew it, I was stuffed to the gills and crammed into the living room for a classic McAllen family game night. We laughed and laughed after rounds of Crimes Against Humanity and Exploding Kittens.

Our parents were the funniest to watch playing the latest trendy game. I couldn't stop laughing.

As I fell into bed again sometime after midnight, my cheeks hurt from smiling so much.

Finally, fall break was going the way I'd planned. But how long would that last? Tomorrow was our first sacred stone training session. And I had no idea what I was doing.

CHAPTER FIVE

The west side brownstones blurred past my window as Felicia maneuvered the car through the maze of yellow cabs and black cars that clogged the roads. Though I'd lived in this area for all my life, Manhattan never truly felt like home. Not since Mom died. She'd provided a happy childhood home on Long Island while my dad "worked" in the city, climbing the corporate ladder—only later to find out it was all thanks to his power in the Watcher Corps.

Sure, Dad was gone all the time. But no one minded. On the rare occasion he did come home, we were always on high alert.

I winced at the memory of cowering behind my mom as he screamed at her for letting us leave our bikes out.

My sister turned down Fifth Avenue headed for the east side of Central Park, and I blinked the nightmare away.

Why did this city always remind me of the cloud of terror that was my father? Maybe that's why I jumped at the chance to go to Shadowstone Academy. Especially knowing my sister was safe in the ranks of the Guardians.

After Mom died, Dad insisted we move into the city—into a glass and concrete condo monstrosity, no less. The place was cold and impersonal, and I always met my friends in the park or somewhere on the west side of town. Then my sister had escaped to Montrose Paranormal Academy, leaving me in the care of our housekeeper, Marte. Luckily, Dad still rarely came home.

"Don't worry." Felicia reached out and patted my shoulder as she pulled into the condo's underground parking garage. "He's not here. He'll be out of town for your whole break."

"Good." I collapsed into the seat, shutting my eyes against the burning sludge of terror that filled my veins.

Relax, Eric. One breath in, one breath out. After a few minutes of deep breathing, the panic subsided.

Felicia parked the car in our numbered spot, and I hopped out, almost reaching for my luggage. Then I remembered, we'd had to leave it at the airport. Hopefully, my battered navy blue suitcase would be returned to me soon enough. That six-year-old piece of luggage was one of the last things my mom got for me.

We took the elevator, and Felicia pressed the lobby button. "What? I've got to check the mail."

I smirked at her. "Such a grown-up now."

"Someone's got to be responsible, little brother." The tired lines on her face eased into a full-on grin as we walked across the marble-tiled lobby to the mailboxes.

She slid her key in and grabbed the mail, then we headed toward the main bank of elevators.

"Miss. Excuse me, Miss Morales." The bell-capped man at the front desk waved an arm at us. "You have a package."

She stopped in her tracks and squinted at me. "Are you expecting anything?"

I shook my head until it dawned on me. "Could be my lost luggage from the airport." I raised my eyebrows, trying to silently communicate the need to play it cool.

She nodded once, the corners around her sharp eyes softening. "Right. Might be needing that."

My fingers itched to touch the worn leather handle. Mom even had my initials engraved on the handle. At the age of ten, the small gesture had made me feel so grown-up.

We strolled over to the front desk, and the little rotund guy rolled my navy blue suitcase over to us.

I almost leapt for joy.

"Thanks, Carson." Felicia smiled at the concierge. "You know airlines, always losing people's luggage."

He tipped his cap at us. "Sounds like you got lucky this time."

"Indeed." She waved, and I rolled my luggage to the elevator.

A lump welled in my throat.

As soon as the door closed behind us, I grinned at her. "Way to play it cool."

"I'm glad you got Elmo back." She eyed the tattered luggage. "I'm just surprised they returned it so quickly. Sounds like quite a fiasco you had this morning."

Right, the airport incident. How had that slipped my mind even for a second?

I nodded, studying her face. She really was playing it cool. If anyone was watching us on some kind of hidden elevator cam, they'd have no idea we were talking about something other than lost luggage.

"International travel is always a crapshoot." I kept my gaze front until we reached the forty-seventh floor.

At last, the doors opened, and we slipped into our condo.

The moment the door shut behind us, Felicia wrapped me in a big bear hug. "I'm so glad you're okay. When Sed called and said Paige had a premonition on the plane, I was so worried. But I'm glad we had Steve there to help us deliver what you needed."

I pulled back, studying my sister's face. "Don't tell me it was your idea to send tasers."

She grinned and released me. "Sure was. I know how the Watchers operate. They're too much like Nexis was, relying on the sacred stones. You need real weapons to take them down."

"Noted." I took a good look around the sterile condo.

The walls were gray, along with the giant sectional in the living room and the matching chairs. The only color came in the form of two bright teal pillows and a light blue blanket.

"Someone's making this place more livable." I slipped out of my jacket and hung it on the coat tree by the door.

Felicia sighed, dropping her purse on the gleaming marble kitchen island. "Dad's been gone for six weeks, and it's been nice. But Sed and I are still getting our own place close to headquarters."

"Whoa, that's a big step." I blinked at my sister, who suddenly looked years older.

But the gold flecks glimmering in her light green eyes and the huge smile on her face told me all I needed to know. She'd finally found someone who could make her happy. And even better, she was getting out from under my father's thumb.

"I'm happy for you, sis." I looped one arm across her shoulders and wrapped her in a side hug.

She used to be taller than me, but I'd grown a few inches in the last year and could now rest my head on top of hers.

"Thanks, bro." She grinned up at me. "I find that I quite like being a normal girl. Makes me wish you'd join the same club."

I gritted my teeth, letting my arm drop as a protest simmered in my throat. "Maybe once I'm on my own, away from Dad like you, I'll be able to drop my guard. But until then, I'm gonna use every weapon I can find to protect myself against him. And the people I love."

She folded into a padded stool at the island. "I guess you heard about all the ladder-climbing going on with the Watchers."

Cringing, I nodded. "I heard Sherilyn is climbing the ranks, and I'm sure Dad is nipping at her heels."

Her lips twisted. "Yeah, that's why he's been gone so much. Part of me wants to know what he's up to, just so we can stay ahead of him."

I crossed my arms over my chest. "Part of me doesn't want to know."

"Same." She glanced up at me.

A door down the hall squeaked open, and out popped our house-keeper, dressed in all black like a true New Yorker.

"Eric, my boy. You're home." Marte practically raced toward me, squeezing me in a giant hug. "I'll make your favorite pierogis tonight. Then you tell me all about Switzerland."

With a slight grin, she hurried into the kitchen and went to work making dinner.

That was about as much emotion as Marte liked to show. I smiled at the woman who was like a second mother to me. Normally, I'd help her with the pierogies. But my eyelids were drooping. Jet lag was starting to catch up to me.

"I'm going to catch a nap. See you for dinner, Marte. Sis." I winked at her and rolled my luggage down to my room.

Maybe Felicia and Sed would have a spare room for me. But what would happen to Marte? One thing at a time. I had my own problems to worry about.

Pulling out my phone, I thought about texting Paige. Then I drifted off to sleep.

PAIGE

At this rate, I'd never see the sun on the skyline of New York. If headquarters was ten stories below ground, the training room was five stories more.

But my crazy siblings and future sibling led the way down too many flights of stairs like it was no big deal. While I did my impromptu Stairmaster routine, I typed out an update to Stella, Brooke, and Owen.

Day 1 of sacred stone training. Fingers crossed.

Two beeps trilled out, echoing from somewhere behind me. I whirled around to find Eric and Felicia half a flight up.

"Hey, guys." I waved up to them, then rammed into Lucy's back.

"Nice one, Squirt." Will shook his head.

"We're here." Lucy turned and steadied me, and we all watched James type a long, complicated code into the keypad.

"You'd think the door would just magically open for the head honcho," I mumbled at my sister's back.

Eric and Felicia finally reached us, and I could feel his presence beside me like a live wire. Tingles zinged up and down my spine at his nearness.

Now that we weren't running from Watcher soldiers, we might actually get some bonding time in. That'd be nice for a change.

A girl could dream, right?

The door clicked open, and James strolled into a dark room, flicking on the lights.

One by one, the fluorescent lights overhead hummed to life, illuminating different sections of the massive underground training room.

The whole place was a giant black rubber mat. Even the walls were covered in black rubber. In the far right corner sat a boxing ring, surrounded by punching bags and all things related to boxing.

The far left corner housed a row of practice dummies made of black foam and more hanging bags. It must be the kickboxer's sparring section. Along the entire back wall lay a massive set of free weights worthy of any gym.

"This is the officer's training room. I figured we'd want to test out the sacred stone powers without an audience." James led us to the center of the room, free from all fighting implements.

Lucy walked to his side, then turned to face us. "We're gonna test out Paige's new gift on some sapphire pieces our not-so-little friends left behind."

With a gleam in her eye, she reached into her hoodie pocket and pulled out six sapphire necklaces.

James held out one hand and waved me forward, *Matrix*-style. "Paige, why don't you tell us how this whole thing works."

Gulping back the acid rising in my throat, I took a few tentative steps forward and joined my siblings. "Well, last time I did this on the fly. But an angel came to me and told me I could imbue whatever powers I wanted into each sacred stone. It all happened in such a blur I barely remember exactly how I did it. Or if my angel did the power transfer, or in what order ..." I stammered off, staring down at my shoes.

Great start.

Lucy's hand landed on my shoulder. "Why don't you close your eyes and reach out to your angel for guidance?"

"Okay?" I grimaced at her but closed my eyes anyway.

Okay, Angel Dude. Kinda need your help here.

A spray of warmth trickled across my arms like a shower of sparks.

You called? Angel said in my head.

I resisted the urge to open my eyes and break the spell. *How do I use this new gift you've given me, you know to give powers into these sacred stones?*

A gentle wind wafted across my face. *Good question, little secondborn. Use your inner gift to direct each stone to display the ability of your choosing. And remember, the power you imbue to each sacred stone is yours to give and take away.*

Suddenly, a cold breeze slammed down at me from above, almost as if my angel had just shot through the ceiling, leaving a void in his wake.

I snapped my eyes open and snagged a necklace from my sister. "Here goes nothing."

In my mind, I called up my pink lightning and shot it into the stone, willing the power of invisibility to flood the sapphire.

Then I handed the stone to James. "Here. Put this around your neck."

"Okay." James took the necklace and hung it over his head. The instant his head slipped through the hole, it turned invisible. Then when the chain settled around his neck, his whole body disappeared.

Poof! Just like magic.

"Whoa!" The whole room erupted in cries of disbelief.

"What, guys? What happened?" James' voice resonated from beside me, where his body should've been.

"Dude, you completely disappeared." Will's eyes were wider than I'd ever seen.

"Cool," came his invisible response. "Can I turn it on and off at will?"

"I don't know," I shrugged, shooting a glance at Lucy. She just shrugged. "Try holding it and thinking *not invisible*."

Suddenly my brother appeared out of thin air, clutching the necklace.

"Cool. I wanna try." Eric turned to me, those normally murky eyes lit up with excitement as he grinned at me.

I tried not to grin back. "Sure. What kind of power do you want?"

"Hey, you didn't let me choose. And I'm the section chief." James blinked in and out of existence as he played with his new power.

But a storm cloud dampened the joy on Eric's face. He was back to scowling and scrunching his eyebrows together.

He rocked back on his heels. "That's a tough choice. On the one hand, super strength would be cool, if that's even possible. But when I had powers before, I had red lightning like my sister, which came in real handy. But I also love Will's shield. That'd be pretty cool to have. I don't know." He scratched his chin as his gaze roamed my face.

"How about we stick with lightning power for now?"

His face split into a grin. "Perfect."

Gripping the sapphire in my hand, I closed my eyes and thought of the one power he needed right now.

He took the necklace from me and slipped it on. "Thank you, Paige."

His words were soft, but I felt the full meaning behind them. I knew how much this power meant to him. He'd almost killed himself a few months ago in a desperate attempt to restore his powers.

"I'm just glad I could help." I squeezed his shoulder. "Now go test it out."

That boyish grin was back, doing funny things to my insides. Then he trotted off to the other side of the room to test out his new blue lightning.

I gave the same power to Felicia and Will, then imbued the remaining stones with protection shields. Lucy and I could use all the protection we could get for sparring with a bunch of newbies.

We went around the room, practicing putting up shields and shooting lightning.

I was super glad for the extra shield to compensate for my own pathetic lightning powers.

James clapped his hands until we all ceased fire. "Hey, guys. I have a great idea. Why don't we try these things out in the real world? Test out if we need to be near Paige for them to work or not."

"Field trip." Will slapped my brother's hand and raced out of the room with Lucy in tow.

The rest of us filed up the stairs behind him.

Felicia opened the door to the parking garage then turned to me. "Why don't you go with Eric? James and I can test if your cute little stones work without an active Chosen One, or secondborn, nearby."

James opened his mouth to protest, but Felicia shot him a glare.

"We'll be careful." I waved goodbye and walked with Eric to the subway.

"This should be interesting." Eric took my hand and led me into the depths of the New York subway system.

CHAPTER SIX

Paige

"Next stop, 59th Street, Columbus Circle." The garbled announcement blared through the grungy subway car.

A man sat across from us on the orange bench, eating falafel and stinking up the entire car.

I inhaled the smell of grease and exotic spices.

Ah, New York.

Eric and I sat side by side, tapping our feet against the dirty floor, not saying a word. He just stared straight ahead and wouldn't even look at me.

Awkward.

"What's going on with you? Why are you so quiet?" I elbowed him in the ribs, keeping my voice low.

He glanced over at me with those stormy blue-green eyes. I almost melted into a puddle on the orange subway seat, but I held my ground.

Clearing his throat, he leaned in. "I just found out my dad is moving up the ranks of the Watchers. Quickly. And I'm just worried about what that means."

"You mean, for you and Felicia?" I angled his way, studying the way his jaw twitched.

He stiffened. "And you, too."

"Me?" My hand flew to my chest as I reared back, my elbow bumping the subway car wall.

"Yes," he grunted out as if the word cost him something. "My father always finds a way of hurting the people I care about."

"Oh," was all I could say. Fireflies sparked a blazing trail from my stomach to the back of my throat.

As the train pulled to a stop at Columbus Circle, he finally grabbed my hand. "Follow me. I have an idea."

His voice was gruff in my ear, sending a shiver down my spine as he led me out of the subway car.

I bit into my bottom lip and did as I was told.

For once in my life.

Together, we navigated through the maze of people entering and exiting the Columbus Circle station.

When we hit daylight, I gasped. A giant roundabout with a park in the middle diverted traffic across from us.

Eric tugged me through the crosswalk toward the entrance to Central Park. Then a glint of gold caught my eye, and my jaw dropped.

Suddenly I felt like I was in a movie. I'd never been to Columbus Circle before, let alone Central Park in the fall.

A towering statue stood at the entrance to the park, with grayish beige Greek-looking statues at the base of a giant pedestal that towered several stories high. On top of the pedestal sat a lady made of gold in a flowing dress with horses around her.

It was the most beautiful statue I'd ever seen. I'd been to New York several times and somehow never saw this statue.

The best part was the most colorful fall leaves dotting the landscape behind the stone carving.

I slowed my steps, craning my neck and staring at the awe-inspiring gold statue. Could I ever make something that awesome?

Eric tugged me to the corner, and we hurried through our last crosswalk into the relative quiet of the park.

Wow, was Central Park beautiful in the fall.

The wind turned crisp as we passed the statue, the breeze clearing away the car exhaust for just a moment of fresh air.

Red maples, orange-trimmed sweetgums, and yellowing ash trees loomed large all around me. I slowed to take in the beauty, the grandeur, the slice of peace in a city of chaos.

Eric planted his large frame in front of me, crossing his arms over his chest. "Quit gawking like a tourist, and let's go. I've got the perfect spot for our little experiment."

I narrowed my eyes at him. "Can't we just slow down a sec? You know, enjoy our fall break for like five minutes?"

He narrowed his eyes right back at me and growled. Like, actually growled at me.

"Five minutes," he ground out through clenched teeth.

I rolled my eyes and started walking at my own pace, probably a snail's pace to him.

The air smelled crisp and clean, with just a hint of city smog. A chilly breeze blew a pile of leaves across the sidewalk. Bending down, I captured one of each color—red, orange, and yellow—and tucked them in the pocket of my hoodie.

"Now can we go?" Eric's snarl had lost its bite.

I knew who was really in charge here. I wanted to pat his head and tell him good boy, but that'd only make him protest again.

"Yes, fine. Show me your secret hideout." I gave him my hand once again and let him lead the way.

"Thank you." The edges of his mouth tipped in the barest hint of a grin.

Eric quickened the pace, and I struggled to match his long strides.

At last, we reached some kind of bridge that arched over the path.

He glanced around, waiting for passersby to walk out of sight. Then he walked up to the base of the bridge and found a rock with a little circle and wavy lines carved into the stone—the Guardian symbol. He leaned against the stone, trying to look casual until a little door popped open.

"I can't decide whether that's cool or creepy." I peered into the dark opening as a dank smell wafted to my nose.

"C'mon. We don't want anyone seeing this." Eric yanked on my arm.

I tumbled through the black hole, my arms flailing as the door scraped shut behind me.

Complete blackness was all I could see as my hands hit something solid and warm. My throat went dry, and my lungs constricted as all the air leaked out. I didn't like total darkness. Not one bit.

Reaching into my pocket, I pulled out my phone and instantly relaxed as the soft glow of the screen hit my face. Then I tapped on the flashlight feature, just as Eric did the same.

"Don't ever do that again." I punched his chest where my hands had landed. Fireflies swirled in my belly.

"Ow." He rubbed his pec, his face awash with shadows from my phone. "Why'd you do that?"

"I hate the dark," I mumbled to my shoes, hoping he couldn't hear me.

"Oh." His hand slid around my waist, pulling me close. "Sorry." His breath feathered across my face.

I blinked up at him, letting his warmth soothe my pulse back to a normal rate.

"What is this place anyway?" I shined the flashlight around the small room about as big as a walk-in closet.

"It's a safe room for the secret societies, usually used for dropping or exchanging intel." Eric's warm words wafted across my cheeks.

I stared at the strange shadows dancing across the planes of his face as if they could tell me what this hulking, broody guy in front of me was thinking.

His eyes softened around the corners as he stared down at me, and that telltale muscle in his jaw was twitching away again. Maybe he was nervous.

"So you wanted to do this little sacred stone test somewhere that wasn't so public, right?"

His Adam's apple bobbed in the light. "I want this power back so badly it hurts. And I'm afraid of what will happen if it doesn't work for me."

One hand flew to my hip. "You mean like you'll go all beast-mode and take a swipe at people in the park?"

A chuckle rumbled from his chest. "No. Worse than that." His voice broke on the last word.

Air clogged in my throat. Of course, he was worried he'd break down in front of dozens of people. Why hadn't I figured that out before now?

I wanted to slap myself in the forehead.

When it came to Eric Morales, there was a lot I still had to learn. Whatever his dad did to him must've been traumatic for him to act like this, even in front of just me.

"Well, what're you waiting for? Let's try this baby out." I took a few steps back and gave him some room. "Whenever you're ready."

"Okay, here goes." Eric wrapped one hand around the necklace, and it suddenly began to glow blue.

Then he held out his hand, and an electric current crackled from his upturned palm, swirling into a ball.

"Yes!" I pumped my fist in the air. "I worked."

Pale blue light danced in Eric's eyes. "I can't believe it worked. This is awesome."

Suddenly the sparkling blue orb winked out of existence.

"What're you doing?" I aimed my flashlight at his face.

He shielded his eyes. "We have one more test to do. And you're not going to like it."

"Just tell me," I huffed.

"I want you to go outside and walk toward the nearest bench."

"What?" I jerked my head at him. "Why would you want me to walk away right now?"

He paused and exhaled a breath, running a hand through his hair. "Because I need to see if this only works with you around or if the stone carries this power all on its own."

"Oh, so you think I'm an amplifier or something?" I gulped, my throat suddenly going dry.

He leaned in and grabbed my hand. "I know you are. At least to me."

Tingles shot up my arm at his touch. I tilted my head at him, but the shadows made his expression unreadable. "So, what? You want me to go find the nearest bench and wait for you?" I tapped my toe against the stone floor. "For how long?"

Maybe it was selfish of me, but I wanted to see him come into his full powers.

"Just give me five, ten minutes tops. That should be enough time for my little experiment." He backed into the far corner of the room.

"Fine. Have it your way." I turned my light toward the door and found my way out.

Eric

I inhaled a breath, the musty air tickling my nose as darkness surrounded me. Paige's scowl as she left said it all, but I needed to find out the truth. For me.

Did I have my old power back? Just like that, no questions asked?

An image of my father's menacing face flashed into my mind, but I slammed it back to the depths where it belonged.

Okay, this little testing wasn't only about me. It was about protecting the ones I loved.

I flexed my hand at my side, then held it level with the ground, palm up. My muscle memory knew what to do. It was almost like old times, back when I had my secondborn Messenger power.

Without touching the sapphire around my neck, I focused on my internal energy first. Except this time, I came up blank.

No power coursed through my veins like it had before. My Messenger gifts were long gone.

My pulse thudded in my ears.

"Okay, don't panic. Time to try something else," I whispered to the blackness around me.

Placing my hand on the stone, I willed it to give me its energy. The sapphire warmed in my grasp, lighting up the darkness with blue light.

Next came an onslaught of electricity, flowing down my arms like a river—like the energy knew exactly where to go.

Sparks shot from my fingertips, unbidden. Closing my eyes, I directed the bits of lightning into a swirling sphere that grew bigger and bigger in my palm.

"I guess that works." I stared at the writhing blue light in my hand, letting it grow bigger and bigger until the sphere touched the ceiling.

Tendrils of blue light fanned out across the rocky surface overhead, shooting lines of blue light down every wall and even across the floor.

"That's new. It's like the *Matrix*, only blue." I laughed at the new-found power at my fingertips.

With a blast of wind and daylight, the door burst open. Paige slipped through the opening, her two-toned hair blowing in the breeze. Then the door slammed shut behind her.

"If you were trying to keep a low profile, it didn't work, dude." Paige's cute little nose scrunched as she scowled at me for the twelfth time today.

"Wh-what do you mean?" I stammered, studying her face in the suddenly low light.

"I was like fifty feet away, and I still saw the blue light flashing on the underside of the bridge like a strobe light."

"Seriously? That's not good." I dropped my hand from the sapphire, and the energy left my body. "How is that even possible? I thought this room was sealed tight."

A trickle of fear slithered down my spine. Central Park always had spies of every society persuasion patrolling the area. What if one of the rogue Watchers had seen my little display?

She put her hand on her hip, wrinkling her nose. "Okay, maybe I was exaggerating a little bit. But there's definitely a crack under the door because I saw a thin ray of blue light like a laser."

I huffed out a cross between a laugh and a sigh of relief that came out more like a strangled snort. Of course, she was exaggerating. I should've known. Part of me was annoyed at her, but part of me wanted to grab her and pull her close so we could laugh about it together.

She didn't seem to notice I hadn't said anything. "Luckily, most New Yorkers don't seem to care about strange lights in Central Park.

"Good," I huffed out, taking a step closer.

"Doesn't mean I'm not curious about what happened." She aimed her blinding phone light at me again. "C'mon. It obviously worked just fine without me. Show me what you've got."

She tilted her head and tipped her chin at me in that adorable way of hers. A different kind of electricity tingled down my back.

"You asked for it." I clutched the sapphire again and let the lightning flow.

In hyper speed this time, electricity bubbled from my hand, then touched the ceiling, and zipped across every surface of the room.

"Awesome. It's like the *Matrix*, only blue." Paige's full-watt smile rivaled the light.

"Yeah, that's what I said. It's pretty cool, huh?" I called the light back into the palm of my hand. "And it wouldn't be possible without you."

"Don't worry about it." She waved a hand in front of her face like it was no big deal.

In two steps, I closed the distance between us, my eyes roaming her face. "I'm serious, Paige. You have no idea what this means to me—you giving me my power back. I'm so much more than grateful."

She stared up at me, those luscious lips catching my eye. "Why don't you show me?"

That was all the invitation I needed.

I released the lightning and wrapped both arms around her, pressing her body into mine. Then I took a quick taste of her lips before devouring them completely.

How could this strong, powerful girl really be into *me*? I wanted to ask, but I didn't dare point out the obvious. I just held her tight and kissed her until I saw stars.

Or was that something else swirling into focus behind my closed eyes?

Suddenly, the Shadowstone Academy campus came into view, the Swiss Alps jagged across the nighttime sky.

I was with the Sacred Stone Squad, Paige on my right and Will on my left. Stella, Owen, and Brooke were all fanned out beside me—in fight stance.

Dark silhouettes appeared on the horizon, marching across the snowy field toward us.

Everyone in the SSS dug their heels in and called up their powers, forming a few layers of protection and invisibility bubbles around us.

And still they came, the unknown army of shadows. We were outnumbered ten to one. Then I realized we weren't alone. We had a whole army of SA students behind us. Professors and teachers too.

Even though our powers were ready for attack, each member of the SSS carried a weapon of some kind.

Huh. That's interesting.

Finally, I caught a glimpse of the approaching army. Fear curdled in my stomach. It was my father, leading an army of Watchers against us.

How had it come to this?

And how was I even seeing this?

Suddenly, the scene cut to black, and I opened my eyes, back in the real world with Paige's face inches from mine.

A flutter rippled through my middle.

"What was that?" she whispered, her words feathering across my lips.

"I, I don't know." Shaking my head, I took a few steps back.

I needed to think, and she was too close for my brain to do anything but revel in her nearness.

"Was it a premonition or something?" She blinked and blinked at me like she'd seen the whole thing.

"I was hoping it was just a bad dream. But if you saw it, too, then maybe it really was a premonition." I ran my hand through my hair, pacing back and forth in the tiny park hideout. "How is this even possible?"

"Maybe the sapphire amplifies your powers. It is supposed to be the illuminating, all-seeing stone, right?" My flashlight bounced around the room, revealing her eyebrows scrunched in thought.

I stopped pacing and took two steps toward her. "Or maybe it's you who amplifies this new power you've given me."

"Maybe." She gnawed on her bottom lip, sending a flicker of flame curling inside me.

I drew her close, daring to kiss her again. She melted into my arms, but the scene threatened to return again.

And I couldn't have that. I didn't want to see my father marching on my safe haven, my refuge.

So I pulled back. "Either way. We have to tell the others."

"I know." She planted a quick peck on my lips, then turned and opened the door.

Even the gray sunlight was blinding after being in utter darkness for so long. Blinking, I let my eyes adjust.

Back to the real world and my real problems. At least I had someone by my side this time.

I reached for Paige's hand and squeezed, leading her out of the park. She'd given me so much, and yet somehow, it was all too much.

Chapter Seven

Paige

I couldn't believe what had just happened. Would Eric and I see visions every time we kissed? This was really starting to get weird.

We didn't speak as we walked through the park back to the subway. All of the beautiful sights of New York in the fall had lost their luster after that awful vision. Were the Watchers actually going to march against Shadowstone Academy?

Unreal.

On the entire subway trip back to headquarters, Eric was silent as a statue. But he still held my hand, even as his blue-green eyes clouded over.

Having your powers stripped away, then suddenly reappearing, would be a lot for anyone to handle.

And I was starting to figure out that Eric was the silent, brooding type.

Me? My leg bounced with the need to talk, to move, to do *something*. But I restrained myself.

His mercurial gaze flashed to my jiggling knee.

"What?" I shrugged one shoulder, shooting him a sly grin. "This is me giving you time to process."

"Oh, thanks." He puffed out a laughed, squeezing my hand as our stop was called.

We filed out at a less busy stop with a few other professionals in business suits, one of the benefits of hiding headquarters in the financial district.

Entering through the main entrance felt like a scene from a mundane version of *Get Smart*. The gadgets weren't as flashy—only an elevator with a secret code that sent you down instead of up—but still a hidden entrance housed in plain sight.

We entered the nondescript office building lobby, got in the elevator, and Eric punched in the special code of floor numbers to take us to the HQ reception area.

Still, nothing but silence. Eric must need a *looong* time to process.

The perky blonde receptionist greeted us with, "Captain McAllen asked you to reconvene in the training room."

"Yes, ma'am." I saluted her with a smile.

Her lips ruffled, then returned to normal.

Eric grunted something unintelligible and led the way down the three flights of stairs to the officer's training room.

Blue light flashed under the door, and I rushed into the room, fists clenched.

James and Felicia were on opposite sides of the training gym. Felicia shot blue light around the room, and James deflected with some kind of shield strapped to his arm.

Then he touched the stone around his neck and went invisible.

"Cool," Eric uttered his first word in thirty minutes.

An idea popped into my head. "Grab your sapphire, and see if we can find him."

"Good idea," Eric's eyes lit up for the first time since we were in that tiny little under-bridge hidey-hole.

I wrapped my hand around my amethyst, pouring my energy into it.

Suddenly, James popped back into existence, crouching across the room towards Felicia.

"Watch out!" Eric reached out one hand and sent a bolt of blue lightning zinging into my brother's shield.

"Hey, that's my brother you're shooting at." I elbowed Eric in the ribs, biting back a giggle.

He raised his eyebrows at me. "That's my sister he's sneaking up on."

"Relax, bro. I can see him too." Felicia held up the sapphire in her hand. "But at least I know my acting isn't half bad."

"Dang it." James dropped his invisibility cloak. "We're going to have to find a way around that or get multiple sacred stones so we can have more than one power."

"I like that idea." A smile stretched across Eric's chiseled face, and a dimple on his cheekbone popped out.

"Guys, no fair. You started without us." Lucy and Will burst into the room, laughing.

"Please. We were just waiting for you two lovebirds to return." James unstrapped his shield and motioned for all of us to gather around. "Okay, we've all had our little power field trips. Time to report in on your success. Felicia?"

She nodded her red ponytail swishing. "Since neither of us are Chosen Ones, anymore at least, we thought it would be fun to try out James' invisibility in Times Square."

"You didn't!" Lucy gasped, with a gleam in her eye.

Felicia's eyebrows arched, and her mouth pulled into a grin. "That's right. We totally went and bugged tourists and street vendors."

Now I couldn't stop the giggles from bursting out.

My brother's face lit up with glee. "I swiped people's hats, made an umbrella stand topple over into a crowd of tourists with matching shirts. It was epic."

"Epic, huh?" I shook my head as my giggles died off. "Sounds like the kind of pranks you used to pull when we were kids."

"Exactly." He pursed his lips at me. "Still epic."

We all laughed at that.

"At least we know the sacred stones work without a Chosen One present." Felicia's jaw twitched, making me wonder if she felt the same confusing swirl of emotions her brother seemed to be dealing with right now.

James clapped her on the shoulder. "Nice to know you've got your powers back, kid. And it's pretty cool actually having one myself now, like I wondered for eighteen years if I would."

Lucy reached out and squeezed his hand. "We decided to test out the extra powers theory. Would we have more powers with the stones? So we went back to Montrose, looking for trouble."

"You went all the way to the Bronx? My sister the rebel." James grinned at her.

"I'm sure that was all Will." I shot my future brother-in-law a smirk.

"Yeah, he threw down some money and Ubered us over." She shot me a knowing grin.

Will threw up his hands. "What? It's not like the campus is in operation anymore. It was completely desolate. The perfect place to see if Paige's stones heightened our Chosen One powers."

"Needless to say, it totally worked." Lucy glanced at her boyfriend, eyes dancing. "You should've seen this guy flinging lighting around the Nexis Tower."

"I bet that felt good," Felicia muttered.

"Yeah, it sure did," Will nodded, with the biggest smile I'd ever seen on his face. "What about you guys?"

Everyone turned to us, and I turned to Eric.

He cleared his throat. "I took her to the dead drop spot in Central Park. Figured we didn't need an audience for our power test."

"Good thinking." James bobbed his head at Eric.

He folded his arms over his massive chest. "I had the same thought you guys did. So I tested my powers out with Paige in the room, then had her walk a hundred yards away. And they still worked. No difference at all." His eyes went wide as his normally hard features softened in a look of awe.

"Wow. That's awesome, baby brother." Felicia reached out and punched his shoulder. "I know you had it as bad as I did when we lost our powers. Must feel nice to have them back."

"It sure does." His face split into a grin. Eric turned to me, and his grin faded. "I know I've already told you this, but you have no idea the amazing gift you've given us."

My throat clogged with some unnamed emotion.

Felicia took a few steps closer, her green eyes sparking. "My brother is right, Paige. You made an amazing choice to share your gifts when most people wouldn't have. We'll be forever grateful."

Aw, crap. Now tears welled up in my stupid eye sockets.

James edged around Felicia and took my hand. "As someone who's always wanted a Chosen One power and never had the chance, I'm going to side with Eric and Felicia. This choice you made is going to impact a lot of people. Maybe even change the outcome of the war that's coming. You should be really proud of yourself right now."

"I, uh ..." I couldn't choke out another word as a tear rolled down my cheek.

To me, it hadn't really felt like much of a choice. But now that I could see the people who were empowered by these new powers, I knew I'd made the right decision.

My brother's phone buzzed in his pocket, and he read the screen, eyebrows scrunching. "Uh, guys. We've got a problem. Looks like we're needed at Shadowstone right away."

"What? But we have four more days off." I couldn't keep the pathetic whine out of my voice.

James shook his head. "I know, but this conflict between the Guardians and the Watchers is escalating quickly. Apparently, there were a bunch of rogue Watcher attacks this afternoon all around the world. The Guardians are saying that it's coordinated and are calling for the Neutrality Committee to enforce the Nexis Ruby War Treaty sanctions. And they want the meeting on neutral territory."

"Great," Lucy muttered. "So much for peace."

James gulped, turning her way. "This might be our last chance to fight for peace. If the Neutrality Committee can't solve this, we might be headed for another war."

"I'm so sick of war." She huffed, stamping her foot into the rubber mat.

"I know, Tiger. We'll figure it out." Will wrapped one arm around her and pulled her close.

I wanted to reach for Eric, to have someone hold me close too. But I had no idea where we stood.

Just like the fate of the Two Societies, apparently.

Were we in a relationship or not? Eric and I definitely needed to talk. Soon.

Eric

I blinked, and somehow we were back in a private jet with a horde of Guardians flying across the Atlantic Ocean.

Could this day get any weirder?

Earlier today, I was playing with sapphires and testing out their powers. And now the sky was dark outside the plane window as I watched the girl of my dreams twitch in her sleep.

Was this really happening to me?

I ran my hand through my hair. How in the world could I be lucky enough to get my powers back and be about to start something with the secondborn Seer?

After the train wreck my life had been for the past few years, such happiness was almost too hard to imagine.

Paige McAllen could have anyone. The fact that she chose me, even let me kiss her....

Suddenly the air clogged in my lungs. I cleared my throat and inhaled a deep breath.

There was only one problem. I kept having crazy visions when I kissed Paige, but this last one was the craziest of all.

I smacked myself in the forehead.

"What? What's happening?" Paige jerked awake, her eyes all sleepy and her hair all over the place.

Still adorable.

"Nothing. Sorry, go back to sleep." I slipped an arm across her shoulders, drawing her close.

She smiled up at me. "Obviously, something's bothering you. People don't slap themselves for no reason."

That girl. "You're right. I just remembered something. We forgot to tell your brother and sister about that weird vision I had."

"You're right." She sat up straight, eyes darting around the cabin.

"Hey, it can wait." I patted her shoulder, scooching her closer.

She blinked those big mocha eyes at me. "But it was at Shadowstone. Shouldn't we tell them, just in case?"

I flinched at her words. "Yeah, but my dad was in it too. So maybe it wasn't a vision. Maybe it was a nightmare."

"Oh, that was your dad?" Those beautiful eyes widened. "I hadn't thought of that."

I ran my hand down her silky hair. "Why don't you go back to sleep? It's a long flight. I promise we'll tell Lucy and James as soon as we land. Okay?"

She shook her head. "I can't get back to sleep until you and I have a little talk. About us."

"Oh." I gulped, a lump of daggers rising in my throat.

Those big brown eyes lifted to meet mine, and my heart skipped a beat.

Then she fluttered those eyelashes at me. "I feel like we're in a relationship. You act like we're in a relationship. And yet, you've never asked me out or called me your girlfriend."

I froze at the word girlfriend. If my father knew I had a girlfriend, let alone the secondborn Seer, he'd find a way to hurt her. And I couldn't let that happen. But I cared about her too much to leave her hanging.

"It's complicated," I cleared my throat and leaned in, lowering my voice. "Maybe I haven't said the words out loud, but I want you to be my girlfriend. There's only one problem. My father."

As soon as the words left my lips, a cold shudder shivered down my neck.

"I see." She blinked, her hopeful smile falling.

I nuzzled her temple with my forehead, breathing in her sweet scent. "I can't let you get hurt because of me."

She pulled back, her expression unreadable. "Don't take this the wrong way, but I have a feeling your father is coming after me whether or not we're together. For some reason, Sherry Montrose is after me. Not my sister. Me. And I assume that extends to her henchmen too. Including your father."

My jaw fell open as I stared at this girl who was just as smart as she was beautiful. "You're probably right about that. But you don't know my father. If he knew we were together, he'd make it his personal mission to use you against me somehow. He's twisted."

Hatred spewed from my lips that I had to admit to her the truth. My fingers curled into fists.

Instead of rearing back like I feared, she leaned in closer to me, cupping my cheek. "I'm sorry you have a father like that. You deserve so much better."

"So do you," came my gut reaction.

Her hand moved to the back of my neck. "Did you ever stop to ask what I want? Maybe I don't care what kind of baggage you come with. Maybe I wanted to be your girlfriend anyway."

Something like hope buoyed inside my chest. I hadn't felt this feeling in so long, I almost couldn't believe it.

So I did something I never thought I'd do. I turned to her and laid my heart bare. "Do you want to be my girlfriend?"

Her eyes light up as her face split into a huge grin. "Yes, I want to be your girlfriend. Especially if that makes you my boyfriend."

"Okay then." I couldn't help but laugh.

"It's official then." She lifted her chin and closed her eyes.

Goosebumps tingled up my arms as I pressed my lips into hers, reveling in the soft warmth of her mouth against mine.

I didn't dare close my eyes. I couldn't let another crazy vision of my father at Shadowstone ruin the ecstasy of kissing my girlfriend.

Paige was probably right, and everyone needed to know about the vision—that my Dad might be preparing to march on Shadowstone Academy sometime in the near future. But part of me hoped it was just a nightmare, not a premonition.

I'd had plenty of nightmares about my father over the years.

Paige pulled back, her eyes fluttering open. "Thank you for being honest with me."

"I'm glad we cleared the air." I couldn't stop staring at her flushed cheeks.

"I'm sleepy now, boyfriend. Wake me when we get there." She rested her cheek against my chest, the warmth sending a tingle of electricity down my spine.

I rested my head on top of hers, letting myself drift off along with her.

An announcement blared over the speakers, and I jerked awake.

"... landing in fifteen minutes," the captain said.

I blinked, opening my eyes. Sure enough, shades of pink lit up the sky outside the plane window.

Strands of Paige's hair were stuck to my jaw. Great. So I'd fallen asleep and drooled on her. Hopefully, she wouldn't notice.

She slept soundly, her mouth half-open, as the flight attendant went around and checked the cabin.

I uncurled myself from Paige's exquisite warmth and tiptoed down the aisle toward James and Cosette, cuddled in the back of the cabin.

"Hey, man. Can I talk to you for a sec?" I gave him a tight smile.

"Sure, bud." He grinned back, a gesture that reminded me of his sister.

"I'll just go powder my nose." Cosette rose and slipped past me.

"Thanks," I whispered as she walked down the aisle, then I settled into her still-warm seat. "Listen, there's something I forgot to tell you about our trip to Central Park."

James jerked his head and squared his shoulders at me. "Is it something I should be worried about?"

"No, it's nothing like that." Heat sizzled across my cheeks. "Well, maybe a little. See, I had this vision about an army marching against us across the back field at Shadowstone."

"Oh, great." James dropped his head into his hands. "Did you see any faces you recognized?"

I grimaced. "Yes. My dad was leading the charge."

My heart pounded in my ears as I watched the range of emotion flicker across James' face. Disbelief, to anger, to something like determination.

"Dang it." He punched the seat in front of him. "I was afraid he was involved in these attacks."

"What? Really?" I choked out the words.

He pursed his lips together. "I'm afraid your dad has been on our radar for a while. Felicia told us about his six-year bid to climb the Watcher ladder. And his six-month absence recently. Power always comes at a price."

"Don't I know it." I raked my fingers through my hair again.

"If your vision was a premonition, it confirms our theory. We think he's making a play for section commander." James leaned in, lowering his voice. "But obviously, this stays between us. Okay?"

"Yes, sir." I nodded, pressing my lips together.

James clapped a hand on my shoulder. "Thanks for telling me. I know it wasn't easy."

"You bet." I rose to my feet and hurried back to my seat as the plane's landing gear screeched out.

I clicked my seatbelt closed as Paige opened her eyes.

She yawned and stretched, blinking those long lashes like crazy. "Are we there yet?"

"Almost." I tried to muster a grin, but it probably didn't work.

She tilted her head at me. "You're acting weird. What'd I miss?"

I chuckled under my breath. "You're too smart for your own good. I just told your brother about the vision."

"I see." She nodded, reaching for my hand. "That must've been hard."

I laced my fingers through hers. "It's better that he knows."

"Agreed." She squeezed my hand as the plane dipped sharply toward the runway.

With a roar, wind rushed past us outside as the plane landed with a jerk and braked to a stop.

I bit back the little bomb James just dropped on me. I promised not to tell anyone, and I needed to figure out how to protect the girl of my dreams from the father of my nightmares.

If my vision were truly a premonition, he would be coming for my girlfriend. I had no doubt of that.

Chapter Eight

Paige

When we stepped off the private jet, we were greeted by a team of shiny black Escalades waiting for us on the tarmac.

I leaned in and whispered in Eric's ear. "I could get used to this Guardian royal treatment."

"It probably won't last for long." His lips twisted into a rueful smirk.

What's that supposed to mean? Now probably wasn't the time to ask.

Everyone seemed on high alert here. Burly-looking bodyguards exited the fancy SUVs and opened the doors for us.

I was ushered into a car with my parents, James, Lucy, and Will. Eric and the rest of my friends were bundled into another SUV.

The regional airport was full of private jets and chauffeured cars heading in the same direction. An ominous feeling hung in the air that had nothing to do with the gray clouds skirting the mountain peaks. This private airport was closer to campus than Geneva, so we arrived at Shadowstone in twenty minutes despite the line of cars before and behind us trailing up the mountain roads like a line of black ants.

When our Escalade pulled into the circle drive at Shadowstone Academy, I was not prepared for the sight that greeted us.

I blinked and blinked at the crazy mass of people swarming the campus.

It was like the entire school came back from fall break early and brought their entire families with them.

Ten black SUVs lined the circle drive in front of the SA gates, but our driver paid no attention to the line. He doubled-parked right in front of the gate.

Dad swirled around from his seat in front of me. "Stay behind me, kiddo."

He leveled his gaze on me like he meant business and wouldn't look away until I bobbed my head in agreement.

Beads of sweat popped out on my palms, and I smoothed out the plane wrinkles from my black slouchy slacks and my pin-striped, boat-necked blouse. Now I couldn't help but wonder if I was dressed too casual for this emergency meeting of the Neutrality Committee.

Outside my tinted window, a swarm of people of all ages streamed through the gates, dressed in everything from business suits to ski gear. It was a madhouse on the Shadowstone Academy grounds.

The driver stepped out to open the side door, sending a cacophony of sounds screeching toward me.

Dad climbed out first, followed by Mom, then Will, Lucy, and finally little old me.

The noise around us faded as everyone in the crowd stopped to stare at us.

My jaw fell open, and I stumbled.

Lucy grabbed my arm. "Just keep walking. Don't say a word till we get there."

I opened my mouth to agree, then clamped my lips shut and nodded at my sister.

Following her lead, I stayed close to my parents as the crowd parted for us. All kinds of people stared at us, with all kinds of emotions on their faces.

Some scowled, squinting their eyes until I could practically see steam coming out of their ears.

Others stared at us in awe, as if my family was the key to some un-known solution to the whole conflict between the Watchers and the Guardians.

The driver was met by a squadron of black-clad bodyguards who led the way through the gates, around the crowded fountain, and toward the press of people headed for the assembly hall. Of course. Where else could my school house a crowd this crazy out of control?

Two groups of people faced off in front of the assembly hall—waving signs in English, French, German, and Spanish. And yelling at each other in all languages.

On the left, the group was dressed in various hues of blue with Watcher logos on their shirts, holding signs that read *No More Lies! Stop the Propaganda! Boycott Tyranny!*

On the right, another group clad in purple tones with Guardian symbols on their shirts held up signs that said *Stop the Attacks! Protect the Repositories!* and my favorite. *What are they looking for?*

Our band of bodyguards led us through the screaming crowd into the auditorium and straight down the center aisle to the front row of seats.

As of right now, the seats of the auditorium were empty. The room was eerily silent, like the calm before the storm. This place would be pandemonium soon.

The stage was set with two long black-clothed tables facing each other and little gold nameplates and microphones at each chair. A gleaming, mahogany podium was set up in center stage, with a microphone on top. I didn't envy whoever had to mediate this mess.

One of the bodyguards moved closer to my dad. "Commander McAllen, if you'll come with us, please, sir. Your family can sit here in the front row or wait backstage in the greenroom if they're uncomfortable."

"You guys have a greenroom?" Will cocked his head at me.

"I guess so." I shrugged, making a face at him. "I had no idea."

Dad pursed his lips, then turned to us. "It's up to you guys. Are you going to be okay out here on your own?"

"I'll protect them, sir." Will puffed out his chest and stood a little taller.

"Very well. I'll see you after this whole thing is over." He flicked his eyes at the guards and held two fingers at his side.

The head guard nodded and pointed at two of his men. They stayed behind with us while the remaining four guards escorted Dad backstage.

"Smooth, Dad," I whispered to his back. He seemed to be adapting well to his role as a section commander.

"So much security. This can't be good," Mom whispered as she took a seat in the middle of the front row.

Lucy and Will sat on her right, and I sat on her left. Her eyes glazed over as she fiddled with her purse, but the lack of color on her face had me worried.

The rest of our plane crew shuffled down the aisle toward us, most veering off to sit one row behind us. Eric kept walking and slipped into the seat beside me.

I fought the urge to grin. That would *so* not be appropriate right now.

"This is crazy," he mumbled in my ear.

"Tell me about it." I glanced over my shoulder as the auditorium filled with people.

Watchers sat on the left, and Guardians sat on the right as if there were clear delineations of sides.

I had a sinking feeling that Mom was right, for once. This couldn't be good.

I scanned the crowd for Stella, Brooke, and Owen. Finally, I found my roomie's face in the crowd, and I waved her forward. She was with both her parents, being escorted by a half dozen bodyguards like we were earlier.

One of the guards cleared his throat. "Commander Mamertus, we need to get you on stage now."

"Bye, Dad," Stella hugged her father around the neck.

He held a clear resemblance to Stella with his clipped-short dark hair and sharp eyes.

"Be careful, Manu." Stella's mom kissed her husband on the cheek.

"I will." He nodded and followed the bodyguards to his spot on the stage.

Stella turned to me, her dark eyes glistening. "Sorry, Paige. This is my mom, Dipti Mamertus."

"Nice to meet you, Mrs. Mamertus." I shook the petite woman's caramel hand.

She gave me a strained smile. "I'm sorry we have to meet under these circumstances. But I've heard many good things about you, dear."

Stella squeezed past her mom and wrapped me in a hug.

"I missed you, girl." I hugged my friend tight and sniffed away the sudden onset of tears.

Behind us, my mom was being the consummate hostess and making introductions to everyone. But I didn't care.

Right now, with the world on the verge of falling apart, I needed my bestie.

Stella arched back. "I was going to say I missed you too, but it's only been like four days."

"This is bollocks," Owen shook his head as he made his way toward us, light green eyes flashing.

Brooke wasn't two steps behind him, with Bryan and Abby in tow. "What a madhouse, huh? So much for fall break."

"It's so good to see you guys, even under the circumstances." I held out my arm and pulled all three of my friends into a group hug.

The lights dimmed, and I scurried back to my spot between Eric and Mom. But with my family and my friends' families, we pretty much took up the whole front row.

It was amazing how many families of the Two Societies were here.

Headmistress Militano walked up to the center stage podium and tapped the microphone. "Visitors, guests, and friends, you are most welcome at Shadowstone Academy. Please take your seats as this session of the Neutrality Committee is now open. Committee members, please take your seats."

Dad walked in with Stella's dad, Captain Beatrix, and Commander Mukebo in tow, both officers I'd met once or twice before, during my brief stint in the Seer's Army during the Nexis Ruby War. Which, to be frank, wasn't all that long ago.

The headmistress cleared her throat. "Shadowstone Academy, please welcome the Guardian delegation of the Neutrality Committee. Commander McAllen of Sector One." A roar went up from the right side of the auditorium, namely the American Guardians. "Commander Beatrix of Sector Two." A cheer erupted from the European Guardians and most of the Guardian-affiliated academy students.

"I can't believe they made her a commander," Lucy hissed from two seats down.

I'd almost forgotten Beatrix was only a captain the last time I met her.

"Commander Mukebo of Sector Three." A tribal drumbeat rang out from the African Guardians.

"And Commander Mamertus of Sector Four." Stella and her family cheered, along with the entire Asian contingent of the Guardians.

As the cheers died down, Militano continued. "Also, welcome two representatives from the Guardian Council: Raymond Harlixton and Isabella Roulette."

"I forgot Professor Harlixton was on the council," Eric whispered in my ear.

I nodded, not daring to speak right now as the left side of the auditorium burst out with boos and jeers.

I studied the ancient, craggy face of the other member of the Guardian Council. She looked familiar, but I couldn't place her.

"Shadowstone Academy, please welcome your Guardian delegation of the Neutrality Committee."

Applause erupted once again from the right side of the auditorium as the Guardians rose in a standing ovation, cheering and whistling.

I felt no need to join the pandemonium. Tension reigned heavy in the room already.

Headmistress Militano waited until the din died down. "And from the Watcher delegation, please welcome Commander Sherry Montrose of Sector One." More cheers, this time from the blue-clad Watchers on my left. "Commander Maxwell Morales of Sector Two." Eric cringed beside me, and someone exhaled loudly from behind us, probably Felicia.

Maxwell Morales was the spitting image of Eric with graying reddish hair and glinting green eyes that glared in our direction.

I grabbed Eric's hand and squeezed. It was awful to see a handsome face wasted on an evil heart.

Militano called out another name. "Commander Cyrus Canaan of Sector Three." The guy glared at the headmistress like she'd mispronounced his name, his eyes narrowing much like my brother. I guess he was James' bio dad after all.

"He should've been the sector two commander instead of my father," Eric whispered in my ear. "I don't know why my dad wanted to be the European commander when Cyrus was next in line."

"That explains why he looks so pissed." I glanced at Cyrus as the Watchers cheered for the commander of Sector Four, whose name I missed.

Then, the Watcher Corps Council members were introduced, a stern-looking old lady with a cane and a smiling Black man.

A final cheer burst from the Watcher half of the room.

Militano held up her hands from behind her podium. "Please, settle down. This emergency meeting of the Neutrality Committee is now in session."

With the crash of a gavel, the real chaos began.

The headmistress paused for effect, then spoke into the mic. "We're here today to address the very serious charges of a breach of the Nexis Ruby War sanctions initiated by this Neutrality Committee at its inception six months ago. The findings of this committee today could lead to criminal charges leading to a tribunal for the parties involved. If charges are not resolved, another war could be at hand. Please proceed with that level of gravity in mind."

Headmistress Militano glanced at every member of the Neutrality Committee, waiting until each nodded in agreement. When her head turned to Sherry Montrose, the commander hesitated.

A hush fell over the crowd as everyone waited with bated breath. Then Commander Montrose nodded, and the headmistress moved on. That was when the murmuring started.

Obviously, the lady needed a little too much attention.

After Militano finished her acknowledgments, she banged her gavel again. "Who brings these charges to the committee?"

Professor Harlixton raised his hand.

The headmistress nodded at him. "The chair recognizes Professor Raymond Harlixton."

"Thank you, headmistress." Harlixton nodded at her. "The Order of the Guardians is charging the Watcher Corps with a breach of the Nexis Ruby War sanctions tantamount to an act of war. On the nights of October 21st and 22nd, twelve coordinated were perpetrated against sacred Guardian repositories around the globe at the same time. Evidence pertaining to the location of the four Guardian Amethysts was stolen, or theft was attempted."

A gasp erupted from the Guardian side with murmurs of protest.

"Twelve attacks, simultaneously?" I gaped and turned to Eric. "Did you know about this?"

He shook his head. "That was the day we flew into JFK."

My jaw dropped, and I turned to Mom.

"It's true, honey." She patted my knee and turned to face front.

Sherry Montrose raised her hand and was recognized by Militano before speaking.

"While an unfortunate event, these burglaries cannot be blamed on the Watcher Corps at large without a shred of evidence." She fluffed out her frizzy red curls and crossed her arms over her ample chest.

"Fortunately, I have plenty of evidence right here." Harlixton held up a folder and waited to be acknowledged.

"Professor, please pass your evidence to the chair to be shown to the committee at large." Headmistress Militano received the file and put the first paper on a light table that projected the document on a pull-down screen behind her. "Please tell us exactly what we're looking at."

"Certainly." Harlixton rose to his feet. "Page one is a list of those captured in the act of breaking and entering on sanctioned Guardian property."

"Oooooh." The crowd murmured.

The professor's lips twitched at the crowd's reaction. "Page two is a record confirming that every single man and woman captured is registered as either a former Nexis member admitted into the Watcher Corps recently or a full-fledged Watcher listed in good standing."

Silence fell on the entire room.

"You can't expect people to believe this—"

Ms. Militano held up one hand. "Commander Montrose, you are out of order. Please sit down and wait your turn to speak."

Sherry clamped her mouth shut and sat down.

"Please proceed, professor."

He nodded. "The rest of these papers are detailed interrogation proceedings outlining how half of those arrested confessed to taking their orders directly from their local Watcher organization. Under the direction of their respective commanders."

With a triumphant grin, Harlixton returned to his seat.

Whispers and murmurs turned into a roar of outcry at this new evidence.

Militano banged her gavel. "I will have order in this auditorium. Commander Montrose, you may now respond."

"Thank you." She dipped her head with an evil glare and rose to her feet. "All of this so-called evidence is propaganda, put forth by the

Guardians to disband the Neutrality Committee and merge the two remaining societies into one society under complete Guardian rule."

The room erupted in yells of protest from both sides.

After a few gavel bangs, Militano said, "Do you have any evidence to support your claims at this time, Commander Montrose?"

"Nothing concrete because I am not willing to fabricate names on a list or arrest reports." She glanced at the list of names on the wall and scoffed.

Snickers filtered through the Watcher side of the auditorium.

Headmistress Militano narrowed her eyes and Commander Montrose. "Since that is the case, please constrain your remarks to address the evidence placed into consideration by Professor Harlixton."

"Certainly." Sherry nodded at the headmistress. "If this alleged evidence put forth by the Guardians is true, what kind of interrogation procedures were followed?"

This time, Isabelle Roullette rose and pointed her shriveled hand at the headmistress. "I believe you asked the commander to address the Guardian charges, not make accusations of her own."

The headmistress banged her gavel. "Please refrain from speaking out of turn, Councilor Roulette. However, your assertion is correct." She turned to address the evil snake Sherry once again. "Commander Montrose, please address the evidence, or you will be removed from these proceedings. How do you plead to the charge of treason against the Neutrality Committee by ordering attacks on Guardian repositories on the nights in question?"

Sherry blanched, swallowing visibly. "The Watcher Corps pleads not guilty."

A cheer erupted from the Watcher crowd, followed by applause.

The headmistress banged her gavel to no avail.

Commander Montrose raised her arms, and the crowd quieted in an instant. "Under the Nexis Ruby War Treaty sanctions, all prisoners are to be treated humanely, without torture. If those captured claim to be Watchers, this committee deserves to know if they were treated fairly."

Militano turned to the right. "Professor, or anyone on the Guardian panel. Your rebuttal?"

"I find it interesting that even though the Watchers claim no affiliation with the members of their organization who carried out these attacks, the Section One Commander of the Watchers is still somehow concerned with their treatment." Harlixton's grin said he was prepared for Sherry's smear tactics.

Chuckles reverberated like a wave through the Guardian side of the room.

Harlixton raised one hand. "However, I have photo and video evidence of one such interrogation that also gives evidence of the real charges at hand."

He passed the headmistress a flash drive, and she brought the videos up on the screen.

Security cam footage showed a team of six attempting to break into a church, only to be captured by waiting Guardians. The tape switched to interrogations, where the prisoner admitted he was just following orders. When asked whose order, he uttered the name, Commander Canaan.

A gasp went up around the room.

"That doesn't prove anything," Cyrus Canaan rose to his feet, going all red-faced. "Someone is trying to frame me. This prisoner could've just as easily said Commander McAllen's name. I've never seen this man in my life. You have no documented proof I ordered him and his team to do anything."

The headmistress banged her gavel. "Mr. Canaan, please sit down, or you will be removed from this proceeding. Do you understand?"

"Yes, ma'am." Cyrus sat back down in his seat, fuming.

For some reason, Maxwell's lips twitched like he wanted to smile. Beside me, Eric shuddered.

"I'm afraid this file and recordings, though circumstantial, must be entered into evidence."

"Is treason the charge under consideration?" Maxwell Morales piped in.

Militano scratched her chin. "Several violations of the Nexis Ruby War Treaty sanctions are being considered."

"That answers that." He rolled his eyes and sat back down.

Pockets of laughter bubbled from the Watcher side of the room.

Harlixton raised his hand again. "I have one more charge to address today. Before this coordinated attack even occurred, there was an attack on a student here at Shadowstone Academy."

I slunk down in my seat, the heat rising to my cheeks. "Oh, great. Here we go."

CHAPTER NINE

PAIGE

Rivers of icy fear dribbled down my throat as Professor Harlixton went through the attack in excruciating detail—like how Rocco stormed my room, tied up my roommate, and dragged me to the old Nexis Headquarters on campus.

Stella gasped from her seat beside Eric. He slid an arm around my shoulder, pulling me closer. I reached across him and grabbed my roomie's hand.

She'd been through the same horror I'd gone through. Her eyes glistened like I'm sure my eyes were right now. Sure enough, I dabbed at the moisture pooling in the corners of my eyes.

Memories flashed through my mind of that horrible night, waking up in a dark room, Rocco's sneering face, and the sense of powerlessness that I'd felt. In that moment, I understood for a second why Eric risked his life to get his powers back. Needles stabbed at my eyes, but I rubbed them away and pushed back the memories. For now.

Harlixton was still outlining the details of that night. My fingers curled into fists. I so wanted to punch his stupid face right now.

"Then, with the help of Nexis work team members and a spy planted on campus, Rocco Rodriguez attempted to do a transference spell on the Watcher's Sapphire."

A collective gasp resonated around the room.

"Is that true?" someone murmured behind me, but I didn't turn to acknowledge their curiosity.

"Then Rocco Rodriguez claimed that he was working under the orders of Sherilyn Montrose." Harlixton paused as more gasps erupted. "He also claimed to be her son."

"That's preposterous." Sherry slammed her fists into the table. "Don't you think I'd know if I had a son?"

Laughter bubbled up from the crowd.

"I think you know exactly what you're doing, Sherry Montrose. The facts are the facts. This Rocco Rodriguez infiltrated the Shadowstone Academy campus, working with another member of the Watcher Corps, Veronica Kingsley. Do you really expect us to believe that these twelve simultaneously coordinated attacks, plus an attack on the secondborn Seer, were all just a giant made-up lie? Especially, when multiple culprits caught at the scene claim the attacks were orchestrated by Watcher officials?"

The entire Watcher side of the stage rose to their feet.

"Yes, Professor Harlixton." Sherry folded her arms and cocked her head at him. "All of your accusations are trumped-up charges perpetrated by the Guardians as propaganda."

Harlixton rolled his eyes. "Are you really going to play that game, Sherry? Denial is not a good look for you."

More laughter, mostly from the Guardian camp this time.

"Enough." The headmistress banged her gavel. "Commander Montrose, would you like to address the charges of attacking minors on neutral campus grounds?"

Finally, the headmistress had the decency to restore order to the back and forth bickering that had my fingernails digging into my palms.

"Certainly." Sherry smoothed her hands down her suit jacket. "I have no idea who this Rocco person, is or how he got his hands on one of our sacred stones, but I absolutely deny this outlandish claim. Did you even perform a DNA test?"

Harlixton snorted. Like, actually snorted. "I find it outlandish that you are a proponent of the Nexis Ruby War Treaty sanctions of prisoner treatment, yet you advocate for breaking them now that's it's convenient for you."

More giggles and protests circled the room until the headmistress pounded her gavel again.

"Professor Harlixton, I assume you have evidence of these charges of kidnapping and treason." Militano held out her hand with a scowl.

"Of course, Headmistress." He produced another folder from his briefcase. "The testimonies of all involved are there, but I think we can all agree that a live testimony in this setting wouldn't be appropriate. Especially as it involves minors."

Headmistress Militano nodded. "Of course. The committee will review the and rule on this thirteenth charge in a private session."

"Thank you." Harlixton returned to his seat, glancing my way again.

I swallowed back the acid in my throat and sat up straighter in my chair. At least he had left out the best part of that fateful night—how I'd been given the gift to bestow powers into sacred stones and beaten Rocco and his goons with the help of my friends.

I guess that would be our little secret, at least until it was time to reveal a fully-trained Sacred Stone Squad.

Mom reached over and squeezed my hand. "I'm sorry you had to go through that again, sweetie."

"Thanks. Me too" was all I could manage.

The Old Lady Watcher raised her hand. "As of this moment, this meeting of the Neutrality Committee has been uncalled for. It seems more like a forum for the Guardians to make false claims and air their grievances."

Headmistress jerked her head at the woman. "Lives were put in jeopardy on thirteen separate occasions in the past few weeks. This type of behavior cannot go unchecked, and it's exactly why the Neutrality Committee was formed. We have every reason to discuss who is responsible for these attacks and bring them to justice."

The woman nodded. "Noted. But I assure you that the Watcher Corps Council never authorized such attacks. And you may have our detailed meeting notes and recordings to prove it."

For once in the past hour, the whole room was silent for a minute.

What would the Neutrality Committee find if they searched the Watcher Corps' records?

Headmistress Militano bobbed her head. "Thank you for your cooperation in this matter. However, if the investigation proves your claims correct, then we may need another session to discuss the existence of a rogue organization masquerading as Watcher agents."

"Yes, indeed." The Watcher Council Lady scratched her chin. "That is most troubling to me."

Professor Harlixton raised his hand. "To prove this theory correct, we may need evidence from more than just council meetings. Section sessions may need to be included as well. Would you submit that level of transparency?"

The older woman pursed her lips, glanced at the other council member, then nodded. "Yes, Raymond. That can be arranged."

Clapping erupted around the room, and my heart buoyed at the thought. Maybe my downfall wasn't being plotted by an entire organization. Just your average power-hungry lady looking to subvert the system.

Commander Montrose looked a little green around the gills for the first time. She sat down with a thud, then leaned over and whispered something into Maxwell's ear.

Yet, I had no doubt in my mind that Sherry Montrose was more than just your average social climber. She just completely denied her own son, then spun the conversation around in circles until you couldn't see straight. She was definitely up to something. And I had a feeling she was making a bid to take over the Watcher Corps.

Headmistress Militano banged her gavel for the twenty-seventh time. "At this time, the Neutrality Committee is unable to decide on the charges at hand without further evidence."

Groans circled the auditorium.

Another bang of the gavel. "The thirteen counts of treason against the Nexis Ruby War sanctions are still open until further evidence can be presented. Once that evidence is received, a private session will be held to determine its validity. If no one else has anything to add, that concludes the twenty-first session of the Neutrality Committee."

She paused, scanning both sides of the stage for objections. No one from either side made a move or uttered a word.

"Excellent. Meeting adjourned."

The crowd rose to their feet, murmuring and complaining about the proceedings. The members of the Watchers and the Guardian delegations were whisked away by bodyguards even as both sides glared daggers at each other.

Yeah, this was so *not* over. Rocco Rodriguez, or Montrose, or whatever his name was, wouldn't get away with kidnapping my roomie and me. We'd make him pay one way or another.

Everyone rose to their feet, filing out of the room and glomming up the aisles.

I ground my teeth together, fuming to myself.

Mom tugged on my hand. "Wait a minute, Paige. Let's wait for your dad, and then we'll both walk you back to your dorm."

"Sure, Mom." I looped an arm around her waist and drew her into a side hug.

I'd almost forgotten she was there, probably stressing as much as me. Or more.

She plastered on a smile and patted my head, but her hand trembled. It must've been hard hearing about the Rocco incident in such detail.

I know it wasn't fun for me.

Stella's mom walked over to mine, and they started chatting.

Stella, Owen, and Brooke crowded around Eric and me.

"So, that was nuts, right?" Brooke's big brown eyes were almost as wide as her black-rimmed glasses.

Owen elbowed her in the side. "Hush up. Can't you see our girl is freaked out?"

I waved at my feuding friends. "Hey, guys. I'm right here. And I appreciate your concern. But I'm okay."

"My strong girl," Eric purred in my ear and grabbed my hand.

This time, I didn't mind his protective instincts. Had he just called me his girl in front of everyone? I guess the secret was out now.

Owen's eyes flashed toward me, zeroing in on Eric's hand.

"I'm just glad we're back at Shadowstone. Together." Stella leaned in with a smirk. "I'm ready to get started with our little project."

She lowered her voice on the last two words, making me smile.

"C'mon, guys. Let's get you settled back at the dorms." Dad had a fake grin on his face, just like Mom.

Yeah, not fooling anyone.

I didn't envy his job, but I was with Stella. Things were going down, and I wanted to be ready for the next fight.

Let the training begin.

Paige

Somehow we all walked back to my dorm as one large group, including my friends and both Stella's and my parents.

Stella's parents huddled in the bay window seat, looking cozy and cute. Stella perched on the edge of the couch where me, Eric, and Lucy sat, with Will perching on her end. My mom sat in the armchair beside Lucy, with my dad presiding over her. While Felicia and Sed somehow shared a one-person armchair, Owen and Brooke sat on the fluffy rug at my feet. I made a mental note to tease them later.

Yeah, fourteen people was a little much for our common room. But we all knew we needed to figure out a plan before the Watchers attacked again.

James stood in front of the TV, commanding attention. "After that crazy circus of a Neutrality Committee meeting, it's definitely time to start the Sacred Stone Squad here at Shadowstone."

Stella leaned in and whispered in my ear. "Sweet. They're taking my suggestion."

I held back a laugh that sounded more like a snort.

My brother glared at me. "Dad and I will be talking with the headmistress tonight about instituting some changes to your course schedule as soon as classes resume."

Stella's dad held up one hand. "If you wouldn't mind, I'd like to be a part of that discussion. Especially as it concerns my only daughter."

"Dad," Stella rolled her eyes, "you act like I don't have three brothers."

"Daughters are special, especially to fathers." Stella's mom spoke in her lilting Indian accent.

Stella's cheeks pinked up, and I bit back another laugh.

"Of course, Commander Mamertus." My dad nodded at his counterpart. "We would be happy to include you in our plans."

"Thank you." The man bowed to Dad.

Brooke rubbed her hands together. "Does this mean we get our own classes and stuff?"

"Possibly. We'll have to see what the headmistress can do with your schedules." Dad nodded at James to continue.

James gestured to Dad. "We've been discussing the best way to proceed. At the bare minimum, you'll need an after-school training regimen."

"Even though we have a few days left in fall break, we could start training now. You know, get a head start." My sister's eyes glinted as she grinned like the Cheshire cat.

Yeah, she definitely had plans for the Sacred Stone Squad.

Suddenly an idea popped into my head. "What if we just had private group sessions of some of our regular classes?"

James furrowed his brows at me. "What do you mean?"

My lips curled up. "Like, instead of regular Combat Training 101, we could have SSS Combat Training. Instead of Sacred Stones and Their Uses, we'd have an AP version of the class just for us."

"That's a great idea, Paige." Dad clapped his hands together. "Keeping the same or similar classes on your schedules would help smooth things over with the headmistress and the school board. Then it would just be a matter of rearranging all of your schedules to match."

"Nice work, lil sis." James shot me his famous goofy grin. "The three of us will get started on that. Lucy, will you head up the first combat training session, like you suggested?"

"Absolutely." Her grin was as wide as our brother's.

For some reason, that hit me hard. Sure, they'd loved my idea about the classes. But Lucy got to head up the training program? I guess that part was her idea. And maybe it'd just be until fall break was over. After all, Lucy had her own classes to attend.

Ugh. I wanted to punch myself. I hadn't been jealous of my sister in ages. Now was not the time to let that flaw rear its ugly head.

"Let's start tomorrow, bright and early. Say eight a.m.?" Lucy glanced around the room, getting nods from everyone. "We did a little test run in New York, and we'd be happy to share the results with you."

James sucked in a breath. "There's only one problem. I don't know if we have enough sacred stone pieces to go around."

Dad tapped his chin. "That could be an issue. And I doubt Militano will want to loan her stash after what happened to the last batch."

Everyone turned to Eric.

He held his hands up in surrender. "Hey, that wasn't me. Anything I touched, I put back. Remember?"

Everyone nodded and grumbled, and Eric lowered his arms.

"Wait, that was you last semester with the dark magic in the gym, wasn't it?" Owen's light green eyes narrowed at him.

"Come on, guys, can we please let that one go already? It was a stupid mistake, and I'll never try it again. I promise." Eric hung his head.

"That's right. Especially not since you have your powers back." Felicia mussed up her brother's auburn mop.

"I'm sure training tomorrow will be interesting." Brooke nodded in my direction.

I couldn't agree more.

CHAPTER TEN

I wanted to hang out in Paige's room forever, but eventually the sun set behind the mountain peaks outside, and people started trickling to their own rooms.

Plus, Mr. McAllen stared daggers at me like he knew all I wanted to do right now was make out with their daughter.

"Ready, bro?" My sister and Sed edged toward the door.

I squeezed Paige's hand and kissed her on the cheek. "I'll call you later."

"You better." She smiled up at me.

I didn't have to glance back to know Paige's dad was glaring at me as I left.

Bits of melted snow dotted the campus as the cold night air bit at my cheeks.

Sed's phone trilled from his pocket and he rushed to answer it. "Hey, Boss. What's up?"

We waited for a few seconds, but then he waved us on.

He leaned in to give Felicia a quick kiss on the cheek. "James has some new intel he wants me to check out. I'll meet you back at Eric's dorm as soon as I can."

"Fine." She gave him a tight smile. "I'll keep an eye on these two."

He flashed her a grin, then headed toward the caf. Or more likely, the secret underground Guardian Headquarters beneath the school cafeteria.

Sometimes I wasn't sure whether I was at an elite academy or a military institution.

Felicia walked with me back to my dorm, with Owen tagging along behind us.

I edged toward my sister. "How long are you and Sed staying in Switzerland?"

Her eyes flashed, and her lips twitched. "Ready to get rid of me so soon?"

"Just wondering where you're staying is all." I let my gaze wander toward the night sky overhead as the moon appeared from behind a blackish mountain peak.

She leaned in and bumped my shoulder. "Always the protective little brother. I'm your big sis. I should be looking out for you."

I had to smile at that. "Every since I grew a foot taller than you, I've been the one in the protector role."

"You are not a foot taller than me, right Owen?" Felicia tossed a grin at him.

"Definitely not a foot. But I know you Americans love to exaggerate." Owen smiled at my sister, then scowled at me.

Did the wind suddenly get chillier?

We reached the dorm, and Owen waved goodbye as he disappeared down the first floor hall.

Felicia and I got in the elevator for the third floor.

As soon as the doors closed, I turned to face her. "What's that guy's problem anyway? He's always so rude to me."

"Ha!" Felicia snorted out a laugh, and I backed up a few inches. Then her face fell. "You really don't know?"

I squinted at my crazy sister. "If I knew, do you think I'd be asking you?"

"Good point." Her eyes flew open. "You seriously have no idea, do you? That boy is jealous of you."

"Jealous?" I reared back, my shoulders hitting the metal bar on the back wall. "Of me? Why? He's going to get his own power soon enough."

She busted out laughing, keeling over in a fit of giggles as the bell dinged. "He likes Paige, you idiot."

My jaw fell open at the bomb she'd just dropped, but she walked right out of the elevator like it was no big deal.

"You're completely clueless sometimes, little bro." She flipped her hair over her shoulder and sauntered down the hall like she owned the place.

Blinking at her back, I trailed her to the room and unlocked the door.

The moment we were inside, I shut the door behind us. I had so many more questions about this insane Owen revelation.

But all my questions died a bitter death on my tongue as an all-too-familiar figure rose from the couch.

"I've been waiting for you." The sinister tone in my father's voice sent a chill down my spine.

Without a second thought, I took two steps in front of Felicia and put my sister behind me.

"What do you want?" Sometimes it was better to rip off the Band-Aid with this guy.

He steepled his fingers in front of his chest. "Straight to the point. I like this change in you, son."

I cringed at the word. I could feel my sister shudder behind me.

"Don't worry. I'm not staying. I've got too much work to do." He drilled me with his black-eyed stare, willing me to crack.

But I didn't flinch. I held my ground and jutted out my jaw, even though my heart was pumping a thousand miles a minute.

"Something big is coming, and I'll want you by my side. Both of you." His gaze flicked to Felicia, then landed on me again.

My fingers curled into fists at my sides. "I wouldn't count on us for much help." I spat out the words.

His scowl curled into a grin. "Believe me, son, now that I have command of this entire section, I have ways of soliciting your help, whether you like them or not."

I bit my tongue, and Felicia sucked in a gasp. With my father, sometimes it was best not to say a word. Why did I keep forgetting that?

Stupid, stupid boy.

He took two steps closer, and he raised his upturned palm, then curled his fingers into a fist. "Shadowstone is mine. It's just a matter of time now. And when the time comes, you better make sure you're on the right side."

With a final glare, he brushed past us in three strides and slammed the door behind him.

Only then did I allow myself to move a muscle.

Felicia slumped into my side. "I hate that guy," she ground out through clenched teeth.

"Me too." I looped an arm around her shoulder. "It sounds to me like he wants to take over the school."

She nodded against my shoulder, trembling like a leaf. "And probably use it for Watcher War Command Central."

I hugged her close. "We can't let him win."

"I know." She straightened, wiping her eyes. "This settles it. Sedrick and I are taking over your crazy old roommates' room."

My turn to bob my head. "Normally, I'd hate the idea of shacking up with my sister and her boyfriend. But it's probably for the best."

"I think so, baby bro." She pulled out her phone and walked into Rocco's old room.

I reached for my phone to text Paige, then froze. Every muscle in my body tensed. Fear curled its nasty claws around my heart, squeezing it in a vice grip.

It was my turn to tremble like a leaf, at least on the inside.

Now I knew exactly what my father meant when he said he had ways of soliciting my help, whether I liked them or not.

Paige.

If I kept seeing her, if my father even caught a whiff of how much that girl meant to me, she'd never see the light of day again.

A hot lump formed in my throat. My father hurt everyone I loved. Why would he stop with Paige? Especially now that he had more power than ever?

Yep, it was official. We were all doomed.

Paige

My alarm blared from my nightstand, and I rolled over and slammed the snooze button.

Why did my sister always insist on early morning training sessions? It wasn't like we were pro athletes or anything. But our lives may be on the line at some point. Maybe I should start taking this stuff seriously.

That thought had my eyes popping open right as my sister burst through the door. Why had I ever given her a key?

"Get up, lazy bum. We're meeting at the gym in twenty minutes." She laughed a little under her breath, giving her ruse away.

I glanced at the clock. Only seven a.m. I still had an hour.

"Nice try, sis. I'm not that out of it." I threw off the covers and stuck my feet into my slippers.

Padding to my bathroom, I splashed some water on my face and eyed the shower. But there was no use in getting all clean and pretty if I was just going to get sweaty in an hour.

I combed my hair into a high ponytail and slipped on my cutest workout gear. I also dabbed on a little bit of tinted moisturizer and some lip gloss for good measure. You know, in case Eric needed a private training session again.

Maybe he'd press me up against a wall and kiss me senseless again like he had in Central Park. Just the thought made my toes curl.

I trudged into our little living room where Stella was waiting with the biggest grin.

"Here you go, sleepyhead." Stella handed me a to-go cup of coffee and a pastry. "I can't wait to get my new power."

I chomped into the buttery goodness. "Did you know you're the best friend ever?"

She grinned at me. "Of course, I know. But you can thank my mom for the food. She's the one who's always prepared."

I tilted my head at her. "Oh, are your parents coming to training too?"

She shook her head. "I don't think so. I'm pretty sure they have meetings of their own today before they head back to India."

"Oh, okay. Cuz it'd be kinda cool to see your mom and my mom kicking butt." I devoured the rest of the pastry as we walked down the hall.

Lucy's eyes gleamed. "We're actually going to be early for a change. Look at you, lil sis. All grown up." She mock-dabbed at her eyes.

I held back a grin. I couldn't let my sister think that kind of behavior was acceptable.

Last night, we'd all agreed to meet at the auxiliary gym and use the less-obvious training facilities there.

But it was so early that I'd forgotten. Now my fancy Nike training shoes were getting all cold and wet from the snow as we trudged across the back field.

"I should've worn my combat boots," I whispered to Stella.

"I know. Tell me about out it." She was gingerly hopping through the snow, just like me.

"I'll race you there," I raised my eyebrows at her.

She arched hers back. It was on.

Eric and Owen were a few paces ahead of us, with Felicia and Sedrick not too far behind.

This would be an interesting crew today.

We picked up the pace to catch up with them, not caring that Lucy and Felicia were snickering to themselves behind my back.

"Morning." I bumped Eric in the hip.

"Morning." He was back to one-word sentences and not looking at me.

"Hey, Paige. Looking good as always." Owen's green eyes flashed at me.

Eric bent down to tie his shoe, and Owen slid closer to me.

I glanced back at Eric, but he just waved me on.

I rolled my eyes. This hot and cold game was getting old. Why was that boy always so much drama?

Owen bounced on the balls of his feet. "I can't wait to get my sacred stone. I wonder what kind of awesome power you'll give me."

I couldn't help but smile at his antics. "Don't worry. You get to choose."

"Are you serious? You're the best." He reached out and wrapped me in a hug.

"Of course." I tried to shrug him off, but I guess getting to choose your new superpower was kind of a big deal.

I patted Owen on the back until he released me with a huge grin on his face. We all walked down the hall together.

A sudden chill slithered down my spine when we got to the basketball gym.

I glanced back at Eric. This was the same place where I'd seen that horrifying vision of him almost dying. He shot me a rueful smirk. He better be glad I saved his sorry butt—and that he didn't have to see what I saw that first day on campus.

Smacking sounds reverberated down the hall, pulling me away from the dreaded basketball courts and into another section of the gym.

Good thing too. It'd be really hard not to see the evil shadows swirling around Eric and tearing him apart if we had to train in there.

Maybe having the Sacred Stone Squad training sessions in this gym would help me put that old premonition to rest. After all, I'd stopped it from coming true.

Lucy led the way to the training room, where James and Will had set up what looked like a sparring obstacle course.

"Hey guys, welcome." James brushed off his palms and motioned us forward. "We're still working out the details of the classes, but you should have your new schedules before you start classes again next week."

"Way to go, Paige." Owen turned around and high-fived me. "That was such a great idea. I'm just glad they listened to reason. And now we get more classes together."

Stella smiled at me from my left side, her lips twisted in a strange look. I'd have to ask her later what that meant.

This was it. I was about to be put on display, front and center.

My brother cleared his throat. "After careful consideration, the Guardians have decided to put Lucy McAllen in charge of the Sacred Stone Squad here at Shadowstone Academy. I have no doubt that her wealth of experience in the Nexis Ruby War will be translated to great leadership for the SSS."

A smattering of applause popped up all around me, but I could feel everyone turn to me.

I had no words. My jaw just dropped open.

It felt like I'd just been punched in the gut. Angel had given *me* the power to share these gifts with people of *my* choosing. So why was my sister suddenly in charge of the squad?

She always beat me at everything. This time, it was just too much.

Stella folded her arms across her chest. "I'm sure Lucy has great experience, and I know she's the Seer and all, but Paige is the one with the power. Why isn't she in charge?"

I tried to smile at my sweet bestie, but my lips just wobbled.

The room started spinning around me.

This can't be happening.

Lucy's face fell as she turned to me. "I'm sorry, sis. It's not like I asked for this job or anything. But I know what it's like to be forced into the middle of a war at such a young age. And I want to save you that. If I can."

"That's a big *if* at this point," Eric spat out, eyes narrowed.

James rushed up to me and took both hands in his. "I'm sorry, Paige. If anything, I thought you'd be relieved."

"Maybe. But you never asked me. My angel gave me this power, not anyone else." Pressure welled at the back of my eyes, but I scrunched up my face to keep the tears at bay. "Sure, it's a big responsibility. But you both had similar responsibilities at my age, and you both turned out better for it. Did you ever think I wanted that opportunity?"

James hung his head. "No. I didn't think that. I didn't even think to ask. I really am sorry."

"I know." I sniffed as the tears threatened to erupt.

I couldn't take it anymore. I raced out of the room. I couldn't let them see me cry.

Chapter Eleven

Paige

I raced into the nearest locker room hoping it was the girl's locker room and plopped onto the first bench I found. Salty water dribbled into my mouth, and I swiped at the stupid tears.

My heart cracked. For what seemed like the millionth time, someone chose my sister over me. Why did I care so much about recognition? Why couldn't I sit on the sidelines and happily dole out powers like a good little girl?

"Because you're not a shy girl who likes to hide in the shadows." Stella tiptoed across the concrete floor in her silent, stealth sneakers.

"Oh, I guess that was out loud." I covered my mouth with my hand, staring up at her.

"Yep." She eased down beside me. "Besides, you're a boss. And don't go thinking you're not just because your sister is technically in charge of the squad. Think of all the headaches she'll have to deal with."

"And the stupid Guardian politics." I huffed out a breath. "I am a boss, aren't I? I have my own Angel who chose to give me this power for a reason."

"That's right, girl. Now you're talking." Stella's face split into a grin as she rubbed my shoulders.

"Funny thing is, I was finally ready to step up and take some responsibility for once in my life. I thought it might actually be good for me." I pursed my lips into a smirk and met her gaze.

She patted me on the shoulder. "That's not funny. That's brave."

"Thanks." I shrugged off her compliment, unsure if I believed her. But maybe she was right.

"Feeling better yet?" She wrapped me in a one-armed hug.

I nodded, wiping away the last watery remnants. "Time to dole out some powers like a boss."

The grin was back. "That's my girl."

We both rose to our feet and marched back to the training room. I squared my shoulders and held my head high.

I wouldn't let this little setback define me.

From the moment we burst through the doors, everyone stared at us. But these were my friends and family. And I needed to suck it up and do the job I came here to do.

James and Lucy both rushed up to me, looking like worried bull-dogs.

I held one hand up to stop the apologies. "I'm fine, guys. Really. Let's get this show on the road. Did you get the extra stones?"

Stella beamed from my side, and my siblings breathed sighs of relief.

James nodded at me. "Professor Harlixton should be here any minute with the stones we need for today."

Just then, he burst through the doors. "I'm here, guys."

Harlixton held a gleaming wooden box in his hands with intricate carvings. "You have no idea what Ambrose and I went through to get this done through proper channels. So please be careful with these."

We all gathered around him as he slowly lifted the lid. I sucked in a breath. These weren't sapphires. Three amethysts the size of an egg gleamed up at us, each with their own silver chain.

"These were used by the Guardian monks back when the school grounds housed a monastery." He smiled lovingly at the jewels like they were beloved friends.

"Wow, that's so cool." Owen breathed, breaking the silence.

I arched my eyebrows at him. "They'll be even cooler when they come with powers."

"That's what I'm talking about." Owen held out his fist, and I bumped it.

Eric leaned in and whispered in my ear. "It'll be interesting to see if the powers are stronger for the amethysts versus the sapphires." He stared down at the jewels with a hint of jealousy.

I bumped his shoulder. "I'm sure it's all the same, but I know my brother will want to test everything."

"What?" James tore his gaze away from the sparkling amethysts.

I blinked and straightened my spine. "Let's get this party started." I rubbed my hands together and closed my eyes.

Okay, Angel Guy. Up for another power session?

A warm cushion of air settled on my head.

I'm ready when you are, little secondborn Seer.

When I opened my eyes, Harlixton lifted the first amethyst off the red velvet lining. "Miss Mamertus, would you like the first honor?"

She bounced on her toes and giggled. "Of course."

Harlixton gently laid the chain around her neck. "Now, what power would you like Miss McAllen to bestow upon you?"

"Oh, geez. So much pressure." Her big brown eyes darted to me. "What are the options?"

I bit back a laugh. "Lighting seems to be the most popular choice, especially for those who like to go on the offensive."

Eric, Felicia, and Will all gripped their necklaces. Laughter erupted around the room.

James cleared his throat. "At least you're giving her an option. You just handed me invisibility without asking."

"Now you know how it feels." I bit my tongue to stop myself from sticking it out at him.

Stella shrugged, staring at the amethyst around her neck. "I don't know. I think invisibility would be cool. What else you got?"

"Well," I glanced at Lucy, "there's always the classic protection bubble. And that's all I can think of. I doubt you want annoying visions or scary premonitions like Lucy and I have."

"True that." Lucy bobbed her head, then turned to Eric. "Your sister had this cool way of using her powers to levitate. I always wondered if that was an extra power or just a truly innovative way to use the lightning power."

Eric's lips curled in a half-smile. "I think it was just her lightning power with her protection bubble power. But she always did like to get creative with her gifts."

I rubbed my hands together. "Maybe you could be like Felicia and create your own power. I can always ask you-know-who." I winked at my roomie.

She grinned at me. "No, I think I want lightning power. Going on the offensive against Rocco was cool. And if I could use it to levitate or whatever, even better."

Harlixton nodded but kept a straight poker face. "All right then, lightning it is. Miss McAllen, will you do the honors?"

"Certainly." I reached for the amethysts and wrapped both hands around it, sending all of my internal energy into the stone.

I squeezed my eyes shut. *Did you hear that, Angel? Time for some lightning power.*

Coming right up came the invisible reply.

An extra jolt of electricity shot through my arms, and the amethyst lit up with a purple glow.

"Wow." Came the collective gasp around the room.

That should do it.

Suddenly, the power in my limbs fizzled out.

I opened my eyes to find everyone staring at me in various states of shock.

A sliver of pride warmed my belly. "Who's next?"

I glanced between Owen and Brooke.

"Ladies first." Owen bowed and held out one arm.

"Thank you." Brook dipped her head at him. "I think I'd like lightning power too."

"That's my girl," I grinned at my friend and watched Harlixton lay the necklace like a mantle on her shoulders.

She grinned back as I took her amethyst in my hands and called up my power again.

More lightning coming right up. Angel's deep baritone echoed in my ears.

The jolt that zinged through my hands was almost familiar now. The stone grew warm beneath my fingertips, but I didn't peek this time. I trusted Angel to do his job.

Thank you. All done now.

I opened my eyes, and the electric current inside me died down. "Owen, you're up next."

"Oh, bollocks. This is tricky. It's so hard to choose." He gnawed on his bottom lip and ran a hand through the short length of his dark brown hair. "I wouldn't mind the power to see the unseen world of angels and demons that you both see."

"Oh right." Stella snapped her fingers. "I forgot about that one."

"But then I'd probably just be a lookout or something." Owen stared up at the ceiling like it held all the answers. "At the risk of being a mimic, I'm going with lightning too."

"Good choice." I smiled at him and let Harlixton do his job.

Then I took Owen's necklace in my hand and closed my eyes once again.

But I held my powers back for a minute. *Hey, Angel. Is there any way I can give my friends more than one power?*

A gentle breeze trickled down my neck. *I'm afraid one power is more than enough for most people. But if the situation is dire, we can have this discussion again.*

The corners of my lips curled as I let my powers loose. This time I didn't even have to ask Angel. He just zinged his power straight into the amethyst.

From all the oohs and ahhs, I wondered if this one was brighter than the rest.

He may be able to switch from one power to the next. But only one at a time.

Thank you, I mouthed to Angel.

You're most welcome, young Seer. Until next time. And then he was gone in a whoosh of sparkles and wind.

Owen's fingers wrapped around my arms, and my eyes flew open. "Did your Angel just fly through the ceiling in a wave of white light and glitter?"

I smiled at him. "Yes, indeed."

His face fell. "So I didn't get lightning powers. You gave me supernatural sight instead?"

"Not exactly." I gulped, bracing for impact. "I asked my angel if we could have more than one power. He told me that one power is all anyone can handle. But then he gave you both powers you requested and said you'd be able to toggle them on or off. At will. Only one can be used at a time, though."

"Seriously? That's awesome." Owen took two steps forward and wrapped his arms around my shoulders, squeezing me into his chest. "I can't believe you'd do that for me."

I hugged him back. "Of course," I murmured into his chest. "It never hurts to ask, right?"

Pulling away an inch, Owen's arms moved to my waist. "You're the best." Then he inched forward, his lips landing on mine.

For a split second, I didn't move. His lips were soft and warm. But then I came to my senses and backed up, only to be greeted by a scowling Eric as he took two steps forward.

Owen didn't seem to notice. He just grinned from ear to ear. "This is the best day ever. Thank you so much."

"You bet." I gave him a thumbs up.

James clapped his hands together. "Well, let's test these powers out, shall we?"

Thanks, I mouthed at him, then turned to Eric. "You know that meant nothing, right?" I whispered to him.

"I know." He nodded, his green eyes glaring at Owen's back. "Did you see any visions or anything?"

I shook my head. "No, not a thing."

"Okay. That's something." He ran a hand through his hair, still glaring daggers at Owen.

This was going to be a long afternoon.

Eric went after Owen with his blue lightning right away, and Owen scrambled to defend himself. Served him right for stealing a kiss from me like that.

Felicia worked with Stella on how to use her lightning and channel it into some form of levitation power. After a while, I glanced over, and Stella was levitating a few inches off the ground and grinning from ear to ear. My heart soared at the sight.

I spent the morning sparring with Brooke, then taking turns with Lucy and Will, who helped us learn to call up our powers quicker and sustain our energy streams for longer.

Maybe my brother had been right to put Lucy in charge. She was a natural leader, whether she liked it or not. And she was great at teaching people everything she knew.

One day, I hoped to be that good at something. For now, I guess I'd have to be content to live in her shadow. The secondborn Seer, second best at everything.

My time would come. Some day.

Paige

After all the drama in the training room today, I didn't have much of an appetite. Instead of meeting everyone in the caf for dinner, I huddled up in my dorm room watching Netflix.

And that was where Stella found me when she flounced into our living room.

"Have you been here this whole time?" She unraveled her scarf and draped her coat on the armchair, putting one hand on her hip.

I gnawed on my bottom lip and nodded. Shame sloshed around like burning acid in my gut, making my stomach growl. But I didn't care. After Lucy was named leader of the Sacred Stone Squad, even though the whole operation was only possible because of my power, I needed some alone time to lick my wounds.

Her face fell, and she plopped down on the sofa at my feet. "I know it's been a rough day. But binge-watching Netflix for the rest of your life isn't the answer."

"I know," I huffed, sitting upright. "I'm just so tired of coming in last place compared to all my siblings. Especially my sister."

"Yeah, I hear that." Her lips twisted into a half smile.

"Everyone always asks me the same question. 'Why can't you be more like your sister?' And I hate it." I could almost see their faces now—my parents, my teachers, even my friends back home sometimes.

She grabbed my hand and squeezed. "Believe me, I understand what it's like to fight tooth and nail to earn your place in your own family. And I've had to do that against three older brothers."

I nodded, squeezing back. "It sucks, doesn't it?"

"It does." Her big brown eyes turned my way. "But what you do with that pain, those preconceived notions will define who you are. Don't let anyone else's comparisons rob you of your joy. Or your determination.

Or your place in the sun. Because you have amazing talents that this world needs to see."

Tears sprang to my eyes at her beautiful words. "Thanks, Stella." I wrapped her in a hug and squeezed tight. "That goes for you too, you know."

She sniffed in my ear. "Thanks."

"No, thank you," I pulled back, dabbing at my eyes. "I really needed to hear that. Thanks for not letting me wallow in my own selfish misery."

Her face lit up in a grin. "Just doing my job, friend. I know you'd do the same for me if our roles were reversed."

"You know I would," I smiled back, feeling lighter than I had in ages.

Funny how a well-timed word of encouragement could make me see through the lies I'd been telling myself for years.

Stella was right. I had amazing talents that the world needed to see.

And soon enough, my time in the sun would come.

CHAPTER TWELVE

The weekend passed by in a blur of training and goodbyes to our families. Apparently, the Swiss didn't care much for Halloween. And Headmistress Militano had canceled all Halloween parties on campus, saying the school was still on high alert until the committee came to a ruling. But Dad took us to a candy shop and bought me a cute outfit before he left, so I was appeased.

Before I knew it, Stella was dragging me out of bed for Monday morning combat training.

"Can't we negotiate all of our combat training for later in the day, like our SSS training?" I groaned, pulling on my workout gear anyway, my muscles working on autopilot.

Stella handed me a mug of coffee. "I'm sure if you were in charge, that's exactly how you'd do it too." She smirked at me.

"Ugh, don't remind me." Suddenly an ache seared through my head.

Or maybe it was a stab of jealousy that I tried to push back. Sure, I knew Lucy was a better leader with more experience. After all, she was the co-leader of the Seer's Army with James, the rebellion that stopped Nexis from taking over the world and ended the Nexis Ruby war. She'd also destroyed all four Nexis Rubies with her Seer power. How could I compare to that? I was just the secondborn Seer, always destined to be less than my big sister.

Just the fact that I'd wanted to step up was important to me. I'd proved to myself I had the capacity to grow and change. Wasn't that a sign of maturity?

For now, I'd just have to embrace my role. I'd be the best co-leader the Guardians had ever seen. That'd show everyone—my brother, my sister, even my parents too.

Speaking of parents, they all flew back to their respective commands yesterday, along with my brother and most of my Guardian friends.

Only Felicia and Sedrick stayed behind to help with the Sacred Stone Squad. Having all three experienced Chosen Ones to help us train would definitely be a great asset. Good thing she'd taken a year off before starting college. Her education hiatus might be more than a year with the war coming on.

Lucy planned to finish out her semester at American University and then reevaluate.

In my regular early morning combat training class, all of my classmates were pretty sore after taking two weeks off. Luckily, Instructor Ambrose went easy on us.

It'd only been a few weeks since I learned he was the leader of the Guardian security forces on campus. It was hard to see him as anything other than Captain Ambrose now.

Stella and I went through the motions of sparring, trying to avoid his gaze. Abby went around checking on everyone as Kellen barked out orders.

After class, I put on my latest school uniform upgrade, which included a layer of gold organza underneath my skirt, making it flare out like a poodle skirt and giving it a bright gold edge around the bottom. What could I say? The statue at Columbus Circle inspired me.

In my sassy new skirt, I flounced down the hall with Stella in tow, hoping to run into Eric and avoid any hall monitors looking to razz me about my uniform improvements.

I found my boyfriend hunched over his locker. "Hey, there." I batted my eyelashes at him until he turned around.

He slammed his locker shut and spared me a glance over his shoulder. "I gotta get to class."

I stopped in my tracks. The boy had dark circles under his eyes and hadn't bothered to shave his stubble. Not that I minded. But he didn't look like himself. Something was definitely wrong.

"You okay, Eric?" I quickened my pace to catch up to him.

He didn't look at me this time, just kept walking. "Yeah, I'm fine. I'll see you later, in sacred stone class, okay?"

Then he picked up the pace to one I couldn't handle in my high-heeled boots without breaking out into a full-out run and looking completely pathetic.

I slowed my pace and turned to Stella. "That was weird, right?"

Her scrunched-up eyebrows said it all. "What's up with that boy? Looks like he got no sleep at all last night."

A lead weight settled in my middle as the realization sank in. "His father must've paid him a visit before he left."

Stella grabbed my arm and whispered in my ear. "That dude is scary. Has he told you anything about him yet?"

I shook my head, my hair swishing behind me. "Not really. Just that he's not a good guy, and whatever happened to him as a kid was pretty bad."

"Yikes," Stella sucked in a breath. "I've heard some rumors from my dad about the things he did to beat Cyrus Canaan out for the job."

"Really?" I whirled around to face my friend. "Do I wanna know?"

"Hu-uh." She pursed her lips together, eyes wide.

"We'll talk about it later." A shudder racked my shoulders.

Sure, my parents weren't perfect. My mom had an illegitimate child and didn't tell my dad until a few years ago that James was really my half-brother. And not the next Seer like everyone thought.

And my dad turned out to be a Guardian spy masquerading as a Nexis member. But they'd never physically hurt anyone to climb the secret society ladder. Which is probably exactly what you had to do to become Sector Two Commander of the Watcher Corps practically overnight.

I stumbled into my next class and let Professor Wisley drone on about Guardian history for an hour. What did I care about Guardian history when I was living it right now?

The bell rang, and it was time for lunch. I figured I'd give Eric one last chance to redeem himself.

So I waited for him in the foyer of the lunchroom. November had arrived today, and it was too bitterly cold to wait outside anymore.

At last, Eric trudged through the caf door. I snagged him by the jacket collar and yanked him into the coat closet.

"Hey, Paige." His eyes flashed at me, darting down to my lips for a second. "How can I help you?"

He reached for me and slid his arms around my waist. My heartbeat kicked up a notch or two. Part of me wanted to melt into his arms. But I stood my ground.

"You look terrible. I'm worried about you." I winced at my words and backtracked. "What's going on with you? Did your father confront you or something?"

"Am I that obvious?" He slumped forward, his head resting on my shoulder. "There's no use in hiding from you. I'll just tell you the truth."

"Please do." I nuzzled his cheek and reveled in the prickles on his jaw and the scent of his cologne.

"My father wants me to do his bidding as usual. And if I don't comply, he basically threatened to harm everyone I love." His eyes flashed at me for a second. "I can't let that happen."

"I ... uh ...." Words clogged in my throat like sharp pebbles.

Was he saying what I think he's saying?

His Adam's apple bobbed as he took a deep breath. "I'm worried that my position on the SSS will be compromised by him somehow."

I shook my head. "But you have your power back, Felicia too. You can fight him like you did before."

"If only it were that simple." He pulled me close again, fingers running through my hair.

I straightened my spine. "You're not alone this time. You have a whole squad of people ready to fight by your side. We can take him. You'll see."

He pressed his forehead into mine. "I've never had so much to lose before. If something happened to you because of me, it'd wreck me."

Then he pressed his lips into mine, kissing me fiercely. I finally let myself melt into his warm, minty mouth. He pulled me tight against him and kissed me until I saw stars.

Then all of a sudden, he was gone, leaving me cold and panting. I opened my eyes to see him edging toward the door.

"I can't let that happen again. Especially not in public." He rested his hand on the doorknob, then turned to me with a haunted look. "You have no idea how much I care about you, how much I *want* to be with you. But we have to take a break for now. While my father is plotting and scheming, he'll do anything—and I mean anything—to make his plans succeed. And I can't let him harm a hair on your pretty little head."

He reached out and cupped my cheek, then dashed out the door.

I just stared after him, jaw dangling as I leaned on the door frame for support.

Did he just break up with me only a few weeks after we started dating? *This can't be happening.*

Students rushed by me, giggling and pointing at the crazy girl stuck in the coatroom. That'd turn into some kind of crazy rumor by the end of the day.

Shaking myself, I hurried into the caf and shoved a random pile of food on my plate. Chicken strips, fries, and some sort of fluffy fruit salad. Not too bad.

Then I hurried over to my usual table with my head down.

"Hey, Paige. There you are." Brooke scooted over to let me into the booth.

I gave her a tight smile, and she flinched.

"Are you okay, girl? You don't look so good." Brooked dropped her fry into a blob of ketchup.

Stella took one look at me and her face crumpled. "What happened?"

"I don't know. It was all a blur." My hand flew to my forehead as an ache formed there. "First we were kissing, and then he was saying he had to stay away from me for my own good. Apparently, his father threatened him, or me, or something. None of it makes any sense right now."

Just then, Owen appeared with a tray of food and sat down. "Sorry, I'm late. What'd I miss?"

"Paige and Eric had a fight." Brooke blurted out.

I elbowed her in the ribs. "Shut it."

Brooke held up her hand. "Sorry, but he's our friend too. Besides, he'd figure it out eventually."

Owen leaned in, putting his elbows on the table. "I know I'm a guy or whatever, but that doesn't mean you can't tell me things. We're friends. That's what I'm here for."

"Really?" I glanced up at him, studying his face.

"Really." His jaw didn't twitch. His eye sockets didn't look ready to explode. He just looked genuinely interested in what I had to say.

Maybe I was wrong about his interest in me. Or maybe he had a crush on me, and now it was over. Either way, I believed him. I knew I could trust him.

"Eric's dad is climbing the Watcher ladder and wants to use him to get wherever he's going." I blurted out the truth and let the chips fall where they may.

Owen winced. "Yikes. That dude is pretty scary from what I hear."

"Yeah, tell me about it." I gnawed on my bottom lip as anxiety rippled through my limbs. "I guess his dad threatened to hurt me if Eric doesn't do what he wants."

Owen slammed his fist into the table. "We won't let that happen. We're a team now, with some pretty cool powers. We'll protect you."

"That's right. And we'll protect him too." Stella sat up straighter with a glimmer of fire in her eyes that warmed my aching heart.

I sniffed, giving myself away. "That's the problem. Eric doesn't think we can stand up to his dad and his army. Not yet, anyway. So he's backing off for now. And whatever we were about to start isn't going to happen anymore."

Heat licked across my cheeks, and I dared to raise my eyes to meet Owen's big green orbs.

"Well, that's balls." He didn't flinch, just held my stare. "Maybe if we can get stronger as a team, we can help him feel better about standing up to his dad."

I couldn't help but smile at him. "Yeah, that's a good way to think about it. At our training session later, I'll focus all this pent-up energy on that."

"That's my girl." His face broke into a grin as his gaze locked onto mine.

My stomach rumbled, so I shoved some food in my mouth, glancing at Owen every few minutes. How had I never noticed how cute he was? Sure, he's wasn't all chiseled and classically handsome like Finn or Eric. Owen's features were much softer, his nose rounder, his cheek more angular than chiseled. But his dark hair and light green eyes made him look oh-so-Irish. And sometimes, personality was more attractive than looks.

I blinked, sitting back in my booth. Eric had just barely broken up with me, and I was already entertaining ideas about my friend? I needed to get a grip. Nobody should rebound so fast it gave them whiplash. Besides, that wouldn't be fair to Owen. Because right now, if Eric came racing in here with flowers and apologies, professing his undying love—I'd take him back in a heartbeat.

Now was not the time to think about boys. Now was the time to lick my wounds and punch something.

Good thing punching things was now on my schedule. Permanently.

Chapter Thirteen

Eric

I couldn't eat lunch today, not if I had to see that sad, beautiful face the whole time. Too bad Paige was like a magnet to me. I'd never be able to ignore her.

So I stomped out of the caf and headed to the library, which had always been a refuge for me.

My stomach rumbled as I snagged a few books and headed to my usual table by the window. But even my sanctuary was tainted by Paige. We'd had our first pseudo-date here and our first kiss in the restricted section.

Why couldn't I just stay away from her? It was for her own good.

Probably because part of me still wanted to rebel against my father, to rage against the tyranny he'd oppressed me with for my entire life. I was my own man now. I had my powers back, too, thanks to Paige. So why couldn't I get out from under my father's thumb?

I punched the book in front of me. Its pages ruffled in protest.

"Sorry." I smoothed out the wrinkles with my fingertips.

Maybe Paige was right, and I needed to stand up to my oppressor. No matter what the cost. If that cost wasn't my future girlfriend, maybe I'd be man enough to stick to my guns. But I couldn't stand the thought of putting her in danger. My gut churned in protest. Just the idea of Paige getting hurt because of my horrible father made me physically ill.

There had to be a solution to this problem. Maybe I'd find it in the pages of my beloved books.

I flipped through the book in front of me that I'd randomly snatched from the Guardian History section. The pages were old and yellowed, making me wonder if it should be in the rare books collection.

Turning to the index, I scanned the table of contents to see if the book had any useful information. My heart pounded when I saw the heading for chapter twenty—*Sacred Stone Powers Explained.*

"What?" I whispered to the ancient tome, flipping to that chapter.

Quickly, I scanned the list of powers, my eyes stopping briefly on a few powers we hadn't thought to ask for. I'd have to make a mental note to tell Paige about this later, in secret.

A sneaky idea came to mind, and I glanced all around me to be sure the coast was clear. Then I pulled out my phone and snapped a picture of the powers page. It might come in handy.

Then I came across an interesting section that read: "In times of great distress, a member of the Chosen Ones or their line, may be gifted the power to imbue these gifts into the sacred stones for anyone wearing the jewel to use. On rare occasions, two gifts could be bestowed into one stone. Allowing the wearer similar powers to that of the Chosen Ones themselves."

"Hmmm," I sat back in my chair, pushing the book away as I processed this new information.

Could someone really have two powers? Owen debated on two powers and was given them to use separately. Could I find a way to use them together? If I had the power to zap people with my lightning and use a protection bubble, then I could worry a little less about protecting the ones I loved.

Chewing on my lip, I rocked back and forth in the chair, thinking about all of these new possibilities.

Maybe there was a way to protect my loved ones after all.

I grabbed the book and trudged to the front desk.

"Everything all right, Eric?" Nancy, my favorite librarian, pushed up her glasses.

My mouth curved into a grin. "It's been a rough morning. But you know what? I have a feeling this day is about to get better."

"Good. I hope so." With a smile, she scanned my card and handed me the book.

I zipped it up in my bag and strolled into the brisk November alpine air with a little extra pep in my step.

My dad would always be after Paige or me. But maybe now I could finally find a way to defeat him.

PAIGE

After my strange encounter with Eric, the afternoon dragged on until our first SSS training session.

Stella, Brooke, Owen, and I ambled across campus through the light dusting of snow that had fallen overnight.

I wrapped myself tighter into my parka. "I don't know if I'll ever get used to Switzerland temperatures. I'd rather be on a beach right now."

"No kidding." Stella shivered, her teeth clattering.

Finally, we reached the auxiliary gym where we would be holding our training sessions from here on out. Sure, I understood the need for privacy and secrecy. But right now, I'd prefer an underground lair to walking two hundred feet across the frozen tundra in the bitter cold.

Owen held the door open for us and waved goodbye at the boys' locker room door. "See you ladies in a minute."

I smiled at him, then ducked into the girl's locker room to change into workout gear with Stella and Brooke.

I turned to the girls. "For as often as we have to work out right now, maybe we should just keep our gym clothes on under our uniforms. You know, start a new trend."

"We'd certainly be warmer that way." Stella's teeth chattered as she pulled on her workout pants.

Both Stella and Brooke busted out laughing as we finished changing. Our giggles carried us all the way into the SSS training room.

Will, Lucy, and Felicia stood in a line facing us, in that order—looking like the fierce Chosen Ones they were.

Our laughter faded into silence.

Lucy arched her eyebrows at us, then cleared her throat. "Today, we're going to teach you about *our* powers and all that we can do with your new gifts."

"Then we'll let you practice out *your* powers to see what you can do." Will chimed in.

Felicia's green eyes flashed. "When you're in a real battle, you'll have to figure out ways to be creative with your power. Especially since most of you just have one power to work with."

"Except Paige and me." Owen piped up, his lips twisting into a smirk.

Eric mumbled something under his breath that sounded more like a grunt.

"Regardless," Lucy shot him the side-eye. "Today is about testing out your powers. And learning from those who have gone before you."

Felicia took a step forward. "I'll start by giving a power demonstration. Please stand back."

We all backed up a few feet, leaving her a ten-foot clearing on the rubber floor. With a twinkle in her eye, she called up two twin balls of purplish-blue electricity.

Her lips curled up. "It's different than my red lightning. Feels stronger. I like it."

Then she held up one hand and shot out a bolt of lightning.

I whipped my head around to find a sparring dummy with a hole through its fake head.

"Whoa. That's so cool," Owen whispered in my ear.

A shiver ran down my spine.

"Keep watching." She shot another bolt of lightning. This one focused into a laser beam. She drilled a matching hole in the practice dummy to the left of the first. Then she arced a beam of purple light into a U-shape beneath the holes.

"It's a smiley face." I couldn't help but laugh.

Everyone else chuckled right along with me.

Felicia drew her lightning back into her body. "If you use your powers right, with lots of practice, you can be that precise too."

"Wow." Stella breathed from my left. "I hope I'm that cool one day."

"There you go, getting all starstruck again." I elbowed her in the ribs and rolled my eyes.

"Thank you, Felicia." My sister nodded at the redhead by her side. "Next up, Will is going to showcase his powers."

Will called up a ball of blue energy and suspended it between his hands. "My power doesn't naturally lend itself to fireworks like Felicia and Lucy. But I have some cool tricks up my sleeve."

The glowing blue orb expanded into a life-sized bubble. With a flash of blue light, Will blinked out of existence.

"Where'd he go?" Brooke's head swiveled all around the room.

Suddenly a zing of blue light lasered into the practice dummy, drawing a diagonal line across his rubber chest, then another.

"X marks the spot." Came Will's floating voice as his face appeared out of nowhere.

Then it was gone in a flash, and blue light zinged across the room, knocking down a pile of dumbbells.

Then a Professor Harlixton burst through the door. "I hope you guys are training your butts off. I'm about to send you on your first mission."

My jaw dropped as my heart pounded in my eardrums. We were nowhere near ready for a mission of any kind. I glanced at my friends, who stared back at me with slack-jaws and wide eyes.

Lucy puffed out a laugh. "Babe, he'd never say butts."

Suddenly Professor Harlixton's scowling face morphed into a grinning Will. "You're right, but I scared them pretty good."

"Pretty cool, huh?" He glanced around the room. "My invisibility is my strongest power, allowing me to even create illusions like the Harlixton you just saw. But I've learned how to siphon off a portion of the energy to create lightning when needed. Too bad it's very draining for me over long periods of time."

Owen clapped. "Still stellar, man. I almost wish I had illusion power now."

Will beamed from ear to ear, clearly proud of himself. "Now it's Lucy's turn to show you what she's got. Give 'em hell, Tiger."

She smiled and promptly punched him in the arm. "I don't have my lightning power quite as honed as Felicia, but I can certainly do some damage."

She held out both hands, and instantly, twin orbs of purple electricity swirled into her upturned palms. Then she arced beams of light around the room in swirling bolts of electricity that zinged and snapped off of every surface.

"And I've learned a few tricks from her too." She glanced at Felicia and winked. Then she lifted her hands up, and suddenly the electricity crackled in a spiderweb formation underneath her feet, lifting her up in the air.

"Not so fast." Felicia turned her hands to the ground and shot electricity into the rubber floor, rising to meet Lucy ten feet in the air.

A chorus of oohs and ahhs echoed around the room. I'd seen some of this before, but clearly my sister had been practicing on her own.

Lucy bobbed her head, then they both returned to the ground, and the lightning died out.

"The key to my power is its longevity. Because I have the Seer gifts, I'm able to sustain the energy longer, long enough to destroy sacred stones." Lucy stated everything so matter-of-factly, like it wasn't the biggest deal in the history of the Three Societies.

Will narrowed his eyes at her. "But even she can drain herself. When she was learning, she used to pass out if she overextended herself."

"You dork, why'd you have to tell them that?" Lucy tried not to smile at her boyfriend. "But seriously, he's right. Today we want you to test out your powers, but not to the limit. We'll save that for another day. For now, you need to build up your strength."

Stella raised her hand. "Are you saying it's like a muscle we have to work out?"

"Exactly." Lucy nodded.

"Aren't you going to show them your other power?" Will winked at her.

"Ugh, fine." Lucy held out her hand, and a glowing bubble of purple light domed around her. "Paige, come at me."

"Uh, do I have to?" I took a step back and cringed.

"I'll do it." Eric's voice came out gruff as he glanced at me. Then he took off running toward Lucy's bubble—and promptly bounced right off. Straight into me, knocking me off my feet.

We tumbled to the ground together, with him on top of me.

I tried to ignore the heat running between us, but I couldn't help but lick my lips.

His eyes darted to my mouth. Then he pushed himself up.

"Sorry." He held out a hand to help me up.

"I'm fine." I took his hand and rose to my feet, brushing myself off. "No harm done."

Everyone clapped and cheered. Eric stood stiffly by my side but didn't make a move to leave.

Lucy released her protection orb and clapped her hands together. "Okay, now everyone will pair up and start training with a Chosen One. Stella and Paige, you're with Felicia. Brooke and Eric, you're with me. Owen and Sedrick, you're with Will."

I tried not to glance over at Eric as I followed Stella to meet up with Felicia.

She held out both hands. "Okay, ladies. Let's see what you've got."

I held out my hands until small pink balls of electricity grew into palm-sized spheres in my hands.

"Not bad, little miss secondborn Seer. Let's see what Stella can do."

We both turned to watch Stella as she held out both hands, her face scrunched up. Finally, she got a little spark to trickle from her fingertips.

Felicia walked up to Stella then glanced over her shoulder at me. "Paige, you work on precision, like I demonstrated earlier. I'm going to work with Stella to get things started for her, okay?"

"You bet." I nodded, focusing on the energy in my palms. Eventually, I got my pink lightning to narrow itself into a beam that I could shoot a few feet out in front of me. Not across the room like Felicia, but it was a start.

"Good job, everyone," Lucy called out over the din. "We'll meet back here tomorrow for weapons training with Sedrick."

"Now you're talking." Owen high-fived Sed with a grin on his face.

Eric didn't look quite so cranky, which was an improvement. Who knew what tomorrow would hold? But I, for one, was ready to kick some butt, Sacred Stone Squad style.

Chapter Fourteen

PAIGE

Today was our first private sacred stones class with Professor Harlixton, and I couldn't wait to get to class for once. I wouldn't let Eric's drama or my sister's new promotion as the Sacred Stone Squad leader get me down today.

I had awesome powers, and I would learn how to use them right along with my friends.

After self-defense training, Stella, Owen, and I walked down the hall like we owned the place. Except, we weren't the only ones turning heads.

Finn's shock of light blond hair stood out in the crowd as he made his way toward us.

"Hi, Paige." He planted his feet in front of me and grinned, like he'd just made my day.

Yeah, right.

"What do you want, Finn?" I crossed my arms over my chest and stared him down.

Stella and Owen flanked me on either side, mirroring my stance and staring daggers at the most popular douche in school. One of the many reasons I loved these guys.

His eyes flicked from Stella to Owen, then back to me. "Can we talk somewhere else? In private?" He leaned forward, eyebrows waggling.

Anger sizzled down my spine, and I curled my fingers into fists at my side. "Anything you have to say to me, you can say right here. In front of my friends."

"Fine, have it your way," he growled, taking a few steps closer and lowering his voice. "I've heard you have an exclusive group training in some pretty explosive techniques, if you catch my meaning." Those eyebrows waggled away.

I sucked in a breath. "Where'd you hear that?" I hissed.

An evil grin curled up his full lips. "It doesn't matter where I heard it. All that matters is this—if you let me in, I'll keep your little secret. But if not …" he trailed off, gesturing around the crowded hallway.

"Get over yourself." I spat out the words, glaring at the audacity of this guy. "If I even had a little group, I'd never let you join. Not after the way you treated me. So you can spread all the unsubstantiated rumors you want. But you and I will never work together."

With that, I flung my hair over my shoulder and walked right past him. Stella and Owen raced to catch up to me.

"That was amazing." Stella's eyes lit up as we made our way to the professor's office.

"You really had him by the balls." Owen stared down at me with a smirk. "I definitely don't want to be the guy who crosses you."

"That's right." I smiled up at him as we reached the professor's office.

When we reached Harlixton's office, Stella knocked on the door like the good little girl she was.

"Come in," came Harlixton's booming voice through the opaque plexiglass.

Owen stopped me in the doorway. "May I say that you're looking particularly lovely today, Paige? Your latest creation is definitely some of your best work."

Warmth singed my cheeks. "Thanks, Owen. I'm putting my brother's birthday present to good use."

Last night I had sewn a beautiful teal peacock print into the lining of my jacket and trimmed the edges and the breast pocket with the same fabric. I'd been waiting for the headmistress or one of the other professors to write me up, but so far, no one had.

"After you," Owen gestured for me to go in before him.

Brooke was already sitting in one of the five chairs lined up in front of the teacher's massive desk.

"Girl, you know how to stand up for yourself." She clucked her tongue at me. "Glad you didn't let that stupid Finn into the SSS."

"As if he ever had a chance." I sank down in the middle seat, my muscles tensing up. "The rumor mill sure works fast around here."

"Tell me about it." Brooke rolled her eyes.

Owen and Stella filled in the seats beside me.

"Welcome to your private lesson on you-know-what." Harlixton leaned across the desk, glancing out the still-open door. "I guess we're just waiting on Mr. Morales."

"Don't call me that." Eric shuffled through the doorway, his shoulders stiff. "I'm here."

"Please close the door behind you, Eric." Harlixton raised his eyebrows. "We don't want everyone to hear us, now do we?"

"No, sir." Eric shut the door and slumped into the last remaining chair by Owen.

"Excellent. Today we will go through all of the powers the sacred stones have awakened over the ages. Tomorrow we will discuss how these powers may be disarmed only by other sacred stones."

As Professor Harlixton handed out some books for us to reference, he asked us to turn to certain pages.

"See, here is the list of all the powers ever bestowed on the three Chosen Ones of every generation. This page has a list of all the Chosen Ones over the ages and all of their known, recorded, or suspected powers."

I scanned the list and brought the book closer to my face. "This can't be right. Some Seers could fly or have super speed. Why don't any of the Chosen Ones today have that kind of power?"

Harlixton rubbed his glasses. "You may be the only one in the room who can answer that question, Paige. Each Chosen One is given their specific gifts for a reason, by their own guardian angel."

"So you're saying I'd have to ask my angel?" Sometimes I forgot to turn to my angel, except when I needed him. Maybe I'd have to fix that.

He nodded. "Why were you given the power to give sacred stone gifts to others? That's a brand new power that's never been recorded before. In fact, your powers are on a level never before seen by a secondborn in any line of Chosen Ones."

"Really? That's kinda cool." I couldn't help but smile.

Owen slid his arm around the back of my chair. "That's because you're special."

"Or maybe this generation is special." Harlixton piped in. "Even the powers that Eric had were an anomaly before the last ruby was destroyed."

"Huh, I never thought about it like that." Eric leaned forward, resting his elbows in his knees. "But I've read about secondborns only having limited powers, like visions. I was surprised when I had manifested similar powers to my sister."

I tried to lean around Owen and catch Eric's eye, but he kept his face forward. Probably had something to do with the fact that Owen still had his arm around draped over the back of my chair. A muscle in Eric's cheek twitched as if he could see it too.

Did he even care? After all, Eric had broken up with me, but only because he cared too much. This was all such a mess.

Harlixton drone on with some cool insights into the powers the Chosen Ones had displayed over the ages.

But I couldn't focus. All I wanted to do was wrap Eric in a big hug and tell him everything would be okay—that his father couldn't touch him.

The problem was, I had no idea if that was true.

Eric

Boy, was I ready for this. After watching Owen hang over Paige all day, in sacred stones class, in the caf, in the hallways, I was definitely for SSS training.

My fingers itched to punch something. And if I got to use weapons, even better.

Staying at least twenty feet behind her, I watched Paige walk with her friends and that Owen guy across the snowy field to the back gym. The funny thing was, that gym was the place where Paige saved my life. Where I first started falling for her.

But that was months ago. Today, things were totally different, even though she still wore my birthday present, like maybe I still meant something to her. I hated leaving her hanging like this, not telling her how I really felt.

Images of the coatroom flashed into my mind. Her big brown eyes blinking up at me in confusion. All I told her was that I cared about her.

Even now, it sounded pathetic. But if I said the three little words I wanted to say, she'd been doomed for sure.

This was all my own fault, and I knew it. But I'd rather be miserable and have Paige safe than risk putting her in danger. Learning to wield weapons was just another way to keep her safe.

I tried not to gag as Owen bumped her hip or brushed snowflakes off her cheeks. Could the guy be any more obvious? Hopefully, I'd get partnered with him for sparring practice today. If so, Owen was going down.

I made it to the locker room without ripping anyone's head off. Luckily, Will and Sedrick were there or who knew what might happen to the little prick.

I changed in silence and marched to the training room without glancing at Owen. If I could just get through this session, I could go back to my room and lick my wounds.

Sedrick had a weapons rack set up at the side of the room, and he motioned for us to gather around.

"Today, we're going to be learning how to fight without our powers." Sedrick pulled out a tall spear and twirled it around like a baton. "If any of you have been out in the field like most of you have, you know that the Watchers can use their own sacred stones to bypass our powers. Your best play is to disarm them of their stone, but that isn't always possible. So weapons training will come in handy."

Felicia cleared her throat. "Today, we'll have you training with non-firearms weapons."

"I doubt they could get that approved on campus." Owen leaned closer to Paige, and they shared a laugh.

I cringed on the inside.

Felicia turned to Owen. "You're right about that. We won't be able to train with guns and such on campus. But we will eventually test out tasers and crossbows."

"But for today, we're going medieval." Sedrick's eyes lit up, and he swept his arm toward the display of swords, spears, daggers, and such. "Swords and spears are good for keeping an opponent at a distance. But if that doesn't work or you get disarmed, your dagger can be your best friend." He pulled a small dagger from his boot and snapped it across the room at the lasered-up practice dummy.

"Poor sparring Steve. He never seems to catch a break." Brooke's bottom lip jutted out in a pouty face.

Lucy, Stella, and Paige cracked up.

"Don't tell me you named the poor guy," I muttered under my breath.

Will and Sed snickered before Sed clapped his hands to regain our attention.

"Now it's time to choose your weapons. Spears first." Sedrick and Felicia helped us pick out spears that matched our height and weight.

"Now, we'll practice the basic moves. Block, parry, and lunge." Sedrick demonstrated first for the guys, then Felicia demonstrated the same moves for the girls.

"Now you try. Everyone. Block. Parry. Lunge." Felicia flipped her spear in a rhythmic dance.

We all repeated the movements after our twenty-something teachers until we'd worked up a little bit of a sweat. Some of us more than others.

"Okay, now let's partner up and try our hand at sparring. I'll pair you up by size." Sedrick pointed out the partners. "Paige and Stella, Brooke and Lucy, Eric and Owen. Felicia and Will, be my helpers and check everyone's form."

"You got it, boss." Felicia pecked Sed on the cheek, and I tried not to gag.

Owen faced off with me, spear ready. I couldn't help the bubble of giddiness rippling through my muscles. Now was my chance to make this dude pay.

Sedrick called out the commands. "Block, parry, lunge."

And I obeyed with a vengeance. I blocked, parried, and lunged with all my might. Owen backed up after the first sequence, and I kept advancing. And advancing. It felt good to see him all flustered. I kept lunging until Owen hit the back wall, and I had him pinned with my spear.

"Are you smiling right now? That's messed up." Owen wiped the sweat from his brow.

"Eric!" Felicia screamed, racing toward me. "What are you doing? Are you hurt, Owen?"

The guy shook his head, refusing to look at me.

My sister punched me in the shoulder. "Why are you being so aggressive right now?"

"What?" I ground my teeth together and shrugged my shoulder. "Sed told us to block, parry, and lunge. That's all I did."

"Good thing we're wearing practice pads. You could've hurt the poor guy." Felicia grabbed my hand and tugged me across the room.

But I didn't feel bad, not even for a second. Owen needed to know exactly who he was messing with.

Chapter Fifteen

Paige

After breakfast, Stella and I walked to class, gabbing about yesterday's training session, Eric's stupidity, and Owen's weirdness.

Finn was standing right outside my next class with his arms folded across his muscled chest.

He wore a scowl on his face that deepened the minute he saw me. "Can I talk to you?"

"I, uh, gotta get to class." I edged toward the door, hoping he'd get the hint.

Instead, he grabbed my arm and dragged me down the hall to the nearest empty classroom.

"Ow, you're hurting me." I pawed at where his fingers dug into my arm. That'd probably leave a mark.

Electricity tingled down my arm, and I itched to zap him, but we were too exposed. Anyone could walk by and see me blasting him with pink electricity.

Not that he didn't deserve it right now for going all he-man on me.

"I'm not letting go until you tell me what I want to know." Finn's jaw jutted out as he leaned toward me.

Maybe I should carry my taser to class from now on. Then I'd have a logical explanation for electrocuting this jerk.

"You have no right to manhandle me like this." I squirmed in his grasp and kicked his shin.

"Nice try, little girl. But you're no match for me." Finn just dug his claws in deeper. "I want to know what this Sacred Stone Squad is and why I wasn't invited."

"Ha! As if I'd tell you after this." I elbowed him in the ribs.

He winced but didn't release me.

Stella shot through the doorway with Owen in tow.

"You let her go." She kicked him in the side, and he doubled over his grip, loosening.

"What's your problem anyway? Sure, you've always been an entitled, world-class douche bucket. But this is a whole new low, even for you. Who are you working for?" I felt the energy bubble up inside me, and I was this close to zapping him.

"That's none of your business." He growled.

"Then neither is the SSS." I shot back.

He lunged for me again, except this time Owen blocked his path.

"You'll have to get through me first." The Irish brogue did nothing to hide the venom in his voice.

"That can be arranged." Finn grabbed Owen's collar and shoved him out the door.

Owen tumbled into the hallway, greeted by shouts and protests from the other students.

"That's it. I've had enough of your bullying." I called up my energy and was about ready to zap him when a muscled guy came flying into the room.

"Why don't you pick on someone your own size?" Eric's protective tone sent a tingle through me.

"Oh look, the whole SSS is here. Maybe you can tell me what I want to know. Or else I'll hurt your girlfriend and her friend." Finn took one step forward.

In a flash, Eric popped him in the face with a jab. Finn reeled back, and Eric hit him with an uppercut straight to the jaw.

"Don't you ever threaten my girl, or any other girl, ever again." Eric grunted, then punched Finn in the stomach.

Finn dropped to his knees, muttering to himself.

Eric hustled Stella and me out of the room. Stella rushed over to help Owen, but I stayed behind to talk to Eric.

"Thanks for that." I rested one hand on his bicep and leaned in to whisper in his ear. "So I'm still your girl, huh?"

He turned to me, his green eyes murky. "Just because things are complicated between us right now doesn't mean I don't care about you."

"But I—"

He held up one hand. "But nothing. I'm only staying away to protect you. Don't you get that by now?" His arm slipped around my waist as if it had a mind of its own.

I inhaled the scent of him. "I just think you can protect me better if we're together. That was exhibit A." I gestured to the empty classroom where Finn still writhed in pain.

He nuzzled my cheek. "You know he's just a Watcher lackey following my father's orders. Believe me. It can get so much worse than that."

My insides melted as my limbs turned to mush. "I get it. I just wish you'd let us face him together."

He ran his hand through my hair and pressed his lips to my forehead. "If only that was an option."

Then he pulled away and marched down the hall, never looking back.

"That boy is so clueless." Stella gave me a sad smile. "Can you help me get him to the nurse?"

"Sure." I wrapped one arm around Owen, and we all limped down the hall. "Sorry, you got beat up because of me."

"Eh, I'll live." He smiled up at me like I was the sun and moon to him.

Too bad Eric was right, and things were complicated right now. Maybe one day, I could return Owen's obvious affection. But right now, I still had feelings for somebody else.

What was happening to Shadowstone Academy? Things were getting out of control. And I was starting to wonder if the Sacred Stone Squad would be enough to even make a dent in this war that loomed on the horizon. Because war was coming, fast.

PAIGE

I was on edge after the altercation with Finn. How could have I ever thought he was cute? That was beyond me at this point.

But there was one thing I knew for sure, I was ready for SSS combat training. I was ready for the day when I could unleash my powers on tools like Finn and not have to hide who I really was.

Maybe that day would come sooner than later.

"You okay?" Stella nudged my shoulder as we headed into the girl's locker room.

"Yeah, I'm okay, physically." Though when I unbuttoned my stupid uniform shirt, sure enough, Finn's fingerprints were bruised into my flesh.

I quickly pulled on my workout top and hoodie to cover the marks.

"How about emotionally?" Stella gave me her best impression of my worried bulldog face.

"Emotionally, I'm trying not to freak out right now. Eric is right, Finn is just a henchman of a bigger, badder dude. And I don't want to tangle with someone like that."

"That's the funny thing about having powers. There will always be people who want to take them away from you." Stella held the door open for me.

"You mean from *us* now." I bumped her hip as we walked to the training room. "Are you sorry I gave you a power?"

She shook her head, her black ponytail flying. "Never. I'll always be grateful for this gift."

"Good." I smiled at my bestie, and we walked into the training arena together.

Lucy stood in the middle of the room, tapping her Fitbit like it was a watch. "You're late."

"Been a rough day," I mumbled under my breath.

"So I heard." Her tone was softer now. "Either the Watchers are frustrated by this little team or they're on the move."

"Or both," Felicia huffed out.

"Probably true," Will nodded at her.

"That's why today's session is going to be different. I'm going to have each of you show me what you've learned and test out the true extent of your powers."

"Awesome. Perfect day for that." Owen waved his bandaged wrist like a white flag.

Lucy clapped her hands together. "Okay guys, time to show off your stuff. Eric, front and center. Show us what you've got."

Eric eyed Owen and shot him a scowl. In a flash of light, twin blue orbs shot from Eric's hands and zinged around the room with abandon, zapping every practice dummy in the arena in rapid succession.

"Nice." Will and Sed both clapped and bobbed their heads.

"Wow. Impressive." I gave Eric a small smile, and he smirked back at me.

"Way to be creative with your powers," Lucy cheered.

"Nice work bro." Felicia beamed from ear to ear.

"All right. Stella, you're next." Lucy nodded toward my bestie.

"We'll see whose creative or not." Stella planted her feet in the center of the room. Fire flickered in her eyes as her features twisted into a scowl, and her fingers curled into fists at her side.

"Argh!" She let out a mighty roar, and purple lightning shot from her hands, crisscrossing around each and every one of us like laser beams.

No one dared to move an inch.

Finally, she released her death rays, and we all breathed a sigh of relief. While everyone else applauded and cheered, I gaped at my roomie.

"Wow, girl," was all I could say as she flounced back to my side.

"What can I say? Anger and years of pretending to be the good girl are what fuel my energy." She grinned, her eyes sparkling with glee.

Okay, so my jaw might've been on the floor. I felt a little safer the next time Finn tried to manhandle me.

"Brooke, you're up." Lucy snapped her fingers and pointed to the center of the room. "Don't be shy now."

Brooke flashed her an evil grin, then wiggled her fingers until tiny bolts of lightning sizzled from each fingertip. She spread her hands wide and waved her arms like a dancer in sweeping motions. Electricity showered in undulating waves around her.

"Pretty and deadly. Your brother and sister would be so proud." Felicia grinned at her.

"And jealous," she quipped and tamped down her energy.

Everyone cheered for Brooke.

Owen stepped up next. "Here goes nothing." He clapped his hands together, and balls of electricity shot from his hands in rapid fire. Then he clapped his hands together, and a purple dome appeared around him.

Will lunged for him and came back wincing. "Bet you wish you could've used that today, huh?"

"You have no idea." Owen gave him a rueful smile, then pulled his energy back into himself.

"Still pretty cool, man." Sed clapped him on the shoulder.

"Okay, Paige. Your turn." Lucy shot me a look that said *pull out the big guns.*

Why did I want to run and hide all of a sudden? I gulped down the nervous bubble rising up my throat, then took my place in the center of the room.

First, I called up my own energy, then directed it to channel through the amethyst at my throat like my sister had been teaching everyone else.

Suddenly, my hands sprouted pink fireballs, and a pink dome appeared around me.

Lucy reached for me and winced. "You still there, Paige?" She put one hand on her stone. "Oh, you're right there. That's pretty cool."

"What?" I literally had no idea what she was talking about.

"It seems like you've managed to turn your protection bubble into an invisibility bubble too."

"Huh. That's kinda cool." I glanced at the amethyst around my neck. "I just channeled my regular powers into the amethyst. Way to go, buddy."

Everyone laughed, and we spent the next hour sparring with our powers.

Who knew when we'd be called up for our first mission. But war never waited until people were ready. So we needed to get our butts in gear before it was too late.

Training with my friends, and funneling my power into the amethyst, made my gifts stronger than they'd ever been.

In a real life or death battle, I just hoped my training would be enough.

Chapter Sixteen

Paige

Blurgh, blurgh, blurgh. A screeching sound ripped through my eardrums, and I shot up in bed.

Everything was dark, too dark. After that night in the Watcher's underground lair, I'd started hating the dark.

My lungs constricted as panic set in, burning through my veins until my hands trembled.

Flashes of light blinked under my door as the god-awful screeching continued.

Stella burst into my room, sporting penguin pajamas and a lopsided messy bun.

"Paige, get up. The fire alarm is going off." She scurried up to my bed with my rain boots and parka in her hand. "The RAs are banging on doors saying this isn't a drill."

I shook myself awake. It'd be an exhilarating and draining day of practicing my sacred stone powers. I'd gone to bed at eight o'clock and slept like a baby. Until now.

Rubbing my eyes, I slipped my feet into the rain boots, tucking my fuzzy PJs into the tall rubber. Then I pulled on my parka and followed Stella out of the room.

Sure enough, girls were streaming down the stairs, all in various states of delirium and undress.

We all gathered on the snowy front lawn, our Resident Assistants organizing us by floors and taking a headcount.

The wind was biting, and I huddled into my parka for warmth. Then I snuggled up to Stella when they still wouldn't let us back in.

Girls were starting to grumble.

"I don't see any flames," a second-floor girl called out.

"Yeah, where's the fire department?" her friend chimed in.

Murmurs erupted as people grumbled about how there was no smoke, or this was just another stupid drill.

An uneasy feeling settled in my bones.

Something strange was going on here.

A group of adults in black cloaks tromped through the front door, one with a shiny silver briefcase in hand.

They turned our way for a brief second, and I caught a glimpse of their faces—Sherry Montrose, Maxwell Morales, and Cyrus Canaan.

"What are the Watcher Commanders doing here?" I hissed at Stella.

She followed my line of sight until her eyes went wide. "You've got to be kidding me. I bet they're looking for the sacred stones."

My muscles seized as fear curdled in my gut. They couldn't get their hands on any SSS sacred stone, or who knew what might happen next.

I patted my chest, silent, asking if Stella had hers.

She blinked and tapped her chest in return.

I breathed a sigh of relief, praying that everyone else on the SSS slept with their sacred stones on.

This was starting to get crazy.

Headmistress Militano exited the dorm, waving her hand in the air. "All clear."

Everyone started chattering and making their way back to their rooms. But I had a bone to pick with the headmistress.

I marched straight up to her and folded my arms over my puff coat. "Don't tell me you just let the Watcher's raid our rooms."

The night shadows weren't kind to her lined face. "The Neutrality Committee authorized the raid. I assure you, everything is above board."

Stella narrowed her eyes at the headmistress and leaned in. "You may be scared of those Watchers, but I have no doubt you didn't consult both sides before you let them raid our rooms. Believe me when I say, you'll be hearing from both of our fathers."

The lines on Militano's face deepened. "Oh, I believe you, Miss Mamertus. I have no doubt I'll be hearing from them soon."

Stella pointed her finger at the woman. "You better start considering whose side you're really on. When the time comes, you'll have to choose."

"I'm sure you're right. Now girls, please return to your rooms."

I was so in awe of Stella's little display that I almost forgot about my own. "You have no right to invade people's privacy without warning, Neutrality Committee or no Neutrality Committee. This is no way to make us feel safe in our own dorms."

Headmistress Militano leaned in. "I fear the time for any semblance of safety is coming to an end. You and your friends best be on your guard. There is only so much I can do to protect you from my position."

For a moment, we locked eyes. I knew right then that she was on our side. A Guardian through and through. Maybe she didn't want to reveal her hand just yet.

I nodded at her to let her know I understood. Then we both went our separate ways.

What were things coming to if the Headmistress of Shadowstone Academy was forced to do things even *she* didn't agree with?

I pulled out my phone and texted Lucy.

My dorm was just raided by the Watcher Commanders. Be careful. They may be coming for you next.

Stella tugged on my arm. "I'm freezing. Can we go in now?"

"Yeah, let's go." I followed her back into the warmth.

My phone buzzed in my pocket.

Thanks for the heads up. I'm calling an emergency meeting of the SSS. 1 hour before classes start tomorrow.

I rolled my eyes as I trudged up the stairs.

Peachy, I texted back.

It was two in the morning now, which meant I only had five hours to try and get a decent night's sleep.

As if I could ever go to sleep after what went down tonight.

As soon as we were back in our room with the door shut, I turned to Stella. "Lucy called an emergency meeting at seven a.m. tomorrow."

"Great." She rolled her eyes and pulled out her phone. "I'll be sure to get you up at six."

I pulled her into a hug. "We'll figure this out, okay?"

She nodded, her eyes glistening with tears. "I'm still putting a chair in front of the door."

"Good call."

Together, we pushed an armchair in front of the door and locked it.

Then I trudged back to my room and tried to sleep, even though I knew it'd be an impossible dream tonight.

PAIGE

Eric was pacing across the rubber mats of the training room as Felicia and Sedrick watched with worry lines etched into their faces.

As soon as I walked in the door, Eric rushed up to me.

"Are you okay?" He ran his hands along my shoulders, his auburn hair mussed and his blue-green eyes rimmed in red.

"I'm fine, you big oaf." I cupped his cheek and grinned at him.

I was too tired to care that he was still being all hot and cold with me right now.

He grinned back, the light returning to his eyes.

Lucy and Will burst into the room, with Owen right behind.

"I just spoke with Harlixton. Tonight, we're going on our first mission." Lucy dropped the bomb.

Brooke and Stella both leaned in, chattering at once.

I couldn't help but glance over at Eric, who stiffened at the news.

"What kind of mission?" Sed asked.

Lucy glanced at Will, who bobbed his head. "First, please tell me you all still have your sacred stones."

"Right here," I patted my chest.

"Check." Eric mimicked my gesture.

Stella, Brooke, and Owen all gave a thumbs up.

"Good job, guys." Will beamed at all of us.

Lucy inhaled a deep breath, then let it all out with a whoosh. "Last night's raid on Shadowstone was planned. But luckily, we knew about it ahead of time."

"Say what?" My hand flew to my hip, and my jaw dropped open. "You think you could've warned us?"

"That wasn't possible. You see, we were testing out a theory that, unfortunately, proved to be correct."

Grinding my teeth, I glared at my sister. "Okay, what in the world are you talking about?"

Will took a few steps in front of Lucy. "We have credible intel that someone on campus is spying on us and leaking intel to the Watchers. So we planted some unactivated sacred stones in each of your rooms to catch the culprits. Stones that the Guardians had just sent in case this trial program proved successful."

"Trial program?" Stella mouthed to me.

I barely resisted the urge to roll my eyes. Of course, the Guardians would want to take my little team and make it bigger and better. And I wasn't shocked that Lucy hadn't told me yet. Just part of the Guardian politics that came with her new title.

"Luckily, we got tipped off by a double agent before the theft occurred." Will's eyes gleamed with mischief.

"There are spies everywhere," Brooke whispered in my ear.

"So we placed a tracker on the stones." Lucy rubbed her hands together and turned to address all of us. "Your mission is to retrieve the stolen amethysts using the tracker by any means necessary. Your full powers will be in play on this mission."

"Full powers!" I pumped my fist in the air. "Now we're talking."

"What if it's a trap?" Felicia's gaze flew to her brother. "If my dad's behind this, we can't rule out that possibility."

"That's why we're not going alone. We'll have a full Guardian backup team." Will's face projected calm, but a little muscle in his jaw twitched.

Eric narrowed his eyes. "So this is more of a sting operation then?"

"Yeah, kind of." Lucy gnawed on her bottom lip, her biggest tell.

"All right, out with it. What's really going on here?" I tilted my head and shot her the stink eye.

"Ugh, you can read me like a book." Lucy threw up her hands. "Okay, so here's the deal. Negotiations have stalled with the Neutrality Committee. The Watchers, especially Sherry Montrose and Maxwell Morales, are spreading propaganda about how the Guardians are really behind all of these raids on Guardian repositories. They claim the Sacred Stone Squad's mission is to confiscate all sacred stones. It's complete crap."

"It's complete crap because that's really Sherry's true plan." Will rested one hand on her shoulder and cleared his throat. "Unfortunately, we're on the brink of another war. This mission tonight is about gathering the evidence we need to expose the Watchers' true intentions."

"Whoa, that's a big mission for the first SSS strike." My knees wobbled, and I suddenly felt the need to sit down.

A strong arm wrapped around my waist, but when I glanced over, it wasn't Eric. It was Owen.

"Hey, it's going to be okay." He tried to give me a reassuring look.

"Thanks, but I should be saying that to you." I stared at the bandage over his eye.

He laughed as if it was the funniest joke ever.

I was gonna be sick.

We were really about to go on our first mission.

-----><-----

Paige

The day dragged on as I went through the motions of stumbling through my classes. Harlixton gave us all a pass on our less than enthusiastic participation in our private session. No doubt, he was in on the whole raid booby trap.

At dinner, I filled my plate for appearance's sake because all eyes were definitely on me. After that debacle with Finn, people were starting to talk. I couldn't help but giggle when he stomped into the caf with a black eye. The guy deserved it and much worse.

At last, the sun set behind the mountaintops, and night finally arrived. A nervous tingle rippled through my body. Tonight was the first mission of the Sacred Stone Squad.

We all met in the training room to gear up. Lucy and Will insisted on Kevlar vests and weapons to the hilt. I was sporting just a taser and a dagger as I found the larger swords a bit unwieldy for my small frame.

Lucy came up to me and slapped both hands on my shoulders. "You ready for this, lil sis?"

"You bet?" I plastered on a grin.

She had a wild gleam in her eye like she might actually relish barging into the campus Watcher's headquarters and stealing back our stones.

We were about to raid another creepy underground lair—much like the one Rocco had dragged me to a few months ago in a failed attempt to steal my powers.

So yeah, I wasn't exactly pumped for this mission. But going into battle with my friends at my side was a good start.

Eric's hand brushed mine as everyone loaded up with weapons and gear.

"Watch your back, princess." He rasped in my ear, sending fireflies sparking down the back of my neck.

Then he squeezed my fingers and promptly marched off without another word.

My body didn't know what to do with that. Tingles flew around like crazy while I ground my teeth together. He hadn't called me princess in ages, and I wasn't sure how to take it.

"Just great," I mumbled under my breath and rolled my eyes.

"What's the matter, Paige? Eric got you all hot and bothered?" Brooke flashed a saucy grin at me.

"Hush up, you." I lowered my voice, pointing my finger at her. "I don't have time for distractions right now. I need to focus."

Brooke arched her eyebrows, then washed the guilty grin off her face as Owen approached.

"You guys talking strategy?" He blinked those jade-green eyes at me.

"That's right." I nodded, staring pointedly at Brooke. "Just basic stuff, like stick together at all times. But if we have to split up, I thought it'd be best if you and I paired up with Stella or Brooke. You know, since we both have multiple powers."

He nodded as his face lit up. "Good thinking." Then he turned to Brooke. "Don't worry. I'll protect you."

He slung one arm around her shoulder, glancing back at me to see my reaction.

"My hero." She fanned her face like a damsel in distress, then elbowed him in the ribs. "Please. I'll be taking care of you."

They bantered for a while as Stella waddled over to us, laden with gear.

"You ready for this?" Stella arched her eyebrows.

I gulped and nodded. "Ready as I'll ever be."

"Ha!" She snorted out a laugh. "I feel exactly the same way."

Lucy clapped her hands together. "Gather around everyone. Time to go over the plan."

We all obeyed and made a circle around her and Will.

"Tonight's mission is about retrieving the stolen amethysts. But it's also about testing out the teamwork and skill of the Sacred Stone Squad." She glanced around the circle. "That's why Sedrick, Felicia, Will, and myself are going to be on recon and mission control. We will clear the path, and the rest of you will be the ones to retrieve the amethysts."

"Whoa," I breathed as I looked around at the faces of my friends.

Stella was grinning, her eyes gleaming. Brooke too. Owen looked like he might be sick. Eric glowered, but when he glanced at me, I saw a flicker of fear in those blue-green depths.

My mouth suddenly went dry.

Lucy lowered her voice. "I know you're all young, but I also know what it's like to be thrown into the fray at your age. Without backup. While I know, it was a learning experience for me and all of the veterans here. I want to do better by you guys. So I'm giving you this responsibility, this chance to prove yourself, your powers, and your teamwork abilities. But always remember, you're not alone. You have us as backup. We have your back if anything goes wrong. Got it?"

"Yes, sir." Owen raised his hand to salute.

We all lifted our hands to our foreheads to salute my sister, which felt more than weird.

But she was absolutely right. She'd been through much worse than this with her friends by her side.

Now it was our turn.

CHAPTER SEVENTEEN

"Okay. Let's move out." Lucy and Will started marching down the hall toward the back door with their tracking device in hand.

When the Guardians set a booby trap, at least they went high tech.

We all fell in line two by two, with Eric bringing up the rear.

Even though I had no idea where I stood with him right now, I knew one thing for certain—he'd protect me with his life tonight if he had to. Which, ironically, was a heavy weight to bear.

My mission tonight was not only to retrieve those amethysts, but to make sure Eric didn't have to sacrifice himself for me.

"Masks up," my sister hissed as we filed out of the auxiliary gym into the frigid Alpine night.

Lucy had insisted we wear these black ski masks that covered our entire heads, only leaving a hole for our eyes and noses. Obviously, I protested because the skin-tight polyester would mess my hair up beyond recognition. But, of course, I was overruled.

Night had fallen outside, and the cloudless sky held no moon overhead. Just as planned.

We were all dressed in black, and with the ridiculous masks, we blended into the night. All nine of us ninja-walked across campus like we'd been taught in our combat training classes.

Lucy led us on a path through the forest. Luckily, there had been a light dusting of snow recently to cover the fallen leaves. Ninjas hate crunching leaves.

As the forest up ahead thinned, Lucy held up her fist to signal a full stop. "Okay, guys, we're almost there. From the looks of it, we've found some kind of back entrance to the Watchers' Headquarters on campus. That means we have no idea what we're up against. A-team, we'll go in first to make sure all is clear."

Will, Felicia, and Sedrick all nodded.

Lucy leveled her gaze on them. "You know what that means, guys. If we run into Watcher forces, we'll have to create a diversion. Even if it means us getting caught to save our friends. You still with me?"

"I love it when you get all bossy," Will smirked and gave her a salute. "Besides, you know Harlixton will get us out."

She narrowed her gaze at him, her lips twitching. "Is that a go for mission?"

"Sir. Yes, sir." Will tapped his hand to his forehead in a real salute this time.

"Yes, sir." Felicia and Sed shouted in unison.

"Keep it down, guys. We don't want to announce our presence just yet." Lucy chuckled under her breath, then turned to my friends and me. "After A-team clears the way, B-team, you'll enter, follow our markings, and proceed to the tracker coordinates as planned. Understood?"

We all nodded silently.

Lucy turned to me. "Paige, you will lead the charge once you get my signal. Eric, you bring up the rear flank and be on the lookout. Got it?"

"Yep." I locked eyes with my sister and nodded.

"Yes, sir," Eric whispered from somewhere behind me.

Lucy squeezed my shoulder, then signaled her team to race across the open field toward a stone-block tool shed on the far edge of the campus.

Will entered first, then they all disappeared inside.

Whatever that place was, it wasn't a tool shed. Maybe Lucy was right, and this rundown shack was the secret back entrance to the Watcher's Headquarters.

A shiver ran down my spine. Was it the same place Rocco had taken me only two months ago? I hoped not.

Owen stepped up beside me, his gaze intent on the target. "How long do you think we'll have to wait before they clear the path?"

As if in answer, a green laser beam blinked on his chest three times.

"Not long, it looks like." I grinned at him, then turned to my friends. I held up five fingers, then counted down.

Five ... four ... three ... two ... one ....

Then I pointed toward the shed, advancing as fast and as silently as possible across the snow-dusted field.

My heart pounded in my ears every second until I hit the shed. Then I pulled the door open and motioned everyone inside.

Stella, Owen, and Brooke all raced past me. Eric motioned for me to go before him, then shut the door behind us.

I was surrounded by complete darkness.

"Night vision goggles," Eric whispered in my ear.

"Right," I breathed, reaching for my forehead and flicking the strange contraption into place over my eyes.

I blinked at the green light that filled my vision, then waited for my eyes to adjust.

Owen had found some kind of door at the back and pointed out the faint chalk mark on the edge.

That was the marking. They'd gone this way.

Now it was my turn to step up.

With a gulp, I dashed to the door, then opened it. Spotting the next chalk mark on the wall, I led my friends down a dusty old stairway.

The air was dank and musty. Just perfect. Another underground lair deep in the mountain.

Bile rose in the back of my throat, but I swallowed it back. Now wasn't the time to give in to panic, no matter how rational.

We descended into the depths of the alps until my ears popped, at least ten stories.

Then, at last, we came to an ancient stone-carved door. The recon team had done its job and left the door cracked.

We easily breached the perimeter of the Watcher repository without so much as a peep.

Again, I searched for chalk marks and found chalk arrows lining the corridor of the stone-walled cave. The hallway opened up into a massive room with four lichen-encased stone columns and a statue of a girl in a flowing toga. It must be the most famous Interpreter or some other Watcher icon.

But there were no marks on the columns, only the walls. So I led my crew around the perimeter of the room.

Stella came up beside me with the tracking monitor, pointing to the little red dot, then the wall to my right.

I held up my fist to signal stop. Sure enough, there was a giant chalk circle around a Watcher's symbol carved into the wall.

I pressed my hand into the symbol, but nothing happened. My heart sank like a lead weight in my middle.

Then I got an idea. I pulled out my amethyst necklace then stuck the stone into the hole. Still nothing.

I breathed out an exasperated sigh, holding my hands up in silent frustration to my friends.

Eric wove his way through the group, then pulled out his own necklace. The moment he slipped the sapphire into the center of the Watcher's symbol, the crest turned like a dial. Metal clanked, and stone scraped as a section of the wall started moving, enough to open a doorway.

Smiling, I reached out and squeezed his hand.

Then I motioned for my crew to follow me into the room.

Whatever lay ahead of us, we were on our own in here. No more chalk marks or pre-planned routes. We had to do this on our own.

PAIGE

We all crept into the room on our tiptoes. Silence reigned loud as I scanned the walls for any kind of safe or repository or something.

In here, there were no chalk marks to guide me. I had to figure this out on my own.

Good thing I had four helpers with me. And an angel to boot.

My gaze landed on another intricate Watcher symbol carved into the floor in a giant dais.

"Eric," I hissed, motioning him over. "Try your little trick again."

His eyes went wide, and he knelt to the rough-hewn stone floor. There was an opening big enough for his egg-sized sapphire to slide right in.

A perfect fit.

The dais beneath our feet started turning, and we scrambled to the edges of the room.

A spiral staircase descended from the dais revealing a swath of inky blackness.

I gulped and adjusted my night vision goggles to the highest setting.

"Here we go," I muttered under my breath.

Then I took the first step on the newly-emerged stone staircase, descending into the depths of the unknown chamber.

My team followed close behind, giving me a measure of reassurance. My pulse still jangled like a tambourine in my ears.

Luckily, these stairs didn't go ten stories deep, more about ten feet this time. Once I hit the landing, I realized we were in some kind of treasure room.

Even though the room was small, the walls were lined with stone shelves full of dusty treasures. Some books, a few cases, and intricately carved boxes that begged for further exploration. But my gaze stopped when I saw a gleaming wooden case that didn't have a speck of dust on it.

"This is it, guys." I rushed to the case, feeling the amethysts' power surge toward me as I approached.

I eased open the case, and sure enough, six gleaming stones stared back at me.

"Okay, guys. We've got the package. Get ready to move out in case this thing is booby-trapped." I motioned for them to start making their way back up the stairs.

Of course, Eric stayed behind with me, lingering at the base of the stairs.

Inhaling a deep breath, I grabbed the case and ran up the steps after Eric.

Sure enough, alarms blared in the distance, and the staircase began to retract. No way. I froze for a second as the realization hit me. The room was collapsing in on itself.

Eric grabbed my hand and pulled me up faster than my own feet could ever move on their own.

We reached the main room, and I crumpled into his arms as the dais slid back into place.

Floodlights had flicked on, throwing the room into so much light it burned my eyes.

I slid off the goggles and stared at Eric until my eyes adjusted. He looked like he was a breath away from saying something or kissing me senseless.

Then the screech of scraping stone grated my eardrums.

The door was closing.

We both raced for the opening at breakneck speeds, barely slipping through to the other side.

"That was too close." Brooke panted, keeling over. "We've got to get out of here."

My gaze darted around the room, but there were no guards yet. Which meant our intel had been correct about this being an unmanned repository.

Even still, footsteps thundered down the stairs we'd come from.

Then I caught a flash of chalk on the wall past the treasure room trap.

"Guys, look at the walls. I think they found a backup exit." Without another word, I started racing down the hall.

My throat constricted, and my lungs heaved for air. My body knew what my brain didn't have time to process. It just felt wrong going deeper into the repository.

But I knew my sister would find a way out for us. And I had to trust that.

Rounding corner after corner, we finally found our way to another circle on the wall with a Watcher's symbol. Eric wasted no time with his sapphire, and the door slid open with a pop. This room looked just like the last room, except there was a dais on the ceiling.

Suddenly, Eric slipped his head between my legs and hoisted me up on his shoulders.

I barely had time to gasp before he handed me the sapphire.

"Try it. Hurry." He barked up at me.

Blinking like crazy, I took the stone and fitted it into the opening. The dais started spinning downward toward us, revealing another spiral staircase.

Eric backed up toward the wall, then lifted me off his shoulders and lowered me down to the floor as if I weighed nothing at all.

Butterflies dive-bombed my stomach as I turned to face him.

His hands slid to my waist as he tightened his hold. "It had to be done."

Behind me, the stairway clanged into the stone.

"Come on, guys." Even as more footsteps thundered behind us, Stella led the charge up the stairs.

We raced up the stairs to find a rickety wrought-iron elevator that looked like it was from the 1920s waiting for us.

"Up we go, I guess." I approached the thing and pulled on the door, but it wouldn't budge. "Does anyone know how to work this thing?"

"Let me see what I can do. Eric, you close up the dais, okay?" Owen didn't wait for a response. He just went to work.

"Good thinking," Eric grunted behind us.

Owen pulled on some latch, and the doors popped open.

Stella and Brooke piled in first while Owen held the door for me.

"Come on, Paige." He reached for my hand just as three black-clad guys bumbled up the stairs.

"Eric!" I screamed, wriggling out of Owen's grasp and lunging for my man.

"Paige, no!" Owen reached for me again, but I knew it was too late.

I kicked him inside and slammed the doors shut.

"Go, Stella. Don't let them take you." I locked eyes with my bestie, and she nodded, her eyes brimming with tears.

"Paige!" Owen screamed, grabbing the bars of the elevator and shaking them.

Stella pushed aside a distraught Owen and fumbled with the controls until the elevator started squeaking upward.

I called up my power and turned to face my attackers, but there were too many now.

Three guys had already subdued Eric, and the remaining six were coming for me now.

I held up one hand to zap the leader, but he held up a sapphire right in the line of fire.

The lightning bolt zinged right back at me, electricity pouring into my body.

I crumpled to the ground in a heap, reaching for Eric before everything went black.

Chapter Eighteen

Paige

When I came to, my head rested on something warm but solid. I was in a dark room, with someone stroking my hair.

Then I heard his voice.

"I'm sorry, Paige. I'm so sorry." Eric's muffled words came from somewhere above me.

Then the warm object beneath me moved. I was resting my head on Eric's lap while he rocked back and forth, hyperventilating and stroking my hair.

I rubbed my eyes, but I still couldn't see anything. Something hard and bumpy, like stone, bit into my hip. The air was heavy and with a dank, musty odor. We must still be in the repository, somewhere.

All of my weapons were gone, even my night vision goggles and my Kevlar vest. I patted my chest. Luckily, I'd worn enough layers and tucked my amethyst into my bra well enough they hadn't found it.

"It's still there," I whispered, trying to sit up.

Eric stilled, sucking in a sharp breath. "You're awake."

"Yep." I eased into a sitting position, fumbling around in the dark so I could still feel his warm, solid chest. "Where are we?"

"I don't know. Still the repository, in some kind of holding cell, I think." Eric wrapped one arm around my shoulder. "I'm so sorry I let this happen."

"Well, I couldn't let you get captured by yourself." Even though I tried to laugh, I knew the words were true as they left my lips.

"You should've gone with Owen and the others. Sometimes I wish you weren't so brave." Then he wrapped his other arm around my waist and pressed a kiss into my temple.

"Yeah, me too. How long have I been out?" I leaned into his lips, cupping his jaw and running a hand down his stubbled face.

He winced like my touch hurt him. "I don't know, not too long. Less than an hour, maybe."

I sat up straighter. "Good. Then we still have a chance of getting out of here. Or getting rescued."

"No, we don't. I overheard one of the guys saying they were going to take us to my father. We don't have a chance." He banged his head against the stone wall behind us.

"Shush, don't say that." I pressed one finger to his lips. "We still have a few tricks up our sleeve."

"Really, Princess? Like what?" His breath was warm on my cheeks.

"Like this." I slid my hand to the back of his neck and pulled his face toward mine.

My mouth crashed into his, sending a delicious heat sizzling throughout my body.

Suddenly, the darkness morphed to gray and then into a scene that played out before my eyes. Eric stood between his father and me, in some kind of office bathed in firelight. Maxwell grabbed my arm, much like Finn had, then backhanded me across the face. I crumpled to the floor as Eric huddled over my prone body.

"See," he whispered against my mouth. "It can always get worse."

The vision vanished, but Eric's lips were still on mine. Pulling back, he wrapped his arms around me and squeezed me into his chest.

"Don't worry. I won't let him lay a finger on you." He dug his fingers into my massive snarl of hair.

The door slid open, and a crack of light filtered into the room.

"Okay, lovebirds. Time to see the boss." Four guys entered the room and dragged us to our feet.

I guess they weren't taking any chances with us. But I still had one more secret weapon.

Eric

Sure enough, just like Paige's vision, we were dragged into a cushy, mahogany and leather-steeped office with only the glow of a roaring fire to light the way.

Part of me wished Paige had never kissed me in that dungeon. But the other part of me would rather be prepared for what was coming next.

My fingers clenched into fists. I wouldn't let my psychotic, narcissistic father lay a hand on my sister—and I wasn't about to break that streak by letting him anywhere near my girlfriend.

"At last. Good of you to join me, finally. Leave us," came my father's gruff voice from the recesses of the room.

The Watcher soldiers nodded and shut the door as they left.

I immediately stepped in front of Paige, putting her behind me.

My father walked over to us as I edged us closer to the door.

"Almost seems like old times, doesn't it, son?" The firelight danced in sinister shapes across his hawk-like features.

"Like hell it is." I grounded out between clenched teeth. "I'm not a kid anymore. You can't intimidate me."

"Oh really? Wanna bet?" He lunged toward me with a growl.

I didn't move an inch. Then he reached out for Paige.

I cringed and backed up.

He threw his head back and let out a cackle reminiscent of a Bond villain. "You know, you have good taste, son. You picked exactly the girl I would've chosen for you." He sat on the edge of his desk, interlocking his fingers in front of her. "I have big plans for your girlfriend, you know. She will usher in a new age where all Watchers have the powers of the Chosen Ones. Under my command, of course."

The stupid, almost cartoonish behavior only brought me back to that fateful night four years ago.

I could see it like it was yesterday. Hear Felicia's cries from the basement like I was back in our old townhouse.

My father had been acting strangely ever since our mother passed away when I was ten. He'd gotten more gung ho in his pursuit of power among the Watcher Corps, even going so far as to play both sides by pretending to be a double agent spying on Nexis. Deep down, I knew the truth. He'd do whatever it took to gain the power he wanted, the power to control his own destiny. So what happened to Mom would never happen again.

The only problem was that he saw Felicia and me as tools on this quest instead of children to protect. We were special children, destined to inherit the powers of the Messenger that he never had. We were his ticket out of Watcher mediocrity and into the limelight of all Three Societies.

It didn't matter that we didn't want to be his puppets. He'd make us fall in line if we disobeyed.

He'd recently made Felicia go to Montrose Paranormal Academy and forced her to join the Order of the Guardians there. While he played the Watcher/Nexis angle, he had her batting for the other team. But we were all his pawns. One day, I'd be expected to join the ranks too. I was only twelve, and I already hated the Three Societies. But more importantly, I hated how he bullied my sister, and I wasn't strong enough to stop him.

I came home from soccer practice early one night to shouting voices in the basement. My sister was yelling, actually screaming at my dad—which was something we *never* did.

I raced downstairs as fast as I could.

"I can't believe you want me to spy on the president of the campus Guardians. He's my friend." Felicia was practically sobbing from somewhere in the basement.

Her words floated to me, and I knew I had to find her. My heart pounded as I fumbled through a maze of storage tubs strewn about the room. My pulse ratcheted up a few thousand RPMs. Dad was all about order and cleanliness. The fact that the storage tubs were thrown haphazardly around the room told me more than I wanted to know.

There had been a struggle. Maybe he'd already hurt her.

The blood boiled in my veins at the thought.

I didn't want to know what was about to happen to her if I couldn't find her in time.

I turned the corner, and my heart jumped into my throat. Dad had Felicia cornered in the laundry room, backed up against the washing machine.

Her shoulders were hunched like she knew what was coming. But her chin jutted out in defiance.

That was my sister, always lashing out. Always poking the bear. Trust me—the bear didn't need any help, especially not lately.

Dad growled and raised his hand high. "I don't care if he's your friend. You will do as you are told."

He lowered his arm, and before I knew it, I was standing in front of Felicia, fists raised.

"Enough, Dad. We've had enough of this. You better back up, or I'll call the cops." I gave him my most menacing glare.

And he just threw his head back and laughed. "Yeah, right, Eric. You're just a boy. Let a man teach you to obey your father."

He raised his hands again, except this time, bolts of red lightning shot from my fists. They zinged straight into Dad's bulging, six-foot-two frame. I didn't let up until he crumpled onto the concrete floor.

Once I knew he was down, I turned to Felicia. "You okay, sis?"

Tear tracks stained her face. "Eric, that was incredible. I had no idea you had the same powers I do."

Her face lit up as we each packed and headed to her dorm room at Montrose. She snuck me in over spring break, and we talked all night about our powers and how we'd never let Dad intimidate us again.

I almost smiled at that thought until I blinked, and I was back in the creepy firelight office with my father looming over me once again.

Shadows danced across his face. "I bet you remember the last time we tangled, and you got the best of me. But I don't think that's going to be the case this time, son." He held up one hand, and my sapphire dangled from it.

Of course, he'd take my only hope at protecting Paige. I swallowed back the bile rising in my throat.

"Now it's your turn to feel the wrath of the sacred stones." Father slipped the chain around his neck, then gripped the sapphire with one hand.

Stretching out his free arm, he called up a ball of sapphire lightning and zinged me with a bolt.

Electricity jiggled through my body, sending pain across every surface. I crumpled to my knees. I was a failure. I had failed.

PAIGE

I blinked and blinked, but the scene in front of me didn't change. Maxwell Morales was electrocuting his own son—and it didn't look like he was going to stop anytime soon.

Rage like I'd never seen boiled in the man's eyes. And there was only one person who could stop him now.

Without a second thought, my own energy bubbled to the surface. In a snap, bolts of pink lightning streamed from my fingers and slammed into Maxwell's head. That was where everything had short-circuited—in the guy's brain. It needed to be rewired.

Still, the moron wouldn't stop jolting Eric.

Angel, a little help here. I called out silently to my secret weapon.

A whoosh of wind barreled into me from above, followed by a clap of thunder.

White lightning sizzled into a floating angel form, then zapped the chain free from Maxwell's neck.

His eyes lit up with my pink lightning, and he dropped to the ground in front of his son.

I knew Eric would hate being so close to his dad. So I rushed over and dragged his heavy body across the room.

"Thanks, Angel," I breathed to the white form. "I always forget to go for the stone."

"You're welcome, child." Angel's voice threatened to break the room apart. "Might I suggest you heal this boy so you can get out of here before his evil father awakes?"

"I can do that?" I croaked at him.

"Of course, you can. You're the secondborn Seer. You have many of the same powers as your sister, this being one of them." With that, he rocketed through the ceiling, leaving a show of sparkles in his wake.

I blinked at his exit but didn't have time to argue. The only thing I could do now was try.

Putting my hand to my chest over where I'd buried my amethyst, I willed healing power to emerge from my hand. A warm tingle shot down my arm, and I pressed my hand into Eric's chest. His body lit up with a pinkish glow.

Then his eyes fluttered open. "Paige? Are you okay? What happened?"

I shot a few more jolts of healing energy into him. "It's okay. I'm okay. He's down, and we have to go."

"Oh," he reared back at the sight of his father laying on the floor. "Okay, let's get out of here. Then you're going to tell me everything."

"Fine. Whatever you say." I grabbed his hand and dragged him toward the door, but my movements were sluggish. I guess healing power was kind of draining.

I opened it a crack, but the hallway was dark. Then a shower of silvery sparkles danced along the ceiling to my right.

"Thanks, Angel," I muttered and followed the sparks all the way back to the surface, ready to zap any Watcher that crossed my path.

But Angel must've been leading us away from the soldiers.

"Thanks for saving my butt again." Eric wheezed out from my left. "I just wish you didn't have to."

"I hope I'm always around to save your bacon. And vice versa." I squeezed his hand and kept going until we tasted fresh cold night air.

We'd have a crazy story to tell when we got back. Right now, my only job was to get us back to our team in one piece.

Chapter Nineteen

Paige

Heart pounding in my ears, I raced as fast as I could across the open field, dragging Eric as he tried to keep up.

Luckily, the team was waiting for us at the edge of the forest.

"What happened?" My sister was the first to come up and squeeze the life out of me.

"I ... uh ..." I grunted, my knees buckling as Eric sagged against me.

Felicia and Sed rushed up and took Eric's weight off my shoulders.

"Thanks," I breathed out a smile. "Didn't these guys tell you?"

Lucy nodded, her eyebrows furrowed. "Yes, right up until you two got captured. Sometimes I wish you weren't so brave."

"That's what I keep saying," Eric wheezed out.

Puffs of laughter filled the night air.

"Can this wait until we get somewhere safe? And warm." I rubbed the frozen tip of my nose.

"Yeah, I guess that's the professional way to do it. Let's head back to the gym and debrief." She leaned down and pressed a kiss to the exposed part of my cheek. "I'm glad you're okay. Don't scare me like that."

"Sorry," I shrugged, but everyone had to know I wasn't one bit sorry.

I'd go down protecting my friends any day of the week. Maybe that's why Angel gave me this power and not someone else.

We all limped back to the training room together.

As soon as the door closed behind her, my sister whirled on me. "Okay, spill. Tell us what happened."

"Fine." I gave them the abridged version of events, how Maxwell Morales took the sapphire from his son then used it against him. "Then he tried to turn it on me, but I used my inner power to defeat him. With a little help from Angel."

"Wish I could've seen that," Eric mumbled from the weight bench.

Owen started pacing the room. "This never should've happened."

"What do you mean?" I turned to him, narrowing my eyes as I studied his face.

It was a strange thing to say right now.

He ran a hand through his dark, curly mop. "We were right there at the elevator. You could've easily fit in with us. I should've just grabbed you."

I reared back like the boy had slapped me. "And leave Eric to face his dad alone? I don't think so."

Stella walked up to Owen and patted him on the shoulder. "I think what Owen means is that it was hard watching you being taken away—both of you—and there was nothing we could do about it."

Brooke gulped and flanked Owen's other side. "You made the choice to sacrifice yourself and go back for Eric. We respect that. But it doesn't mean it wasn't hard for us too."

A lump welled in my throat. "I know, guys." I couldn't believe I'd found such great friends in such a short amount of time.

Owen narrowed his eyes. "I feel like we could've done more. We have these powers, but we don't know how to use them yet, not in every situation, to their fullest potential."

"Sounds like we need to get back to training. First thing Monday morning, we'll start running battle scenarios." Lucy made her way to the front of the group. "You guys completed the mission, even if it wasn't perfect. You deserve a day off."

"Gee, thanks." I wanted to roll my eyes at my sister, but I knew she was right. "Before you go, there's one more thing."

I glanced at Eric and nodded.

Clearing his throat, Eric turned to address the whole group. "My dad said something about using Paige's power to usher in a new age. I have no idea what he meant, but we should definitely be on the alert. This is only the beginning."

Lucy pursed her lips, hands moving to her hips. "Scratch that. Sounds like we can't even afford one day off right now. See you guys tomorrow for a full debrief and more power training."

Everyone groaned, but I knew my sister was right.

We needed to keep training. We'd only just learned what our powers could do. Now we needed to learn how to use them in real-life situations.

Because our enemy wasn't about to go easy on us. Maxwell had big plans, and for some reason, they involved the Sacred Stone Squad.

PAIGE

I fell into bed that night and went right to sleep.

Who knew how long I'd been asleep when suddenly the peaceful blackness behind my eyes morphed into a dark scene I'd do anything to unsee. If only I could turn off my stupid powers.

The scene playing out behind my eyelids opened on young Eric, about twelve, frantically searching for something in a storage room. Then, he walked in on his father with his arm raised, about to hit a younger Felicia. All of a sudden, Eric was in front of his sister. His fists were raised, and red lighting burst from his hands. In a flash, Eric was jolting his dad with beams of red lightning. Much like Eric had been jolted by his own father earlier tonight.

My stomach curled in on itself. Maxwell Morales was trying to recreate this scene, only in reverse. Even though Eric was only twelve at the time and was just trying to defend his sister.

My heart broke for the fear and anger smothering Eric at such a young age. But mostly for a little boy whose heart was broken by his monster of a father.

My stomach churned, and I willed myself to wake up from this awful nightmare. But the scene just switched to something else.

Two figures stood close together in a dark forest. The trees reminded me of the woods that surrounded the campus. The shadowy figures were whispering in low tones.

"That's not how that was supposed to happen." A black-clad guy was yelling at the other.

I squinted and tried to see the guy's face, but it was so dark outside, and there was no moon. Wait, tonight was a new moon. This had to be something happening tonight. Was it a premonition?

But why would I see Eric's memory alongside a premonition?

"We got what we wanted, didn't we?" The other man's voice was unmistakable.

Maxwell Morales.

Icicles of fear stabbed at my chest. What exactly had he gotten tonight that he actually wanted?

"That's not the point. You weren't supposed to harm Paige. That wasn't part of the deal." The man with his back to me spat out.

Maxwell grabbed the dude by the collar. "There are casualties in war, so deal with it. You better get that necklace for me, or I'd hate for you to be next."

The faceless guy held his hands up. "Fine. But I need to go now."

"I'll see you later then. For the grand finale." Maxwell snarled, his face menacing even in the low light. Then he stalked off.

His subordinate turned and walked toward me. I gasped as I finally caught a glimpse of his face.

"Sedrick?" I shot up in bed, rubbing my eyes. Suddenly back in the real world. "That can't be real. There's no way Sed would ever betray us, especially not Felicia."

The room was still dark, and the clock by my bed blinked four forty-five a.m.

I closed my eyes and replayed the premonition in my head. The whole vision was more than strange. First, I'd seen a memory of Eric as a kid, but not from his perspective. Were there black edges around the corners? I should've been checking to see if the whole thing was a fake. After witnessing Maxwell in action, I wouldn't put it past him to be the one who'd figured out how to send me fake visions just like the one I'd had of Brooke on my birthday.

I reached for my phone and dialed my sister. "I just had a premonition, but I don't know if it's true."

"What?" Her voice was groggy. "What'd you see?"

"We might have a traitor in our midst." I hated even whispering the words out loud, but what if part of that premonition was true, just like my sweet sixteen vision about Brooke and the headmistress' office?

"Okay, let me think." Rustling noises crackled through the earpiece. "We only have one option here. You need to get Eric and meet me at my dorm."

"Okay. But why are we doing it this way?" I shoved my feet into my snow boots, fuzzy pajamas and all.

Just like last week when Watchers had raided my dorm, things were going down faster than I'd ever expected.

Lucy breathed into the phone. "Because Will and Eric are the only ones who can see and maybe even interpret your visions. And if there's some kind of traitor, we don't want to alert anyone else."

"Oh. Good thinking. I'm glad someone's brain works this early." I blinked at the phone. How did she do that on two hours of sleep?

"I know. I've had practice formulating plans at all hours of the day or night. See you soon. Be careful." She hung up.

Next, I pulled up Eric's number and hit send.

Five rings later, his groggy voice greeted my ears. "Paige, what's wrong? What happened?"

I swallowed hard and cut to the chase. "I had a premonition, and it was bad. But I'm not sure if it's real or not. I called Lucy, and she says you're the only one besides Will who could interpret my vision. And we need to keep this on the down-low."

"In case there's a spy in our midst. Perfect." Rusting noises crackled from Eric's end. "I'll borrow my sister's rental. Meet you outside in five minutes."

"Can you do it without waking her up?" I squeaked into the phone.

"Yeah, I think so. Why?"

I gnawed on my bottom lip. "I'll tell you in a minute."

"Fine," he huffed. "See you in five."

This was going to be a long night.

CHAPTER TWENTY

I felt like a total jerk sneaking into my sister's purse and stealing her car keys. But Paige said it was important not to let her or Sedrick know what was happening, so I went along with her plan.

Maneuvering down the winding mountain road at night, now I wondered if maybe I should've asked more questions.

"Okay. Now can you tell me why I just stole my sister's car so we can drive in the middle of the night to Geneva?" I spared a glance over at Paige, who looked three shades paler.

"I had a vision." Her words came out soft and stilted. "Part of what I saw might be real, but part of it I'm not so sure about."

"It's okay." I slid my hand to her knee, running my fingers on her fuzzy pajama pants to give her some measure of reassurance. "You can tell me what you saw."

She gulped and shook her head. "The first vision was about you. And your dad."

Suddenly my throat went dry, and my foot eased off the gas. The tires spun slightly, so I put both hands on the wheel to right the car.

I gripped the steering wheel tight. "Let me guess. You saw the night I first used my powers on my dad?"

"How d-did you—" she stuttered out.

I shrugged one shoulder. "I just relived it myself, so I figured it'd be just my luck that you saw it only hours later."

"I can see why you're so protective of me. And your sister. You've had to be on guard since you were a kid ...." Her words trailed off as if she wasn't sure how much to talk about.

I didn't know what to say to that. Instead of talking, I just stared at the lights of Geneva as they came closer. She wasn't wrong about my past. I'd been on guard against my father since I was twelve.

"I'm guessing by your silence, that vision must be real." This time, she rested her hand on my knee.

Warmth shot up my thigh. "Unfortunately, yes. What else did you see?"

"It's too awful to mention, but I know I have to." She squeezed my knee.

"Just spit it out." A muscle in my jaw twitched, but I still couldn't look at her right now.

"Okay, but just remember, I think this is the fake part." She huffed out a breath. "I saw someone feeding information to your father."

"What?" I roared, jerking the wheel too hard to the right. I fumbled to right the car again. "Who did you see?"

Her hand moved to my shoulder. "It was Sedrick."

I blinked as I merged onto the desolate Geneva highway.

The sky was growing pink on the horizon as the day dawned. And I knew the truth, deep down in my bones.

"No way, couldn't be him."

Paige was quick to respond. "My thoughts exactly. That's why I called my sister. She said we could only trust you and Will to get to the truth behind the vision."

I finally dared to glance at her. "Well, that's flattering, I guess. I just hope she's right." My stomach churned at the thought of Sed betraying my sister.

She'd been through so much already. She deserved a little peace in her life.

But it would be just like my father to figure out how to project a fake vision, then use it to undermine Sed.

That had to be the explanation.

I stepped on the gas. I wanted Will to confirm my theory.

The car careened around the streets of Geneva, and we pulled into the parking lot of American University in record time. Hand in hand, Paige and I raced up to Will and Lucy's dorm room.

We didn't even have to knock.

"There you guys are. You made good time." Will ushered us inside.

Their whole dorm room was the size of my living room. Lucy was pacing on the far side of the room in front of the window.

"Thank goodness you're here. Now, let's go to work." Lucy rushed up to Paige and pulled her into the middle of the room. "Will, you take one hand. Eric, you take the other. Now, Paige, you try to remember your vision and let them see whatever they see, okay?"

"Sure. I'll give it a shot." She didn't look optimistic, but she closed her eyes anyway.

That was one of the many things I loved about her. Even if she wasn't a hundred percent sure about something, she'd try it anyway. Especially if she trusted you.

I grabbed her hand and closed my eyes, while Will did the same.

I found myself in the middle of our old basement, zapping my father. At least I'd caught the good part of that memory. Then the scene flashed to a forest at night. By the lack of moon in the sky, I'd guess it was tonight.

I heard the traitor talking to my dad, but I tried to tune out the noise. The scene was so black it was hard to see. But there, around the edges, a faint edge of blackness smudged out the stars—every star on the edge of the sky, in a U-shape.

My heart beat like a caged animal against my ribs. I knew it couldn't be Sedrick.

Sucking in a breath, I followed the black smudge around the edges of the vision.

Sure enough, the black edge continued around the perimeter of the forest and the bottom of the grass too.

Somehow, I was able to zoom out again. A giant rectangular black box ringed the scene playing out in my mind's eye.

I snapped my fingers. Definitely a fake. But how fake? Was there really a traitor at all? If so, it obviously wasn't Sedrick. When fake-Sed turned and walked toward us, there were black edges around his face. Almost like he'd been photoshopped in.

When I opened my eyes, Paige and Lucy were staring at me.

"So? What's the verdict?" Lucy nibbled on her bottom lip.

"That last vision is definitely a fake. I saw a black box around the whole scene and even around Sed's face. Almost like the event really happened, but someone is framing Sed."

Then they both turned to Will.

He cleared his throat. "Eric is right. Sed's not the spy. But I'm afraid the interpretation I got isn't good news. There is a real traitor, and the meetup with Maxwell was true. Unfortunately, I know who the real spy is."

Paige gasped. "Who is it?"

"You're not going to like this." Will pursed his lips together, then exhaled. "I'm afraid it's Owen."

"What?" My hand flew to my forehead as an ache spread there. "Why would he do such a thing?"

"I think I know why." Paige's eyes bulged three times their size. "I had a talk with him the other day. Told him there could never be anything but friendship between us."

"You mean—?" I swallowed back my objection. Of course, Owen wanted more than friendship with Paige. I could see it, well, after my sister told me the truth.

The fact that Paige shot him down made my heart soar, but knowing it led to betrayal made this moment bittersweet.

Lucy rushed to her sister's side. "Just because you rejected him doesn't give him the right to rat us out. This isn't your fault."

"Yeah, Squirt." Will reached out and ruffled her hair. "Your sister shot me down so many times I never thought we'd get together. But I waited patiently for her to realize her mistake."

Lucy smacked him in the arm, but her lips curled into a grin. "That's how I realized he really was a good guy. Even though I'd rejected him a few times, it didn't change the way he treated me. I knew I'd been wrong about him."

"You've only known Owen three or four months, right?" Will's voice softened into the brotherly tone he used only with Paige. "A few months isn't long enough to justify him turning on you."

I snapped my fingers as the realization hit me. "It's all starting to make sense now. My father must be the one behind these visions. He must've heard what happened to Felicia and figured out how to do it himself, somehow."

"Yeah, I'm afraid you're right. And I'm sorry for what your father did to you." Will clapped a hand on my shoulder.

Paige perked up a little bit. "And Owen said something strange tonight like 'This wasn't supposed to happen.' Maybe he wanted Eric to get captured, but not me."

Red tinged my vision. "I'm gonna kill that little turd."

"Now, bro. Hold your horses." Will's hand on my shoulder tightened. "We need to play our cards right here. Because I'm sure your father has something big planned for his grand finale. And we need to find out what it is."

"No prob, I'll take care of it. I'll beat it out of him if I have to." I pounded my fist into my palm.

"Maybe we should try a softer approach first." Lucy turned to Paige. "Do you think you could confront him, maybe even get some intel out of him?"

"Oh, I don't know." Paige backed up a few steps, edging closer to me. "What would I have to do?"

Lucy put one hand on her hip and batted her eyelashes. "You know, do your Paige thing. Flirt with him a little and see if that works on him."

"Worked on me," I mumbled under my breath.

Will snorted out a laugh.

Paige's cheeks pinked up. "But what if it doesn't work?"

"Then I'll be there to grind his bones into dust." I clenched my teeth, slipping an arm around her waist.

Lucy and Will tried to stifle their laughter as Paige leaned closer to me.

"Okay, but you better stay close." She batted those eyelashes up at me.

"Whatever you say, princess." And right then, I knew it was true. I'd do whatever I could to protect the girl who stole my heart.

PAIGE

Sipping on a mug of coffee I could barely taste, I replayed the speech I'd planned out in my head.

I just stood in front of our usual table, staring at the scratched surface. We'd had such good times here. How had everything gone so wrong?

I'd asked Owen to meet me in our booth in the cafeteria. Even though it was just the two of us on a lazy Sunday afternoon when most kids slept in, there were still enough people to make me feel safe. Plus, I knew Eric was hiding out somewhere, watching.

"Hey, Paige. I'm so glad you're okay." Owen rushed up to me and wrapped me up in his arms.

Bile shot up my esophagus and landed in the back of my throat, but I swallowed it back. I couldn't throw up now and give the game away.

"Yeah, me too." I eased out of his embrace and slid into the booth.

Of course, he had to slide in right next to me.

Gag me.

"You said you had something to tell me?" His green eyes looked over at me like a hopeful puppy dog.

"Yeah, I had this crazy vision last night." I leaned in, batting my eyelashes at him like my sister had suggested. "It looks like there's a traitor among us."

I sat back and gauged his reaction.

"What? You're kidding." He reared back a few inches, eyes darting around the room. Then he leaned in. "Are you sure?"

Of course, he wanted confirmation, the little turd. Anger burned me up inside, but I inhaled a deep breath. I still had to play it cool and turn on the charm.

I nibbled on my bottom lip and twirled a lock of my hair. "You know my visions aren't always accurate. But this one seemed at least partially true."

Owen blinked and blinked but wouldn't look at me. "Did you get a good look at who it was?"

"Not really. Do you have any idea who it could be?" I shook my head, inching closer, willing him to spill the truth with every bat of my eyelashes.

He finally met my gaze. "Honestly, I'm just as shocked as you. This is so crazy."

I couldn't take it anymore. I tugged on his shirt and pulled him closer. "You wanna know the crazy part?"

I licked my lips.

His gaze flicked to my mouth. "Sure?"

I yanked on his collar until he was inches from my face. "I know it was you. Don't even think about making a scene right now." I jammed the business end of my taser into his thigh. "Don't make me zap you, you little traitor."

"Paige, I-I can explain," he stammered, his shoulders slumping. "It was just supposed to be Eric who got captured. I was trying to keep you safe."

That really burned me up. "By working for that monster? Nice try. You're not getting off the hook this time, you pathetic little wimp. Just tell me what the big grand finale is and when it's going down."

He leaned closer and whispered in my ear. "Maxwell Morales and the Sector Two Watchers have rallied the Watcher students to start raids all over campus. But it's only a diversion. The Sector Two Watchers are going to march on Shadowstone and take over the campus."

"What?" I tilted my head, a little too close to his lips. "Why would they do that?"

Owen's eyes grew as wide as I'd ever seen them. "He wants what everyone wants, now that the word is out. He wants his own Sacred Stone Squad."

I growled as heat rose to my cheeks. "And you were just going to roll over and let him take over, weren't you?"

"What else could I do?" Owen whined, actually whimpered like a little boy. "He threatened you. He threatened my family. My mom is a captain in the Sector Two ranks in Ireland, but he still managed to capture her and throw her in a dungeon. All because I blabbed about some intel I heard that the Guardians were holding one of the sacred Amethysts here at Shadowstone."

"What?" I leaned in, jutting out my chin. "Where'd you hear that?"

He gulped, eyes going wide. "I overheard Harlixton talking to Ambrose in his office after that fight with Finn. When I asked my mom about it, she said it wasn't a secure line and might be compromised. I'm telling you, Paige. The guy's too powerful to go up against."

My stomach churned at the thought of all the people hurt in Maxwell's pursuit of power. "You could've told us the truth or been a double agent. Or run back to Ireland. Anything but this." I curled my lip in disgust.

"I know. I'm sorry, Paige." Owen hung his head.

"Just tell me when it's going down. When are they coming for the Sector Two Amethyst?" I hissed into his ear.

Leaning in, he cupped my cheek. "Tomorrow night. Please prepare yourself."

Then he planted a kiss on my lips that made me want to scream. My fingers curled around his necklace, and I snatched the sapphire right off his neck.

Served him right for stealing a kiss.

"I deserve that." He stood up and walked away.

Even though I'd found out the truth, this was definitely not good news.

CHAPTER TWENTY-ONE

As soon as I stepped through the cafeteria doors, a strong hand grabbed me and pulled me into the coat closet.

Eric's stormy sea-green eyes were narrowed into slits, his upper lip curled in a snarl. My pulse kicked into overdrive as I took in our surroundings.

Back in the coat closet again. I was starting to think of this as our spot. Silly, I know.

"That's twice I've had to watch that guy kiss you. I can't stand him." Eric narrowed his eye at me. "Why did you let him get away with that crap?"

I held up the amethyst and let it dangle from my fingers. "Does it help that I swiped this from him while he was distracted?"

The storm in his eyes calmed, and his lips curved into a grin. "You took back his sacred stone? That's my girl."

He wrapped me in a hug so tight I could barely eke out a breath.

I wanted to squeeze him back and get lost in his arms, but now wasn't the time for that.

"I'm glad you agree with my logic, but we have bigger problems." I stepped back, holding him at arms' length. "Owen said that your father and the Sector Two Watchers are planning to incite student-led raids that will begin anytime. Then the Watcher army is going to march on Shadowstone tomorrow night. He also said we better be prepared, whatever that means."

"What?" All the color drained from his face. "You can't be serious."

"I'm afraid so." I gnawed on my bottom lip for a second, then gave in to what my gut was telling me to do. "Here. You could use this."

I handed him the amethyst I'd just taken back from Owen.

Eric's lips parted, almost in awe as he stared at the jewel in his upturned hand. "You're giving me another power?"

I couldn't help but grin at the look on his face. "I don't see why not. Angel gave Owen two powers, but he clearly didn't deserve them. You, however, do."

"You really think so?" His eyes lifted to meet mine.

"Of course I do. You've protected me more times than I can count, even if your ways are misguided." I cupped his cheek, running my thumb along his smooth skin.

He blinked at me and shook his head. "And what have I done to protect you besides pushing you away? When you've saved my life more times than I can count."

"I don't know about that." Heat licked at my cheeks as I rocked back on my heels. "But I do know one thing—we are better together. I hope you see that too."

He exhaled, shoulders slumping. "I think I do, finally. I just wanted to protect you from my father. You saw how much of a monster he is."

I nodded, not daring to say a word.

"Sometimes I wish you hadn't seen that, but maybe it's better this way." He dug one hand into my hair. "He always wants to hurt the people I love, so I thought if I pushed you away, he'd lose interest. But obviously, you're way too special for anyone to lose interest."

"Hold up." It was my turn to blink. Did he just say what I thought he said? "Did you just say you love me?"

"Yeah, I guess I did." He reached for my hand, his cheeks turning pink. "I love you, Paige."

"Oh, okay. Great." I was blabbering like an idiot, but I didn't know what to say. Did I love him too? We'd never had enough stability in our relationship for me to even contemplate the idea. But I wouldn't fight this hard for somebody unless I loved them, right?

Suddenly, he put his fingers to my lips. "It's okay, princess. You don't have to say it back. I know I've put you through the wringer. So, let's put a pin in this and come back to it later. For now, we better go tell the Guardians about the coming battle tomorrow."

"Right. Battle. Let's go." I followed him out into the graying light of a cloudy day in a daze.

Tomorrow night, we'd be going to war against the Watchers. And I not only had a boyfriend, but a guy who loved me?

Yeah, things were definitely getting crazy around here.

Paige

Once I pulled out my phone and told Lucy about Owen and his intel, she went right to work contacting the proper authorities.

Eric walked me back to my dorms, and things were already going from bad to worse.

Shadowstone Academy was on the brink of war. The Watchers on campus had already begun their assault. Molotov cocktails were thrown through broken windows into random classrooms. The whole academic building had smoke and broken glass everywhere. Good thing it was a Sunday.

Screams tore from the library as a swarm of students raced out. Eric and I stopped in our tracks, then headed over to help. Half a dozen Watchers in blue shirts raced from the back door, carrying armfuls of books.

"What are they going to do with those?" I asked, huddling into Eric's side.

His mouth hung open. "I have no idea. But that's such a travesty."

Suddenly, the emergency storm sire blared from every rooftop on campus.

Then the headmistress came over the loudspeaker. "The Neutrality Committee has declared a state of emergency at Shadowstone Academy. Students are urged to leave their dorm rooms and seek shelter in their respective society headquarters."

The announcement repeated on a loop.

I glanced at Eric. "Your dorm or mine?"

His eyes were wide as he blinked at me. "Let's go get Stella and Brooke. I'll call my sister on the way and see if she'll pack me and bag and meet us at HQ."

"Okay." I wanted to kiss him right now, just for the gesture of putting me first. But I knew there was no time for PDA right now.

We hurried back to my dorm, taking the stairs instead of the elevator.

Stella was already stuffing her clothes and essentials into a suitcase. "There you guys are. What's going on?"

I reached out and wrapped her in a quick hug. "Owen is a traitor, but he warned us that the Watchers are coming. Tonight."

She blinked at me, her eyelashes fluttering like crazy. "You've got to be joking. Seriously?"

My heart sank as I nodded. "I'm afraid so."

Then Eric held up Owen's amethyst. "I have no idea how long that guy has been working for my dad, but the next time I see him ..."

I rested one hand on his bicep. "At least he warned us that your dad is coming. Tonight."

"What? Are you kidding me?" Stella screeched.

I swallowed hard and braced for impact. "Maxwell Morales and the Sector 2 Watchers are marching on Shadowstone tonight."

I let the word hang in the air.

Suddenly, Stella straightened and started furiously throwing clothes into her suitcase. "What are you waiting for? We've got to get to the situation room. The Guardians are going to need us tonight, and we need to get prepared."

"Yes, sir." Eric saluted Stella, then grabbed my hand and dragged me to my room. "Only the essentials, Paige."

I pulled out my travel makeup bag and swiped an arm across my sink's countertop. Then I found my carry-on rolling suitcase and dumped all my workout gear in, along with some sweaters and jackets. Oh, and a few essentials like underwear and socks.

"Done. Let's go." I zipped up my suitcase.

Luckily, Stella was waiting in the hallway. We rolled our luggage down to Brooke's room.

I couldn't believe my eyes. Brooke was in the hallway, nailing boards across her door.

"What?" She put down the hammer and rolled her luggage up to us. "I don't want those greedy Watchers taking my stuff."

"But how did you—" I gaped at my friend.

Stella dangled her phone in front of my face. "I texted her."

"Let's go then." I turned toward the stairwell.

Eric picked up Brooke's hammer and jogged back to my room. "I'll meet you girls in the lobby."

Then he disappeared.

"Boys," I rolled my eyes and lugged my carry-on with attached make-up bag down the stairs.

Sure enough, Eric met us in the lobby, hammer in hand.

Stella furrowed her eyebrows at him. "What exactly did you do to our room?"

A sly grin curled up the corners of his mouth. "Let's just say, you may need a new entertainment center when this is all over. But your room is secure."

Eric stuck the hammer in the cargo loop of his jeans and led the way across campus to the cafeteria, where all of the student and teacher Guardians were streaming through the main entrance to the underground HQ, under the watchful eye of Ambrose and his security team.

Even ten stories into the side of a mountain, the stark gray Guardian headquarters was buzzing with activity under the industrial fluorescent lights.

We met up with Lucy, Will, Felicia, and Sedrick in the situation room.

"There's only one problem." Professor Harlixton was pacing back and forth in front of a clear, plexiglass screen with a bunch of Xs on it. "The full force of the Sector Two Guardian Army can't make it here until tomorrow morning to help us protect the amethyst. At the earliest."

"But the Watchers are planning to march tonight." Will ran a hand through his golden locks. "At least that intel has been confirmed. Right, Ambrose?"

Captain Ambrose had just rushed into the room with two lieutenants in tow. "I still can't figure out how this all went south so fast. It's almost as if the whole thing was a setup."

I cleared my throat, raising my hand as if I was in class. "I may know something about that. It seems like Owen overheard you and Harlixton talking about housing the amethyst on campus. He accidentally told his mom over an unsecured connection."

"Stupid!" Captain Ambrose roared, punching the nearest object—the plexiglass war board.

The clear plastic vibrated in the now-silent room.

All eyes landed on Harlixton. "The Watchers knew, with our location in the Alps, that the Sector Two Guardians stationed all over Europe would have a tough time reaching us."

"Can't we just hunker down in here until dawn?" Brooke blinked wide eyes at Harlixton.

He pursed his lips and shook his head. "I'm afraid we wouldn't last the night. Our infrastructure isn't strong enough, and there are too many double agents who know our secrets."

Captain Ambrose addressed the room as Guardian intelligence officers started filing in. "The Sector Two Amethyst, and the members of the Sacred Stone Squad in this room, would fall to the Watchers. We need to fight to buy enough time for reinforcements to arrive."

Murmurs rippled through the growing crowd.

I took a step forward. "Does that mean we're on our own from whenever the Watchers decide to march until daybreak?"

"I'm afraid so, sis." Lucy pursed her lips and slung one arm around my shoulder.

Professor Harlixton stopped his pacing and moved in front of our little group. "I need you guys to gear up for anything and everything. I'm talking Kevlar, weapons, tasers—the whole nine yards. Maxwell wants the SSS *and* the Sector Two Amethyst. And we won't let him have either one. Right, Guardians?"

"Sir, yes, sir." The entire room of Guardians shouted in unison.

A chill of epic proportions zinged down my spine as all the hairs on my arms stood on end.

This was it. The war was starting tonight.

CHAPTER TWENTY-TWO

PAIGE

My heart was heavy as I followed my friends to the weapons room. On the way there, I passed way too many familiar faces.

There were faculty, students, janitors, librarians, even civilians from Geneva and other nearby cities who came as fast as they could to help.

So here we were. Gearing up for the apocalypse. Or at least the biggest battle in Shadowstone Academy history.

There were barely enough vests and weapons to go around—and everyone was in a panic.

Orders were barked, and questions asked. None of the civilians really understood why the Watchers, who'd been denying any involvement in the previous attacks, were suddenly starting a war on a student population.

"What could they possibly want here?" One guy asked his friend.

And the friend turned and looked at me. "They must want the Chosen Ones or something."

"You're kidding? This is just like Nexis all over again." He scoffed.

"Tell me about it. This whole Neutrality Committee farce was just a smokescreen to gather their forces."

"Too bad some of us believed them for a hot minute."

I pulled Lucy into an abandoned corner with no one around. "Why do you *really* think the Watchers are marching on Shadowstone?"

Her eyes drifted to my throat. "I think they want the SSS for themselves. Or worse. They want you to make a sacred stone army for themselves."

I winced as horrible images flashed through my mind of Maxwell Morales leading an army of super-charged Watchers. "We can't let that happen. The sacred stones in their hands would be a disaster."

"That's the problem with the gifts of the sacred stones—if you have power, someone always wants to take it away from you. That's just the way of the world, I'm afraid." She tugged on my arm and started walking toward the briefing rooms. "I've called an emergency SSS meeting. I think it's time to get our strategy straightened out."

Sure enough, the entire Sacred Stone Squad was sitting in a dozen chairs waiting for me and Lucy to show up.

Lucy cleared her throat. "Hey guys, thanks for meeting like this."

Sedrick bounced in his seat. "So, what's the plan? I'm ready to kick some Watcher butt."

She winced and took a step back. "I'm afraid you're not going to like this plan. My strategy is to hang back and not get taken by the Watchers."

"What?" Felicia rose to her feet. "I don't think I heard you right."

Lucy pursed her lips. "I'm afraid you did. The plan is to stay back until called upon and protect your sacred stones at all costs."

Eric turned to Felicia and tugged on her arm. "It's why dad's here. He wants our sacred stones for himself. And whatever army he wants to give them to. You know as well as I do that we can't let these powers fall into the wrong hands."

"Oh," Felicia exhaled, her shoulders deflating. "When you put it like that..." she trailed off and slumped into her seat.

Lucy nodded at Eric. "As I was saying, don't dive into the fray, even if you see Owen or someone else you might be tempted to use your powers on. These stones can't fall into Maxwell's hands."

"Agreed," Stella said under her breath.

An idea sprang to life in the corners of my mind, and I knew I had to say something.

I leaned in and whispered in Eric's ear. "Do I have your permission to tell everyone about the premonition you had on the plane?"

Eric's eyes went wide, then he gave me the barest hint of a nod.

I rose to my feet in a flash and stood beside my sister. Then I turned to address the Sacred Stone Squad.

"A few weeks ago, Eric had a premonition about his father marching against Shadowstone Academy." I let my eyes wander to Eric, who held my gaze, giving me the courage to continue. "But it's up to us to prove that we can change that premonition. We've already done it in the past. Tonight, let's use everything that we've got to keep these sacred stones out of Watcher hands. If they take possession of even one gifted amethyst or sapphire, who knows what kind of havoc they will wreak with it."

I wrapped my hand around the amethyst dangling at my neck. "Sacred Stone Squad!" I yelled, throwing my fist in the air.

"Sacred Stone Squad!" The whole team echoed in unison, stomping their feet against the cement floor.

Goosebumps tingled all over my body.

Beside me, Lucy cleared her throat. "Remember guys, we just have to hold them off until dawn. Then the Guardian Army will arrive to waste the Watchers."

"Yeah!" Another cheer went up as I beamed at my friends.

I had no idea what was about to go down tonight. But at least I was going into battle with my friends by my side.

ERIC

Hundreds of Guardians had shown up at headquarters today to put their lives on the line. Most of them had no idea they were protecting a dozen gifted sacred stones from falling into the wrong hands. All most people knew was that the crazy Watchers were starting a war with teenagers. And they came to stop the tyranny.

I just hoped it'd be enough to last until dawn.

For a rag-tag group of people from all ages and walks of life, were as armed as we ever were going to be to hold off thousands of Watchers for ten to twelve hours.

We had a long night ahead of us.

Time to face the inevitable.

I knew exactly who we were battling and what we were up against.

A rock the size of Manhattan rolled around in my stomach.

I had more powers than I'd ever dreamed of. And yet, I couldn't help but wonder—would they be enough? Could I protect the girl I loved against my power-crazed, sadistic father?

I gritted my teeth. Whatever happened today, I was going to go out swinging. What I saw in that premonition was only one possible future—just a small part of it, even.

Just because my father wanted the sacred stones and those who could wield their power didn't mean he would win this fight tonight.

At this point, we could only pray and do our best to hang on until the Guardian reinforcements arrived.

As we emerged from the underground armory, the Guardian infantry fanned out in the quad behind the cafeteria to assess the situation.

The sun was setting over the jagged peaks, and I couldn't believe my eyes.

The campus looked like a war zone. Smoke billowed in the air from buildings with broken windows that looked like they'd been hit with grenades, Molotov cocktails, or some other kind of small, homemade bombs.

The Shadowstone Academy Watchers had already laid the groundwork for their brethren's arrival.

Just perfect.

Silence hung heavy in the air as the makeshift Guardian army assessed the situation.

I grabbed Paige's hand and pulled her off to the side.

"Listen, princess. I know you've got these powers, and you want to protect me, but I'm asking you to protect yourself first tonight, okay?" Something tickled in my throat as her broken gaze locked on me.

Her eyes glistened. "What do you mean?"

I swallowed the acrid lump in my throat. "I mean, if we're being overrun, you retreat when they say retreat."

She blinked those long lashes at me. "Okay. That sounds doable. But what if you, or my sister, or one of my friends is threatened? You don't expect me to retreat then, do you?"

The way she looked up at me, her gaze turning hard, her jaw jutting out, told me all I needed to know. She'd already made up her mind. If she had to, she'd sacrifice herself for anyone she loved.

So why did I hate *and* love her for it?

Because it tore me up inside.

I smoothed my hand down her soft cheek, hopefully not for the last time. "I wish you would just do as I ask. But I know you can't."

She leaned into my touch. "Listen, I know this is bad, okay? I get it, believe me. But I also have to believe that I have these powers for a reason. That *we* have these powers for a reason. So have a little faith that we can figure out a way to outmaneuver your father—together. Okay?"

I blinked and stepped back, all the air hissing from my lungs.

"That's a lot of faith for me," I whispered as my thumbs caressed her cheekbone. "But I have faith in you."

Her lips lifted into a small smile. "I'll take it. Now let's go get some bad guys." She grabbed my hand and squeezed.

Together, we rushed to catch up to our friends.

I'd been on my own, just my sister and me, for so long that I almost didn't know how to work in a team.

But for her, I had to try.

"We can do this," I mumbled to myself more than anyone else.

Then I let my mind wander to this newfound power I had.

Okay, Mr. Angel Guy. If you're up there, and you want me to have this power, too, give me a little sign.

Suddenly, brilliant stars popped out of the dusky blue sky—brighter than I'd ever seen them. And the ground beneath my feet morphed into a churning scene of fire and flame.

Is this really happening?

The scene below faded, but the stars twinkled brighter.

You, Eric Morales, may see the unseen world of the supernatural. But only to protect my charge, the secondborn Seer. I hope that is acceptable to you.

I nodded vehemently. "Yes, sir. I'll take it."

Good. We will be here when it's time.

That last word reverberated through me like a gong. Time.

Because my father and his minions were coming.

And there'd come a time when we'd need extra help from above.

As the day took its last breath and night finally fell, a shadowy army marched toward us in the open field. Just like my vision.

My father's face flashed in the light of the setting sun, leading the charge.

Let the battle begin.

CHAPTER TWENTY-THREE

PAIGE

The Watchers marched on us, in formation, fifty-wide across the open field.

And, of course, their forces went hundreds of lines deep.

Could this really be happening?

It was like watching an ancient battle.

Who fought like this anymore?

I guess when you knew it was thousands against hundreds, you had time to display your power.

The arrogance.

I clenched my fingers into fists and called up my power—ready for when Lucy gave the signal.

She twirled one finger in the air.

Bubbles up.

Will, Lucy, and I called up our bubbles to encompass the entire front line.

Iridescence layers of blue, purple, and pink surrounded our small army, the colors lighting up the night sky in a mesmerizing array of neon, almost like a domed Aurora Borealis.

Blinking, I shook myself and tore my gaze away from the sky. Now was not the time to get distracted. I needed to focus here.

The Watchers threw RPGs and grenades at the bubble, but they just bounced right off in a display of fireworks that lit up the night.

Then they lobbed something funny-shaped at us. It was a Molotov cocktail with a sapphire attached.

"Duck and cover!" Will yelled.

Lucy zinged her lightning at the homemade bomb, and it zinged off into the night sky.

But not before it pierced the bubble.

That small victory seemed to incense the Watcher rabble.

A battle cry erupted from the front line, and they started racing across the field.

"SSS, front and center," Lucy called over the din.

Eric grabbed my hand as Stella and Brooke raced up beside me. Felicia and Sed were already on the front line.

Lucy turned to face us. "Their little test worked. They've got plenty more sapphires attached to different weaponry. We need you guys to zap them out of the sky as fast as you can."

"Like lightning archers. Cool." Stella's eyes lit up.

"But how long can that last?" Brooke looked skeptical, even as she reached for her stone.

Sed clamped a hand on her shoulder. "Remember, we only have to hold them off until daybreak. If this buys us a few hours, then it's worth it."

"When this doesn't work, we'll figure something else out. But it's all I've got for now." Lucy's lips pursed into a straight line.

"We can do this." I planted my feet and stretched out my arm.

The rest of the SSS did the same as lights arced across the field.

Fireballs and grenades were headed straight for us, all with little bits of sapphire strapped to them.

As if on cue, we all let our lightning fly.

Eight bolts of electricity zinged through the air, branching off to intercept more than twenty objects headed our way.

Ooohs and ahhs rang out behind us, but I didn't have time to look.

I had three grenades and three Molotovs to disband and less than three seconds. Zing, I spun left to zap a cocktail that exploded off into the woods. Zag, I twisted right to blast two grenades at once. Ping, pow, I vanquished two Molotovs with one bolt. But I still had to shoot one grenade left. I stretched out my pinky at the last second, and it burst into flames, just on the outskirts of the bubble.

A collective gasp erupted behind me as everyone cringed.

There were only eight of us with powers, and the Watchers were just getting started.

"Advance!" Ambrose shouted, and the front line advanced, guns blazing.

They were trying to buy us time to rest.

My heart soared, and tears pricked my eyes at the gesture. But I couldn't lose focus now.

As the Guardians advanced, the Watchers sent out some kind of SWAT team, a crew with shields that deflected most of the incoming bullets.

I guess they had shields of their own. Literally.

"Hold the line!" Ambrose shouted into the infantry.

Each of the front lines dug in, relying on their side's respective shields for backup.

"Conserve your ammo. Aim for what you can hit." Came the order from Captain Ambrose.

And still, the Watchers kept lobbing firebombs at us.

An hour into the zapping, sweat beaded down my brow.

Two hours in, my knees went weak.

"Don't these guys ever run out of ammo?" Eric and I stood back to back, holding each other up. Stella and Brooke did the same.

It was after midnight now.

"We can't keep this up much longer." Lucy hissed to Ambrose.

"I know, I know." He turned to her. "When your shields fail, we'll retreat."

My heart broke into a million pieces.

We were failing. We were about to let down the army that fought for us.

Minutes later, forty bombs rained on us.

Two broke the shield.

"Look out!" I screamed as a grenade hurled through the sky.

The earth exploded to my left. Thankfully, no one was hurt.

"B-team, retreat!" Ambrose called out. "Fall back."

Lucy grabbed my shirt. "Paige, go with him. Take your friends with you. The rest of us will hold the line here."

"But, I—" I wanted to protest, but Eric tugged on my arm.

"You promised, remember?" He turned a stormy glare on me, and I was a goner.

"Fine, but you take care of yourself." I hugged her around the neck and raced off with Eric, Stella, Brooke, and the rest of the B-team.

PAIGE

That was when all hell broke loose. Since we were toward the front lines, we were on the backside of the mass of Guardian soldiers retreating.

But there was nowhere to go. A gauntlet of terror awaited us in the quad.

The Watchers had been busy while we armed ourselves.

They had laid out minefields, rigged buildings to blow, and set fires between every building.

There was no exit.

"To the woods!" Ambrose shouted and led the charge into the Alpine forest.

All of us weary, battle-scarred Guardians scrambled through the trees as the Watchers pursued with raised fists and war cries.

It was pure chaos.

At last, we reached a clearing in the woods. But all the Guardians stopped short at the edge of the words, standing still as staring off to the east.

My friends and I pushed through the crowd—and gasped.

We were standing on the edge of some kind of stone amphitheater built into the side of the mountain.

And we weren't alone.

A band of heavily-armed Watchers were waiting for us. All the worst ones too.

"You're just in time." Rocco stood in the middle of the stone stage area, with a giant pedestal hidden not-so-gracefully behind his back. Then he barked into a radio in his ear. "Your guest has arrived."

The Watcher soldiers swarmed around us from our front and rear flanks, but the B-team Guardians fought back with an extra dose of savagery.

As I watched these men, women, and teenagers fight to protect me, the world turned in slow motion around me. Pieces of my heart broke at the sight of people I didn't know being cut down on my behalf.

And I knew what I had to do.

The choice reverberated through my bones.

I turned to my team. "Listen, guys, we just have to hold them off until morning. Whatever happens here, however, we have to play along, realize I'll never give in. Okay?"

Stella gripped my hand and nodded. "We'll never give in either."

"We'll do whatever it takes to protect you." Brooke gritted her teeth.

"What she said," Eric rasped out.

The Watcher soldiers broke through the Guardian front lines, one grabbing my arm. "Time to give the rest of us your powers, little Seer. It's share and share alike in the Watcher Corps. At least when it comes to powers."

The disgusting man leered at me like I was a piece of meat. Or was it my power that really appealed to him?

"You keep your hands off her." Eric kicked at one guard and zapped another with his lightning.

It took five guards to finally subdue him.

That bought us ten minutes.

Only four more hours to go.

I dragged my feet as two goons marched me down the stone steps to the stage landing. Stella, Brooke, and finally Eric were right behind me.

"So good of you to join us." Rocco's creepy smile slithered across his face as the Watchers lit two dozen torches around the circular stone dais.

The firelight revealed a stone pedestal with one of the four sacred Watcher's Sapphires on top. Oh goody, another attempt to transfer my powers to a psycho. Did that ever work in the history of the Three Societies? And why did they always bring out the sacred stone they were supposed to protect at all costs? Hadn't the Watchers learned anything from the downfall of the Nexis Society? If we ever got out of this, I'd have to ask Harlixton.

"Rocco," I nodded at him. "Looking creepy as ever. I see you're up to your old tricks. Even if your mommy forgot to acknowledge you as her legitimate son."

He raised his arm to slap me, but Eric lunged at him.

Finn burst through the ranks of the Watchers, lunging for Eric's knees and helping the guards secure his hands behind his back.

"Aren't you two cute?" Veronica sauntered through the circle of torches, chuckling to herself like she owned the mountainside. "But don't worry. No one's getting away this time."

"We'll see about that," I ground out through clenched teeth.

Finn called in two more guards to handle Eric, then put a taser to his temple. "You better obey, Paige. Or your boyfriend gets it."

I shuddered. I didn't know what would happen if they tasered Eric in the skull. Would he die? Be brain dead? Either option was too terrible to think about.

Suddenly, Rocco was at my side, shoving a taser into my ribs. "Put your hands on the sapphire."

I rolled my eyes at him, jamming my hands into my hips. "You can't be serious. Not this nonsense again. What could possibly be different this time?"

Rocco leaned in, his face contorted in fury. "You've got a brand new power, don't you, Paige?"

I pressed my lips together and schooled my expression. Goosebumps prickled up my arms.

His beady black eyes lit up with firelight. "It's time for you to share your power with the people who matter. It's time for the Watchers to have the power of the Chosen Ones."

He raised one fist in the air, and the Watcher soldiers cheered.

"As if you'd share this kind of power with your minions," I muttered under my breath.

Out of nowhere, he slapped me across the face. Pain radiated through my right cheekbone, and for a few seconds, I saw stars.

Eric lunged at his captors, but they held him at bay.

I shook my head, rubbing my cheek. I guess the time for talking was through. Now I'd have to go through the motions to buy us more time.

Rocco grabbed me by my hair and thrust me toward the Sector Two Sapphire. "You know the drill."

"I do indeed." And I was counting on him to follow the same playbook as last time.

So for once, I did what I was told.

"Hello, old friend." I clamped both hands on the sapphire and let its tingling energy flow through my body.

The night sky lit up like a Christmas tree, stars twinkling in the more-brilliant-than usual navy blue.

What looked like a river of lights flowed down from the heavens above.

Everyone around me stared up at the celestial display in the night sky overhead. Ooohs and ahhs erupted from Guardian and Watcher soldiers alike. My plan was working just how I hoped it would.

My secondborn Seer powers allowed everyone around me to see the unseen world of angels and demons around us. A distraction I needed to use to my advantage.

My gaze turned to my friends.

Now, I mouthed.

They all slipped away from their captors and formed a circle around me, each locking hands. I shot out my energy, and a pink protective bubble domed around all four of us.

I closed my eyes and said a simple prayer.

Angel, please give all of my friends the gift of protection, a power not affected by sacred stones.

I bit my lip and waited. Hey, it was worth a shot, right?

A shower of sparkles shot from the heavenly display headed straight toward me.

A warm wind blasted my face. *Little secondborn, you have chosen wisely. I will grant your request. But now, you must destroy that stone.*

I gulped as fear flowed through me like the river of hot lava that suddenly lit up at my feet.

What? I screamed in my head. *I can't do that. I'm not my sister. I'm just the secondborn Seer.*

Suddenly a brilliant white light flashed, enveloping everything I saw in a sea of white. The brightness dimmed a fraction until I could make out a beautiful man in white, flowing robes walking toward me. His eyes glowed like golden butterflies fluttering in the breeze.

"Hello, young Seer. Nice to see you on my plane." Angel's voice boomed through the air, even though his lips didn't move.

"Wh-where am I?" I stammered, gaping at the glistening beauty in front of me.

The boom softened to a dull roar. "Don't worry. You're not in heaven. You still have too much life to live before you join us there. Let's just say you're in another plane, one where we can talk face to face."

"Oh, okay." I had no idea what to say to that.

The whiteness suddenly morphed into a scene of darkness. Maxwell's twisted face appeared from a sea of black-clad soldiers, his eye dancing with shadows.

He tugged on a chain, and a girl stumbled into the middle of the circle with a metal chain around her neck.

That girl turned her head, and I stared into my own haggard, tear-streaked face.

I gasped, my hand flying to my lips.

The roar held a note of dissonance. "This is one possible future, young secondborn. If you choose to cooperate with this man, death and destruction will reign in your realm."

The scene shifted into a sea of black-clad soldiers armed with glowing pieces of amethyst and sapphires around their necks. They all had zombie eyes as they raided towns and villages all over the world. Shots rang out, innocent civilians fell in pools of their own blood, and screams tore through the air as the world descended into chaos at the hands of these sacred stone zombies.

"How can I stop them?" I croaked, turning away from the horror.

The sea of whiteness returned. This time, I welcomed the strange world of brightness after the horrible darkness I'd just witnessed.

"You have to destroy this sacred sapphire and all of the remaining three sacred sapphires." The words boomed like a clap of thunder.

"All of them?" I croaked, blinking at my Angel as if that would help. "But that would paint a huge target on my back. The Watchers would surely kill me then."

"Not if they want your powers for themselves. Which, believe me, they do." Crackling noises rustled through the air.

All the hairs on the back of my neck rose up.

"I know what I have to do." I nodded at him, staring at his golden eyes.

"The choice is yours."

Glowing gold butterflies swarmed from his face, flying fast toward me.

I blinked, and the real world—the battlefield on the hillside of Shadowstone Academy—zoomed into focus around me.

I knew there wasn't a choice. I had to destroy the stone. Right now.

"As you wish," I muttered and nodded at him.

My friends gasped, heads pivoting from the sky overhead to stare at me.

Had they just seen everything I saw?

Maxwell burst through the crowd of gaping soldiers, his lips curled in a scowl. "You idiot. Did you start without me after I specifically told you not to? Your mother is stupid for trusting you with anything."

Maxwell tried to break through my protective bubble, but he couldn't. Then he pulled out a sapphire necklace and tried again. Still nothing.

"Clever girl." He shot me a sinister grin.

"You won't think so in a minute." I turned to my friends. "Guys, I have to do this."

Eric nodded. "We saw everything my father wants to do with that sapphire. Don't worry. We've got your back."

I nodded and poured all of my energy into the sapphire in front of me.

It started bubbling and spewing bits of blue lava.

"No!" Maxwell screamed. "Somebody stop her!"

But it was too late. The stone was melting at my fingertips, even as the shield cracked around me.

Four hands were on me somewhere. All of my friends were giving their energy to me. To destroy this evil stone.

Maxwell lunged for me, grabbing me by the throat. I coughed and sputtered, much like the version of me I'd just seen chained by the throat. As that vision flashed through my mind, it only renewed my determination. My hand never left the sapphire.

Then Eric pushed his father away, standing between me and the evil man who sired him. With a burst of light, he turned his lightning on his father, who returned fire. They were locked in a battle of blue electricity.

How Maxwell Morales got a charged sacred stone, I'll never know.

But I didn't have time to figure it out.

The girls and I had a job to do.

We focused our energy on the stone until it burst into a flaming ball of blue sparks and embers that drifted away on the breeze.

I sank to the hard ground, my energy spent.

"No!" Maxwell screamed, his stone turning to blue dust around his neck. It must've been made from the sapphire I just destroyed. Huh, neat trick.

Eric let his lightning fizzle out and raced toward me. "Are you okay, Paige? Talk to me."

He stroked my hair like he thought I was a goner.

"I'm okay," was all I had the energy to mutter right now.

Angel, can you take care of the rest?

Suddenly, the sky began to lighten as dawn broke.

Don't worry, little one. We're here now.

I watched as the angel armies and the Guardian reinforcements battled it out with half of the Watchers.

Rocco, Veronica, and Finn dragged a twitching Maxwell off into the shadows.

Hopefully, the Guardians would capture him before he got away.

Then the Guardian Army turned toward the front lines and drove the Watchers off campus.

I clutched the amethyst around my neck and wrapped my arms around Eric. We'd done it. We lasted the night and so much more.

CHAPTER TWENTY-FOUR

PAIGE

We'd driven the Watchers out with the help of ten thousand Guardian reinforcements and a few angels on our side.

But the aftermath was devastating.

Half the buildings on campus were uninhabitable, bombed-out into nothing but shells. The back fields were a mess of mines that needed to be defused as if the Watchers hadn't wanted us to re-treat—at least not alive. Our retreat to the amphitheater had definitely been part of their plan all along.

There was one bright spot in all the chaos. Most of the Watchers march had been purely part of a distraction tactic to get me right where they wanted me. You know, so Maxwell Morales could suction off my power.

A fact that half of the Guardians had seen displayed in the sky like a big-screen TV.

The Watchers hadn't really tried to kill anyone. As such, we only had injuries and no death toll.

But this was just the first battle of many.

I'd destroyed one of the eight sacred stones still in existence, let alone the Watcher's Sapphire to boot. Now there were only three Watcher's Sapphires left on earth. And they would stop at nothing to save their remaining precious stones and revenge themselves on me.

I'd forever have a target painted on my back.

We were all bunking at Guardian Headquarters tonight until Shadowstone Campus could be cleared of all the Watcher booby traps.

They set up cots in one of the training rooms for all the female students while the guys got stuck in the war room. At least we had bathrooms nearby.

I sank into my cot with a sigh.

"Why the long face?" Stella plopped down beside me, making my cot squeak.

"I just know this isn't the end. Maxwell and Sherry will have it out for me now. They won't rest until they capture me and force me to give them my powers."

"Well, then we'll just have to find their sapphires and destroy the rest of them. Just like your sister did with Nexis." Stella's eyes softened around the edges. "You were given this power for a reason. You can do this."

"I don't know how she did it, how she lived like this." I rested my head in my hands.

"How I did what?" Lucy came in, her smile drooping. "You okay, sis?"

I shook my head. "Not really. I don't know how you lived with this big of a target on your back. I just want to hide in the shadows and never come out."

Her lips twisted as she perched on the cot across from us. "I know the feeling. But for whatever reason, you were chosen for this task. Not me, not Will, not anybody else. Your angel must see tremendous strength in you."

"No, I'm not as strong as you." I shook my head, my messy bun flopping around. "You did it before. Why can't you do it again?" I was so tired I was practically whining now.

"Because it's a heavy burden to bear, the burden of war. I did it once, but I don't think I could do it again. It'd break me." She squeezed my hand as her gaze went distant. "But you're young and strong, just coming into your new powers. And you have tons of friends with extra powers to help you."

"I guess that's true." I smiled at Stella and Brooke as she walked up behind Lucy. "I also have a sister who's been through the fire and can show me the way."

"That's why I'm not leaving your side. Whatever you need, I'll be right here." My sister's gaze returned to me, and her smile broadened. "I've got your back."

"We all do," Felicia said, drying her still-damp hair as she came in from the shower. "Things are about to look really different over the next few months. But we'll all still be here. The SSS needs to stick together."

"That's right," Brooke chimed in. "We might even get to add some new recruits now that you've shown everyone the truth."

All three of them laughed while still looking at me in awe.

"We know you'd sacrifice yourself for us in a heartbeat. We just want you to know we'd do the same." Stella's smile straightened in a flash, and the truth hit me in the gut. She wasn't joking. She was completely serious.

If I had to go to war, at least I had great friends to go into battle by my side.

Paige

"Let this meeting of the Guardians come to order." Harlixton banged the gavel on the podium so loud it echoed throughout the auditorium.

It was December now, and it'd been a week since the Sector Two Watchers had marched against Shadowstone Academy. So many things had changed in just seven days.

Crews were already hard at work rebuilding the ruined academy. Classes were on hold for the rest of the year, maybe longer if the ruling in today's meeting went as expected. There was talk of suspending all classes here and making Shadowstone a sanctuary for the Guardians as the Watcher's ravaged Europe. Right now, the Guardian soldiers were hard at work setting up a security perimeter around campus.

So something like this would never happen again.

Any remaining Watchers had been interrogated and driven from the campus. Their intel had revealed that Sherry Montrose ordered this attack, just like she'd ordered every other attack, even if she hadn't bothered to show up in person.

Her little minions, namely Maxwell Morales, had managed to escape capture. This time.

The truth was becoming apparent. Sherry Montrose was trying to take over the Watcher Corps.

By whatever means necessary.

Shadowstone Academy had become a safe haven for all Sector Two Guardians. Because Watcher attacks were springing up all over Europe.

Nobody was safe anymore.

The gavel banged again. "Order, order!" Harlixton shouted. "We have three items on the agenda. Then we can get back to base repairs."

Oh, right. Shadowstone Academy was now the new Sector Two Guardian base. Surprise!

"The first item on the agenda is to disband the Neutrality Committee. Headmistress Militano, please commence those proceedings."

"Gladly." The woman rose from her chair and tapped the mic. "All those in favor of seceding from the farce of a Neutrality Committee, raise your hand."

Hands went up all across the auditorium, including mine.

"The motion passes." With a satisfied smile, the headmistress crossed her arms over her chest.

I'd never seen her show so much emotion in my life. We all applauded.

"As of today, the Guardians will no longer participate in the Neutrality Committee. Next item of business, the official status of Shadowstone Academy." Her voice cracked, and her hand flew to her throat. "As you can tell, this school is near and dear to my heart. As such, I will ask Councilor Harlixton to present the verdict on the state of this institution."

She stepped back from the podium and pulled out a handkerchief, wiping her eyes.

Eric leaned in and whispered in my ear. "It's probably not good that she called him Councilor instead of Professor Harlixton."

I glanced at him and nodded, studying his face. Over the past few days, he'd been too busy to shave. A reddish-brown stubble covered his lower cheeks and jaw. And it wasn't the worst thing ever.

I leaned in and nuzzled his cheek. What could I say? After what I'd just been through, I needed all the comfort I could get.

Harlixton nodded at the headmistress and walked to the podium. "As you know, as soon as our defenses are secure, Headmistress Militano and the school board have agreed to open their campus to all Sector

Two Guardians from every country seeking shelter from the tyranny the Watchers are perpetrating around the world right now."

Stella winced by my side.

I grabbed her hand. "I'm sure the rest of your family will be here soon."

She nodded at me with a feigned smile. Her parents had been rushed to the campus by Guardian leaders. But her brothers were scattered throughout Sector Four, putting out Watcher fires.

She gripped my hand tight.

Harlixton continued after a long pause. "First, we will open up the former Nexis section of campus to all refugees. Then the Watcher section. Until those sections are filled, classes will remain in session. At least in some form."

A groan rippled through the student population of the auditorium.

Harlixton's lips twitched. "Some of you may be happy to know that the class schedule will be changed. You will be involved in real-life intelligence gathering, combat training, and other necessary war-time functions. The schedule will be determined in January."

Claps and cheers erupted in scattered bursts, and I smiled at my friends.

"Next year should be interesting."

They all nodded at me.

"Now we come to the final item of business for today's meeting. The declaration of war." Harlixton nodded at all four commanders. "Will all section commanders rise?"

A hush filled the room as my father, Stella's father, and the rest of the commanders rose to their feet.

Goosebumps danced up and down my arms. This was it. Today's declaration would make the Watcher/Guardian war official.

"Will you pledge your troops if the Order of the Guardians declares war on the Watcher Corps?" He nodded at my dad first.

"I will pledge my troops." Dad saluted Harlixton, and a cheer went up.

"I will pledge my troops." The Sector Two Commander also saluted.

"I will pledge my troops." The Sector Three Commander saluted too.

Stella's dad cleared his throat. "I will pledge my troops."

I couldn't help but bang my hands together and cheer as a roar erupted through the room.

Harlixton tried to yell over the noise. "With the four section commanders in agreement with the Guardian Council, the Order of the Guardians officially declares war on the Watcher Corps. We will reconvene tomorrow to discuss strategy. You are dismissed."

This time, as we filed out of the auditorium, a new weight hung in the air.

I knew declaring war on the Watchers was the right thing. They wanted power, or at least their leaders wanted more power than they needed—and they would stop at nothing to get it.

But I also knew my role in this conflict would be significant. And it was a huge burden.

Eric came alongside me. "How are you doing, princess?"

I turned to him. "I don't know yet. Things are getting crazy, and I'm still trying to figure out my place in this."

"Your place is right by my side," he slung his arm around my shoulders.

"And at the center of the Sacred Stone Squad. We will protect you at all costs." Lucy shot me a goofy grin.

"It may be time to widen our little circle. I hope you and James have been working on a list of trusted people to add to our ranks." Whoa, that came out totally bossy, and I didn't even care. Just because Lucy was named the leader of the SSS didn't mean I wasn't also a leader too.

She smiled at me. "That's the spirit. I'll tell Harlixton to round up the prospects. We'll start training ASAP."

"Good." I grinned at her, at all the SSS members around me. "I think we should all take key leadership roles in the new SSS."

"Great idea." Stella high-fived me.

I was ready to expand the Sacred Stone Squad into a force to be reckoned with. If I couldn't hide in the shadows anymore, then I wouldn't hold back my team either.

We were about to step into the limelight. And unleash the sacred stone powers on the Watchers.

Look out, Watchers. Here we come.

Enjoy a FREE Sample from:

SHADOWSTONE ACADEMY

Book 3

Sacred Stone Squad

By Barbara Hartzler

Chapter One

Paige

Branches lashed me in the face, and my lungs burned, heaving for air. But I couldn't stop running. I had to find him before they found me first.

Pine needles crunched on the frozen ground behind me. I spared a glance over my shoulder as the black sky crackled with electricity.

Instinctively, I grabbed the Amethyst around my neck—willing my shield into place. Twin rays of blue lightning fractured off the glowing pink bubble I'd domed around myself.

"Clever girls." I stopped in my tracks, bracing my hands on my knees as I gulped in lungfuls of crisp mountain air.

Stella and Brooke emerged from the snowy pine trees with matching grins plastered all over their faces.

"When did you know more than one of us was following you?" Stella's fingers twitched at her sides, her eyes darting from tree to tree.

I narrowed my eyes at her, keeping my protection shield up. I knew my bestie too well. She was hiding something.

And *he* was still out there.

I raised my arm over my head in a flash and zapped the branch above me.

A hulking figure came crashing through the trees. My heart leapt to my throat, but two streams of light arced out around his feet to slow his descent.

Eric landed just outside my pink bubble, encased in his own blue protection bubble. He punched his fist into the snow, shooting me a sheepish grin that almost melted my insides.

I chuckled at his defeated expression. "You guys act like I haven't seen Jurassic Park. The Velociraptor technique is never gonna work on me."

Eric rose to his feet, brushing off the snow from his battle fatigues. "We'll never know for sure until we try all the possible variations."

Dropping my protective shield, I reached out and cupped his scruffy face. "You know, that's not a bad idea for our team strategy. Maybe we could use this tactic on our sisters and their boyfriends. Or at least a variation *not* straight from the movie."

Eric's cheeks flushed in the moonlight. "I hate to say it, but if you picked up our plan this fast, I'm sure your sister will too."

"Yeah, you're right about that. Too bad we watched all those movies as a family." I shrugged one shoulder. "What if we added some guerrilla warfare techniques in the mix?"

"Didn't Lucy learn guerrilla-style from Commander Curtis in the jungles of India?" Brooke pushed her glasses up the bridge of her nose.

"Shoot, you're right." I slapped my knee. "We'll think of something to beat them. I hate that we always finish tied at the end of our training runs."

Stella shot me a sly grin. "But at least we're learning to master these sacred stone powers. Finally."

Hard to believe it was January, and we'd just celebrated the new year in a strange new world. The Guardians had just declared war on the Watchers—only a year after the Nexis Ruby War ended.

The Watchers had been planning attacks and trying to kidnap me for the past six months. At first, they'd blamed the whole thing on Nexis rebels who hadn't been caught or rogue Watchers. But after the attack on Shadowstone Academy, everyone knew who the Watchers were really after.

Me.

Just me, the Secondborn Seer. Not my sister, the Seer. Or her boyfriend, the Interpreter. For some reason, the Watchers wanted me.

Sherry Montrose wanted to take over the Watchers. And I was the missing piece of her grand plan.

In that horrible battle, we caught a glimpse of the extent the new Watcher Queen would go to guarantee her plan came to fruition.

Half the Watcher and Guardian Army had already witnessed the truth of her crazy endgame. Thanks to the all-seeing power of the Watcher's Sapphire, her plan to use my powers to create her own Sacred Stone Army was broadcast for the entire battlefield to see.

After her minions had invaded Shadowstone Academy in an attempt at a hostile takeover.

What did they want with Shadowstone Academy?

Professor Harlixton and the Guardian Council assumed that the Watchers wanted to steal the Guardian Amethyst and set up a base camp for their new world order here at Shadowstone.

Oddly enough, that's exactly what the Guardians had done instead. So much for that plan, crazy Sherry. At least until she attempted the next trick up her sleeve.

Shadowstone Academy was now a safe haven for all of Europe's Guardians as they fled from the Watcher raids sweeping across the continent.

All the intel the Watchers had extracted from their rogue attacks last year was used to invade every Guardian outpost that had ever housed the Guardian Amethyst. Every sector of the Order of the Guardians was on high alert. One thing was for sure, Sherilyn Montrose wanted the sacred stones. All of them.

Nowhere was safe anymore. War had broken out in Europe, and it would soon spread to the rest of the world.

The only way to stop them was to build an even bigger Sacred Stone Squad.

But my throat constricted at the thought.

This was my gift, and I wasn't sure I wanted to give just *anyone* the power of the sacred stones. How did we know who we could trust?

One of my best friends, an original SSS member, had turned traitor to the Watcher's Sector Two Commander, Maxwell Morales. Also known as my boyfriend's evil father.

Speaking of my boyfriend, Eric slid his arm around my waist. "You okay, princess? You're making that face that says you're thinking too much."

"Am I?" I unscrewed the furrow from my forehead and gave him a tight smile. "I know the Guardians want to expand the Sacred Stone Squad. I just don't know if I want to give away so many powers."

His lips curled as his hip bumped mine. "If they give away too many powers, there'd be no more sacred stones intact."

"Haha. Very Funny. Can you imagine?" I snorted out a laugh at that, even as my insides fluttered at the thought. "But seriously, you know what I mean. What if this power falls into the wrong hands? You know, someone like Owen or a double agent?"

"You know I love you for worrying about this so much. But you aren't responsible for other people's choices." The way Eric looked at me with those stormy sea eyes made me want to sink into his arms and never let go.

I still hadn't been able to say the L-word back to him yet. And he didn't seem to mind. He'd just throw it out casually here and there as a little reminder that we had unfinished business.

For now, I simply rested my head on his shoulder. "You're right. I think too much. But passing on the powers is my choice. So I can worry about it. Just a little."

"As you wish." He planted a kiss on my forehead.

Brooke cleared her throat. "Hey, guys. Are you done being all disgustingly cute? 'Cause, we have incoming at three o'clock." She tilted her head to our right.

Lucy, Will, Felicia, and Sedrick strutted through the forest like they owned the place.

"Who's ready for the deciding training run?" Lucy arched her eyebrows in challenge.

Narrowing my eyes in response, I crossed my arms over my chest as my team stepped up beside me. "We're ready, sis. Game on."

An air horn blasted somewhere in the distance, and both sides took off running in the opposite direction.

We'd find the fake sacred stones first. Then I'd worry about adding any new members to the Sacred Stone Squad.

Paige

Wiping sweat from my brow, I barreled into the training facility, victory in hand.

I hoisted up the squishy rubber sapphire for all to see. A cheer surged around the gym.

We'd been on eleven training runs now throughout the Shadowstone Academy campus and its facilities. But we'd never been on top of the leaderboard before.

Lucy clapped me on the back. "The B Team finally pulls in front of the A Team. Way to go, sis."

I wrinkled my nose at her. "Yeah, it's definitely time to stop calling us A and B teams. We deserve a better title, fitting for a run of three victories in a row."

"Especially the win that put us over the top!" Brooke reached for the trophy and trotted around the room in a victory lap all her own.

Stella eyed me, and I dipped my chin in response. Without another word, we raced to catch up with our teammate. Eric wasn't too far behind.

Felicia beamed at her brother with a hint of pride in her eyes. "Maybe she's right, Lucy. I think they've definitely graduated past the B Team."

"Thank you." I swept my hand out in a mock curtsy.

"We'll think about it." Lucy grabbed a clean towel from the stack and wiped her glistening forehead.

Just then, James burst through the gym doors. "Sacred Stone Squad, listen up!" His eyes darted around the room wildly. "Situation report in one hour, my office. Don't be late."

Then he turned on his heel and marched out of the room.

"Yikes." I glanced at my sister.

"That can't be good." She winced, biting into her lip. "We better just do what he says. Let's hit the showers."

We all gave each other sidelong glances as everyone dispersed to their respective locker rooms.

Stepping into the hot shower, I let the warm water soothe all my aching muscles. I breathed in the humid air, enjoying a much-need moment of quiet.

Now that Shadowstone was the worldwide Guardian headquarters, my school was now teeming with Guardian officers from all walks of life—including my family.

The extra officials had taken up residence in the old Nexis section of campus. Ironic, huh? Oddly enough, most of the battle damage to the academy had been on the back half of the campus, where the outbuilding, extra gym, and the Watcher section were the hardest hit.

The Guardians who'd taken refuge on campus were in the process of repairing the damage. We all knew there would be more refugees soon enough.

Those students still left on campus were allowed to keep their dorm rooms, but many families had moved into the empty suites. Apparently, not everyone wanted to live in a war zone.

At least the Guardians had spared the top floor of my dorm, leaving it open for new Sacred Stone Squad members to come. They'd even moved Felicia, Sedrick, and Eric down the hall from Stella and me, across from Brooke and her sister. The team vibe was fun, but it was a little hard to not be distracted by your boyfriend when he lived down the hall.

Instead of classes, now we had workouts, training sessions, and strategy meetings. And more training sessions.

My muscles were more sculpted and defined than ever because of all the training drills we went through in the past few weeks. At least we'd gotten a day off for a quiet Christmas celebration.

The shower water lost its steam, and I knew it was time to face the music.

Turning off the faucet, I toweled dry and put on my Guardian uniform—a standard-issue set of black canvas fatigues with a gold SSS patch emblazoned on the right breast pocket. Right below my last name.

Between the golden SSS letters were two little diamonds to represent the sacred stones that gave us our powers. At least they let me design the logo.

My shoulders had one golden upside V on each arm. That's right. I was now Private McAllen of the Order of the Guardians, Sacred Stone Division.

Once we added more members to the SSS, they might bump me to Corporal like my sister. That is *if* I decided to dole out more sacred stone powers.

My fingers curled into a fist at my side. I couldn't let another Owen slip through the ranks. I'd just have to figure out a way to vet candidates better this time around.

Brooke and Stella wrapped their hair into neat little buns while Felicia and Lucy pulled theirs into high ponytails. I left my hair down and blow-dried it under the hand dryer. A girl's gotta retain some element of style.

As a unit, we left the training gym and marched like good little soldiers down the gray concrete hall to the Guardian offices.

All of the offices were underground, just in case of invasion. At least my half-wet hair wouldn't freeze in the arctic temperatures of Switzerland in January.

I followed the rest of the girls to my brother's office, and we all took seats at the conference table on the far side of the drab gray room.

How I missed the espresso machine from his New York office right now. But I took the cup of coffee Eric offered to me.

"Hey, this isn't half bad." I sipped on the warm, creamy liquid.

"Thanks," he shrugged and slid into the chair beside me.

Once the guys were all situated at the table, James slammed a stack of files on the gleaming mahogany. "It's time we expand the SSS. The Watcher attacks are getting worse. Just look."

I clenched my teeth but met my brother's glare. "How bad is it?"

Lucy passed the files around the table, and everyone's eyes widened. Outpost after outpost had been invaded, ransacked, or worse—innocent Guardians hurt or killed during Watcher raids.

"It gets worse." He grimaced, no doubt mirroring my expression. "One of the Watcher Council members was assassinated, and Sherry Montrose has taken the open seat."

I gasped, and similar noises echoed around the table from my friends.

Will pounded his fist into the table. "Let me guess. She's saying the Guardians are behind the whole thing?"

"Bingo," James pointed at Will, but a sadness lingered in his eyes.

Will narrowed his gaze. "No rise to power would be complete without lies, false favors, and bribery. I bet the Watchers are congratulating themselves for choosing her."

Lucy sucked in a breath. "That's messed up. There will be no reasoning with the Watchers now."

James pursed his lips together. "I'm afraid not. But there's one thing we can do. It's time to add more members to the team."

For some reason, tears welled in my eyes at the magnitude of everything we were facing. Whether it was Sherry taking over the world or the fact that I had to dole out more sacred stone powers, I couldn't be sure.

"You okay, princess?" Eric's hand found my shoulder as he leaned into me.

I blinked back the sudden emotion and nodded at him. "I'm just not looking forward to giving out more powers. It can be a taxing experience, to be a conduit for that much energy." Then I turned back to James. "How many more people did you want to add?"

"Ten, maybe twenty if you're up for it." His eyes softened on those last words.

A wave of exhaustion rippled through me at the thought, but I wrapped my fingers around the edge of my chair to hold myself upright. If we were going to do this, we couldn't let another spy slip into the squad. I'd had my fill of traitors.

I gave him a quick nod. "I think I can handle that."

"Good. Let's start at the top of the pile." He went to his desk and pulled out another stack of files, placing them in front of me. "This is Laura Brewster. She's a trusted friend of Lucy's from Montrose Paranormal Academy. And she fought with us in the Seer's Army."

Lucy squealed and clapped her hands, smiling at Felicia, who politely dipped her head. But I caught the beginnings of a grin creeping up her face.

James pulled out another manila file. "This is Abby Cooper. You may know her from your self-defense class here at Shadowstone."

Brooke's face lit up. "Looks like we're keeping it all in the family."

James nodded. "I think it's best to tap people we trust first. That's why I'm a little hesitant about the next candidate. But your brother Bryan has been a loyal Guardian for years."

Both Will and Sed winced at that, glancing at each other. I couldn't help but wonder what that was all about, but I knew better than to ask right now.

Cosette leaned over my brother's shoulder and pulled out the next file. "Also up for nomination to the SSS is Malik Jones. He, too, served in the Seer's Army and—"

James cut her off with a slashing motion across his throat as his gaze shot to Lucy.

Cosi's eyes went wide, and she clamped her lips shut.

Lucy's eyes watered at that suggestion, her smile fading a bit.

I'd met Malik briefly when he joined the Seer's Army a year ago. But saying his full name seemed to open up old wounds for my sister. Her best friend, Shanda Jones, died early in the Nexis Ruby Wars—and was Malik's cousin.

My throat constricted as I offered Lucy a sad smile. I couldn't imagine losing my best friend in the awful war. I grabbed Stella's hand and squeezed.

"Sorry, Lucy." Cosi bit her lip.

James cleared his throat, turning to open two files at once. "Raj and Patel Mamertus would also be good additions to the team."

All eyes turned to Stella, whose blush seeped across her caramel cheeks.

"I guess we are really keeping it in the family." Stella rolled her eyes, chuckling under her breath. "They're a little rowdy, but both good fighters. They were instrumental in saving the Genesis Academy from the wrath of Nexis during the war."

Brooke turned to Stella, eyebrows arched. "Are these older or younger brothers?"

"Older. And they're twins." Stella bit her lip.

A grin broke out on Brooke's face. "Nice."

Stella rolled her eyes at our blonde friend. "Let's just focus on the candidates."

"Fine," Brooked huffed, adjusting her glasses.

James went through a few other files, all names I pretty much recognized from Shadowstone students or my brief stint in the Seer's Army.

"Seems like a good mix of Guardian loyalists and Seer's Army rebels," Felicia smirked at her own joke.

Sed leaned forward, resting his elbows on the table. "What's the timeline for training these new members?"

James gulped, thunking back down in his swanky chair at the head of the table. "I'm not going to lie. It's getting bad out there. As you've seen from the files, the Watchers are attacking every Guardian outpost that has ever housed smaller shards of the Amethysts."

Will scoffed, rubbing the back of his neck. "What do they want with the small pieces?"

James shook his head. "I wish we knew. Maybe they want the smaller stones for some kind of ritual. Or maybe they think the intel will lead them to the original four Amethysts housed by each sector. It's hard to say right now."

"But the time will come when they turn their attention to the big stones. And we need to be ready." Lucy's words were low, but her conviction resonated throughout the room.

Around the table, everyone fidgeted or sat up straighter in their chairs.

"We're doing all we can to move the stones around and keep them out of Watcher hands. But this is our next line of defense." A muscle twitched in my brother's jaw as he pointed at the stack of SSS candidates.

Cosette reached out and patted his hand.

As I glanced around the room, I couldn't help but wonder if the vision I'd had on the side of campus last year might just come true—except in reverse.

If I gave more people the power of the sacred stones, what would stop the Guardians from twisting that army into something that served their Order?

Maybe expanding the Sacred Stone Squad wasn't the answer. But even I knew we were running out of options.

Want to keep reading all about the new Sacred Stone Squad and Paige and Eric's new love?

Check out Shadowstone Academy, Book 3: Sacred Stone Squad FREE on Kindle Unlimited or 1-click today!

OR...

Join my mailing list to download your exclusive free copy of Montrose Paranormal Academy, Book 0: The Nexis Awakening today!

Montrose Paranormal Academy

Book 0

The Nexis Awakening

By Barbara Hartzler

Chapter One

JAMES

Here was the funny thing: I was never that guy. The responsible guy. No, I was the guy who froze his younger sister's training bra. The guy who paintballed the Guardian floor of Denby Hall for Halloween open dorms.

Sure, I've been on my own for four years of high school living it up at Riverdale, New York's finest boarding school. And I'm still president of the Nexis Society, for at least another day. Until they find out what I'm about to do.

Because there I was, sitting on the subway, about to break into a church in Harlem.

I had told the heir apparent this was his initiation mission. That's right. I lied to the great Will Stanton, Jr., Golden Adonis of the Nexis Society. The fifteen-year-old boy wonder who'd supposedly usher in the Utopian society Nexis had been engineering for centuries.

It was easy to lie to this kid, but infinitely harder lying to all of my friends, especially my girlfriend, for two months now.

Here's the truth—I was doing the most responsible thing I'd ever done in my life.

I had a plan to protect my kid sister, Lucy. Even if I had to break into a church to do it. You think the cops would buy it? Yeah, me neither. *Let's pray we don't get caught.*

Cocking my head, I glanced across the subway bench at the kid who'd soon replace me. Maybe tomorrow, maybe next week. But right now, Will Stanton didn't know what I knew. He thought this was a Nexis mission like any other.

The corners of my mouth curled. Good. That's what I wanted him to think. It was his family against mine. The Stantons vs. the McAllens. And I wouldn't let them win. *If I'm going down, he's going down with me.*

The brakes squealed as we slowed to a stop. I zipped up my black hoodie and stood up.

"You ready for this?" I asked as the doors slid open.

"You bet," he said with a grin plastered across his face. "I'm always ready for a secret mission."

I fought the urge to roll my eyes. Only a handful of bleary-eyed people walked out with us. Still, every hair on the back of my neck stood up. My blood pumped double-time, but no one seemed to notice two black-clad teenagers on the subway platform. It was midnight on a Thursday, after all. Only in New York.

We booked it up the steps, two at a time, and made our way out to the street without any more naive freshman comments that might give us away. I led our two-man crew around the corner to the next stoplight.

Will pressed the button, and we waited our turn. When the Walk sign lit up, we crossed Third Avenue, ducking into the shadows of the residential side of 104th. Distant sirens and the clunk of our footsteps were the only sounds in the night. Almost in the clear now.

"So, what's this mission anyway?" he asked, breaking up the silence.

"You'll see," I whispered. We had to sneak past the Harlem projects without being seen. Didn't he get that?

The street was darker now. Twenty more feet and we'd be there.

"C'mon man." Will was whining now. "Tell me what's up."

Shaking my head, I kept walking. Five more steps, and I stopped. "Here we are."

Will backed up. "No way. I can't break into a church."

"Some pampered Nexis president you'll be, mama's boy," I hissed at him. Pivoting around to face the wimp, I glared him down. *Think. Make something up.* "Listen, man. This is my last mission as Nexis president. And your first. It's a long-standing tradition to initiate the new guy. But hey, if you can't handle it, I'm sure they'll find someone else." There, that should shut him up.

Sure enough, his eyes went wide. "Are you serious? I'm the next Nexis president? Awesome. Let's do this."

"Welcome aboard." I shook his hand, all official-like and everything. See what I mean? Responsible. Turning back to the church, I pulled my lock pick out of my pocket.

Bing. Bong. Bing. Bong. The church bells dinged as I jimmied the lock. Not helping.

"St. Lucy's Church," Will said slowly, as if he had just learned how to read. "We're breaking into a church named after the first Seer?"

My hands quaked. *Please God, don't let him figure it out. Not yet.* But I kept working the lock. I had to get those documents. My own Lucy needed protection from the likes of people like him. And she needed that stone.

"Don't you have a sister? Her name's Lucy, right?" Will asked.

I flinched and hunched my shoulders, refusing to give anything away. "Yeah, so what?"

"A funny coincidence I guess." He started whistling to himself.

"Yeah, funny." I tuned him out. Thank God he was fifteen and completely clueless. Back to business. I was so close. My palms were sweating now. My heart thumped in my ears. I could feel the lock about to give way. I needed to relax.

Pop. Like magic, the lock clicked and the door cracked open.

"You've gotta teach me how to do that," he said as we tiptoed into the dark building.

"Shh." I put one finger to my lips.

Darkness draped the cavernous foyer in eerie silence like it knew we were here—watching our every move.

My sneakers squeaked across the marble. I slid up against the wall, motioning Will to do the same. He followed my lead as we turned the corner and trekked up a long hallway. Two doors down was the library. I knew because Responsible James had already cased the place.

At the library door, I jimmied the lock again. This one popped open in only a few twists. These guys needed to up their security, especially in this town.

"Nice," Will whispered.

I opened the door, yanked him by the collar, and dragged him inside. Ever-so-slowly, I closed the door until it clicked. Locking it behind me.

"Keep your voice down," I growled at him. "Try to remember we're on a covert mission."

"Sooor-ry." He hoisted his hands in the air. "What're we looking for anyway?"

Gripping his hoodie tighter, I stared him down. "This stays between us, past president to future prez. Can I trust you?"

His eyes were wide, but he didn't flinch or look away. "Of course you can trust me. I won't tell anyone."

"You can't tell a soul. Not Nexis, not even your parents. No one, got it?" I narrowed my eyes at him. "You swear? This is life or death stuff here."

"I swear, James." With one nod he clapped a hand on my shoulder. "I know I'm a Stanton and everything that's supposed to mean in the Nexis world. But I'm your friend first. You can trust me. Tell me what's going on."

I narrowed my eyes at him, studying every nook and cranny of his face. But I couldn't find anything. No telltale nervous tick, or rapid-fire blinking. Will just stared back at me, looking me square in the eye. Could he actually mean what he said?

Will came from a long line of Stantons, the family that had ruled the Nexis Semigod Nations for a century, with no end in sight. But this guy seemed different. I'd watched him all year. He wasn't like every other Nexis freshman looking to climb the ladder. Maybe Will's family hadn't told him about their plans. Maybe he was in the dark like I was once. So I decided to take a chance on this guy.

Pulling two flashlights from my hoodie pocket, I handed him one. "Here's the deal. I'm looking for documents on the sacred stones and their current locations. Think you can handle that, rookie?"

"So that's what this is about." A slow grin curled his mouth. "You're looking for a leg up. Can't say I blame you, either. If I was next in line to be the Seer I'd want to find the Watcher's Sapphire, too. So everyone would take me seriously. But I doubt we'll find a treasure map to their secret hideout in here."

"No, that's not it," I said, shaking my flashlight. "I don't want just *anyone* to be able to see the unseen world of angels and demons. It's not a gift. It's an incredible burden." I had to give this kid credit, though. He knew more than I did at his age. *Figures.*

"So what are you looking for?" he asked. "You know where we keep the Nexis Ruby."

"Do I seriously have to spell it out for you?" I shook my head at him. "There are only three sacred stones. I'm looking for the Guardian Amethyst."

"Whoa." He sucked in a breath. "You've got some balls man. That could start a war, you know."

"Maybe," I said, gnawing on my lip. Now was the time for some major BS. "But not if we do this right. If I shave off a little piece for protection and report its location to Nexis—"

"Nice," he said. "That way no one can touch you and you'll still score some major points."

"Exactly." I shrugged like I couldn't care less. "You'll get credit, too. For helping and all."

"That'll make me a shoe-in to take your place as president. Say no more. I got your back, buddy. Let's see what we can find." He aimed his flashlight at a bookshelf in the far corner and walked over to it, thumbing through the titles.

Now I was the one following Will's lead. Ironic. Maybe he'd been on a few covert missions after all. Flashlights in hand, we searched the cedar shelves, pulled out enormous parchment tomes with interesting titles, and stacked them on a mahogany table in the middle of the dark room. We opened the most promising books first.

Blowing off dust. Poring over yellowed parchment. Page after page after page of nothingness. Pure Nexis propaganda. Outlines for their Utopian world order, aka global domination. Blah, blah, blah. The usual Nexis garbage.

At last, I'd found the two words I'd been searching for. *Sacred stones.*

This section was an overview of the twelve sacred stones of the twelve tribes of Israel. Apparently, the legend of the stones originated from some passage in Exodus. Each gemstone was reported to have its own unique properties—four rubies, four amethysts, and four sapphires. These stones formed the basis for each secret society's beliefs.

Nexis started with an obsession to find the rubies because they have the power to give fallen angels human-like bodies. And the ability to mate with the women of earth and create Nephilim. Yeah, crazy stuff.

This book documented how Nexis found all four rubies by the 13th century. For nine hundred years. they'd been protecting their precious stones and hunting down the other three components of their plan: the Seer, and at least one amethyst and one sapphire.

A chill slithered down my back. They'd been trying to get the Seer on their side for years. This was the closest they'd ever come. I could feel their grip circling me. Slowly tightening the noose around my neck. Waiting until I turned eighteen to reveal their true plan.

Tomorrow, Nexis would know the truth. I wasn't the Seer. I couldn't be. The truth was almost a relief, actually. Except the part about Mom having an affair and the fact that Dad wasn't really my biological father. I wasn't James McAllen after all. A sad story. Pathetic, really.

Two months ago, I needed a passport for the senior ski trip to Canada. Mom wouldn't give me my birth certificate. Said she lost it. So I played the responsible card and went through all the red tape to get my passport on my own. Only to find out I wasn't who I thought I was.

If I wasn't the Seer, then Lucy was next in line. I had to protect her, even if she was only my half-sister. Because tomorrow was my eighteenth birthday. The day that everyone would find out the truth. A truth I'd known for a long time. Longer than two months, if I were truly honest.

I never had the Awakenings, not like the legends say you're supposed to. I laughed it off when people talked about it. Like it was no big deal. I told myself I'd probably be the Seer's dad or grandpa or something. Deep down, though, something always felt off.

I wanted to run, start a new life somewhere. But I couldn't. Not yet. Not until I knew my sister would be safe. If I wasn't the Seer, at least I could be the Guardian of the Seer. Has a nice ring to it, right?

I read on. The next passage was about the purple stone. The stone of protection. Finally. It was all there in black and white. Nexis knew where all four amethysts were—under Guardian control, of course.

Centuries ago, when Nexis started organizing, there was opposition. Naturally, because their plan was crazy. The Guardians came together to protect the world from Nexis. While Nexis combed the earth for rubies, the Guardians searched for the amethysts. From this record, Nexis believed they'd hidden one stone in each of their four primary locations, America, Europe, the Middle East, and Asia.

Over the centuries Nexis tried to steal the amethysts, without success. They'd sent spies into the Guardian ranks, learning approximate locations for each stone. In the 1900's, a spy reported the American amethyst was in New York, but Nexis still hadn't found it yet. The last search was dated a year ago. A spy had heard rumors that the amethyst was hidden in the neutral zone, Montrose Academy. He searched the chapel but found nothing. No notes about any more rumors.

"I've got something," Will said a little too loudly.

"Quiet," I hissed at him. "There could be someone here." Nonetheless, I rounded the table and read over his shoulder.

"Look here," he pointed at a passage. "It's a record of the amethyst at Montrose. Crazy, huh?"

"Yeah, crazy," I whispered. My eyes landed on the passage. Sure enough, a record of the American amethyst. I stopped in my tracks. My heart punched against my ribcage. I was so close to finding it, but I had to be sure.

I skipped to the most recent entry—from six months ago. A rumor of the amethyst buried somewhere in the Montrose chapel library, or a hidden tunnel below it. The next entry was the Nexis plan to dig under the chapel. To get permits.

"A hidden tunnel?" I asked silently.

Click, clack, click.

I froze. Looked at Will. "Go to the door," I whispered. "Check if someone's coming."

My fingers itched. I knew this page was important, so I kept reading. Nexis bribed cable companies and city officials, but each time the city denied their permit. At the end, there was a strange note. A reference to another page in another book.

"Someone's coming," he hissed across the room. "Let's get out of here."

Voices floated down the hall. They sounded far away. Far enough away to give me time to do what I knew I had to do.

Sticking the flashlight in my mouth I scanned all the titles on the table until I found the book I needed. Adrenaline pumped through my body as I sliced through the pages at lightning speed, looking for the right one.

The voices were louder now. Closer. My heartbeat skyrocketed, fingers flying in overdrive.

"Hurry up," Will said, hands flailing like a madman. "C'mon already."

Eureka! I found it. Something about St. Lucia and the stones. *This better be it.*

"Just take the book and let's go," Will hissed, grabbing my collar.

"And have them find a sacred book missing? Not a chance," I hissed back, my heart pounding. No time to read. I grabbed a few pages...and ripped. I ran toward the door, stuffing the pages in my hoodie.

"What did you do that for?" Will held the door open, staring at me.

I ran past him. "No time. Let's go." I took off running up the hall. Churned my legs as fast as they would go.

Will was right behind me. But he wasn't the only one. Someone chased us in the dark.

My brain kicked into panic mode as my legs found a new gear. I rounded the corner and sprinted for the front door.

Then Will yelped. "Hey, get off me."

An old priest had one gnarled grip on the hem of his jacket.

"Keep going." I yanked on Will's arm so hard the priest dropped it.

In a flash, we took off down the steps and raced up the street.

Footsteps echoed behind us. Slowed, then stopped.

Two seconds later we rounded the block. Out of the corner of my eye, I caught a glimpse of the priest in his black garb, keeled over, hands on his slacks. Wheezing like crazy as he pulled his phone out of his pocket.

"That was close, man," Will gasped between breaths.

"Too close. But It's not over yet," I breathed as we jogged up the sidewalk to the nearest subway station. Tumbling down the stairs, we hopped on the next train.

"I can't believe we didn't get caught," he slumped lower on the bench across from me, "and you ripped the pages out of a hundred-year-old book. Must be something good, right?"

"I hope so," I said, stuffing the crumpled pages deeper into my hoodie.

When I saw Lucy tomorrow, I'd warn her. Tell her everything. Until then, I had twelve hours to come up with a plan. Before I turned eighteen and her cover was officially blown.

Want to keep reading Montrose Paranormal Academy, Book 0: The Nexis Awakening for FREE? Read all about how James was banished from Montrose Paranormal Academy ... and when Lucy's visions really started.

Join my mailing list at www.barbarahartzler.com to download your exclusive free copy of the today!

PAIGE'S FAMILY STORY CONTINUES ...

<u>Keep reading for free samples from Book 1 in the NEW, next-generation series, Genesis Academy!</u>

<u>Genesis Academy, Book 1: The Seer's Legacy</u>, is the story of Sophie Stanton, daughter of the Seer and the Interpreter.

Sophie's new powers send her on a collision course to the Guardian reject academy, ahem, Genesis Academy.

Check out the first chapter now ...

GENESIS ACADEMY

Book 1
The Seer's Legacy
By Barbara Hartzler

CHAPTER ONE

Sophie

Would this day ever end? Staring out the window of my third-floor classroom, I counted down the minutes until school let out.

Normally, I loved my chemistry class because it was a key component in my quest to become a forensic scientist.

But not today. Today was the much anticipated Guardian Council elections. Every four years, my grandfather—the great Thomas McAllen—was up for reelection as the Guardian's Supreme Councilor.

Honestly, it was part of my life that I hated. All I ever wanted to be was normal—not a member of the Seer's bloodline in a secret society. The *last* secret society left after the other two had been stamped out in brutal wars. Wars that had to be covered up as terrorist attacks to keep the media, and local governments, from catching onto our secret societies.

And now there was only one secret society left. The Order of the Guardians, or just the Guardians for short. Peace had reigned for twenty-five years now.

Maybe that's why I chose to go to a normal(ish) prep school that wasn't part of the Guardians.

I just wanted to live a simple life where I'd become a forensic scientist or maybe a crime scene investigator. And I definitely didn't want to get some crazy powers dropped on me for my eighteenth birthday, like the prophecy foretold.

But I only had two months left of normalcy. In January, on my birthday, we'd see if any powers to see angels and demons suddenly appeared.

Who knows. Prophecies could be wrong, right?

Tapping my pencil on my textbook, I watched passersby on the street below. There was always someone interesting walking the sidewalks of New York. I preferred to observe and analyze from my safe little perch. For as long as I possibly could.

The bell rang, and I bolted out the door, racing through the front lobby to the town car waiting out front.

"Hey, Julio." I waved and climbed into the backseat.

Yeah, I know. Having a bodyguard/chauffeur wasn't exactly normal. But it was the only way my parents would let me attend Brighton Prep.

Julio dropped me off in the alley behind our cute little West Side brownstone. I waved goodbye to him, hopping the five steps up to the back door.

The minute I walked in, I knew something was wrong. Mom and Dad were just sitting at the kitchen island in the middle of the afternoon, staring at their laptop.

"Hi, Sophie. Welcome home." My mom's smile was a little too bright. And wilting at the edges.

I set my book bag on the nearest bar stool. "What's up, guys?"

My dad ran a hand through the sandy blonde scruff at the nape of his neck. "More lies about your grandfather. This Guardian Council campaign is getting out of control."

I narrowed my eyes at him, studying his face. A muscle in his cheek twitched. Aha! He wasn't telling me the whole truth.

"Okay," I hedged, sitting next to them on the empty stool while shoving my bag onto the tile floor. "What aren't you telling me?"

Mom downed her coffee and rose to her feet. "It's nothing for you to worry about, sweetie."

She ruffled my hair as she passed behind me, heading toward the coffeepot.

"If they're saying bad things about my grandpa, I have a right to know." I wanted to stamp my foot, but I was too old for such childish things. Especially while sitting on a tall bar stool.

Dad swiveled the laptop to face me. "See for yourself, if you want. But it's all lies."

I leaned forward, elbows on the granite countertop as I scanned the webpage on the Worldwide Guardian, our special Order of the Guardians super secret intranet. He had a news page pulled up with an article entitled *Councilor McAllen Funnels Money to Shroudcliff Prison.*

I furrowed my eyebrows at Dad. "What? That doesn't make any sense."

Mom stood beside me, flipping her dark hair behind her shoulder. "Friedrich Vanguard's camp is saying my father is wasting money and doing some sort of experiment at Shroudcliff. It's kind of insane, honestly." Her fingers curled into a fist and she pounded the counter. "I wish the Vanguard family wasn't in such high standing with the Guardians. They're ruthless and will do anything to gain power."

"It's all just conjecture." Dad loved to throw out legal terms, even in everyday life. "They have no proof it was him. The only proof they have is that someone in the Guardian ranks sent extra money to Shroudcliff. They haven't traced it to anyone yet and have no idea what it's being used for."

"But Grandpa is the Supreme Councilor of the Guardian Council. If he's improving the prison system, isn't that part of a Council initiative?" I tried to keep up with Guardian politics, since my parents were so involved. But it was a convoluted mess to me half the time.

"Very astute, Buttercup." Dad glanced at me, eyes brightening with a little extra glimmer.

I cringed at his use of my childhood nickname, but let it slide. Just this once.

Mom sucked in a breath. "Unfortunately, this was definitely unsanctioned spending."

"Wow." I blinked, staring at the screen. My life was all about the politics of the secret society of the Guardians.

My mother, Lucy McAllen, was the infamous Seer who had stopped the Nexis Ruby War and been instrumental in helping my Aunt Paige end the Watcher Sapphire War.

That was back in the time of the Three Societies—three secret societies that each protected a line of Sacred Stones and had their own Chosen Ones with special powers.

My mom was from the McAllen family line. Once a century, their bloodline produced a Seer whose powers were drawn from the Guardian Amethysts, of which only three still existed. She had dreams and visions of the unseen world of angels and demons, and the ability to see that world at any time.

Ever since the secret wars ended, I wondered if she retained her powers. She always told me that her powers had gone dormant when I was born, but I wasn't so sure about that. Every now and then she'd have way too much insight into something she shouldn't know, like how that boy in middle school only liked me because of my Chosen One bloodline.

It was infuriating.

But my mom wasn't the only Chosen One in my family.

Once upon a time, my father, Will Stanton, had his own powers too. The Stanton bloodline produced another Chosen One—the Interpreter. He could interpret my mom's visions and had his own invisibility powers to protect the Watcher Corps' Sacred Sapphire.

There had even once been a third Chosen One, my Aunt Felicia, the Messenger. Her powers were drawn from the Nexis Society's Sacred Ruby and she had the power to see the future, in all its multiple versions. She also had some cool lightning powers that she used to make herself levitate. Pretty badass.

But all the Sacred Rubies and the Sacred Sapphires were destroyed in the wars, rendering both the Watcher Corps and the Nexis Society obsolete, even if old loyalties secretly remained to this day.

The Nexis and Watcher wars left my dad and Aunt Felicia without any powers of their own, since all of their sacred stones were destroyed.

The only line left with any Sacred Stone powers was through my mother.

Ever since I was born and her powers went dormant, both watched me like a hawk. As if they expected me to sprout wings or something.

Never before in the history of the Guardians had there been a child born of two Chosen Ones.

But there had also never been more than one set of Chosen Ones with active powers less than a hundred years apart. And yet, Aunt Paige, who was the secondborn in the chosen bloodline, had received powers only a few years after her older sister. Highly unprecedented.

For all we knew, I was only destined to carry on the Seer's line. And yet, there was this unspoken expectation that I'd somehow have some sort of special power.

I'd turned eighteen in a few months. Hopefully, nothing happened and I'd end up as just an average teenager with a cool family legacy.

Only time would tell.

Dad bumped my shoulder. "Why don't you go upstairs and change? Then we'll head over to headquarters for the election watch party."

"Ugh, fine." I groaned, rolling my eyes and trudging up the stairs to my room.

That meant putting on a nice little dress and pearls to look the part of a perfect family. A part of politics I'd rather pass on, thank you very much.

I usually hated these election watch parties. Grandpa always won by a landslide. But this year, his opponent had waged a nasty smear campaign against him with all of those prison funding allegations.

And this was the first year our family actually seemed nervous about the results.

The only reason Shroudcliff Prison existed was to keep the ringleaders of the last wars locked away for life. Even if one of those baddies happened to be my paternal grandmother.

My father never talked about his mother, the infamous Rosalyn Stanton. But I'd heard Mom and Dad whispering about her now and then when they thought I wasn't listening.

I shut the door to my room and shrugged off my blazer. At least I could get out of this stupid prep school uniform. Why did all the elite college prep schools in New York have to have ugly uniforms? It was obnoxious.

Aunt Paige had helped me add some pizzazz to the hideous monstrosity, but there was only so much we could do without breaking the dress code. She was a busy fashion designer with a husband, my Uncle Eric, and two little kids to wrangle.

But there was one good thing about having a fashion designer aunt. At least when I put the Paige Morales label in a discreet corner of my blazer, the popular kids pretended like they could tolerate me.

I slid the awful plaid skirt to the ground and put on my favorite teal dress with leggings. November in New York definitely had a bite to it, so I added my favorite black boots to complete the ensemble.

Then I slipped on a gold bangle with a peacock clasp. Aunt Paige would surely give me a hard time if I didn't make an attempt to be stylish.

Election night did come with one perk. My whole family would be there. Including my best and only friend Patrick—who was also my cousin. We'd probably have to babysit our younger cousins, which usually made the whole night fun but exhausting.

I hurried downstairs to the living room, where Mom was fixing dad's collar. They both looked like they were about to run for president. Mom in her crisp navy blue dress and Dad in his matching suit, sans tie. Win or lose, we'd all be carted out onstage for a speech. And probably a few interviews too.

Even though the Order of the Guardians was a secret society, they had four sectors across the globe—North America, Europe, Africa, and Asia. This event would be televised in all four sectors, on the Worldwide Guardian closed network, of course.

Dad's phone dinged. "The town car is out front. We better get going."

I resisted the urge to roll my eyes. Really. I did.

Normally, we took the subway when traveling around the city. But whenever Guardian business was involved, the Order sent a town car. Especially on election night.

Outside, the cold air nipped at my nose as the sky turned dusky. The leaves had turned vibrant shades of yellow, orange, and red. But I didn't have time to admire the view from our stoop.

"C'mon, sweetie. Don't dawdle." Mom ushered me down the concrete steps of our family's brownstone.

Dad held open the door for me, and I scooted to the far side. Mom slid in next to me, as Dad took the front seat.

"Hi, Julio." He smiled at the driver. "You know the drill."

"Yes, sir, Mr. Stanton." Julio tipped his cap at Dad and flashed a grin toward the backseat. "It'll be a few minutes to Midtown."

"No worries." The muscle in my dad's cheek twitched again.

Yeah, right. The whole family would be on pins and needles tonight until the results were announced.

SOPHIE

Julio pulled the town car up to a bland-looking office building in Midtown. I'm talking peeling paint and cracked sidewalk kind of bland.

But the windows were heavily tinted for a reason. From the outside, you'd never know this was the headquarters for a secret society.

The moment we stepped through the foyer doors and made it past security, we were ushered into the main lobby of Guardian Sector One Headquarters. Our security team flanked us on both sides as they led us down a roped-off aisle. A horde of reporters with microphones and cameras were lined up behind the barricades all the way to the elevator bank.

At least the Guardian paparazzi had enough sense to keep their chaos indoors.

Lightbulbs flashed and microphones were shoved in all of our faces as Julio and a trio of other bodyguards bulldozed a path through the crowd to the elevators.

"Mrs. Stanton, as the Captain of the Sector One Intelligence team, did you have any knowledge of your father's secret prison experiments?" One reporter asked, shoving a mic in my mom's face.

"No comment." She glared daggers at the pushy man, then dipped her head politely and kept walking.

"Mr. Stanton, as the Attorney General, do you have any defense for the allegations against your father-in-law?" Another reporter angled a video camera at Dad.

"No comment," Dad barked in his clipped lawyer voice.

A perky young woman with a blonde bob had the nerve to shove a microphone in my face.

"Miss Stanton, are you the next Seer or Interpreter? Or Seeterpreter?" She shot me a pointed look, her lips pursed.

My jaw fell open, but no sound came out.

I reared back and tilted my head at the female reporter. That was a new one. I could just see that trending on the Social Shield later tonight. #Seeterpreter. Probably sporting a meme of my *Whaa?* face.

Unfortunately, the super-secret Guardian intranet had its own social media site too.

Mom slid an arm around my shoulders and shoved me between her and Dad.

"No comment." Her words were terse this time, but her smile was still plastered on.

Finally, we reached the elevators, with two bodyguards holding open the doors.

"Your chariot awaits, Stanton family." Julio's lips twisted ever-so-slightly into a crescent moon of a smirk.

He made these secret society events bearable.

We clamored into the elegant car trimmed in gold and mahogany. Once the door shut behind us, the cacophony of questions ceased to exist. For now.

Ahh, blessed silence.

I inhaled a deep breath. Gotta enjoy the little things while you can.

"Seeterpreter?" Dad turned his wide, gray eyes on me.

And just like that, my moment of peace was shattered.

I could only shake my head. "They're getting creative, I'll give 'em that."

Mom tsked at me. "You have to remember to keep your expression neutral if you can't smile."

"Don't worry." Dad patted my shoulder. "She'll learn."

Mom and Dad exchanged a knowing look. Part of me wanted to ask, but part of me wanted them to keep their secrets to themselves.

The bodyguards chuckled under their breath as we descended into the depths of the Guardian's concrete bunker.

About twenty floors down, the doors finally opened to another swanky lobby. This time, there were no paparazzi. The bodyguards ushered us to the green room behind the main auditorium.

Where my entire family waited for me.

This was a family tradition. We all got together on election night to have dinner and await the results.

Tonight, a long rectangular dinner table was set up in the middle of the gray-walled backstage room.

As soon as we walked in, everyone stopped eating to stare at us.

"Here we go." I gritted out under my breath.

<u>Want to keep reading</u> <u>Genesis Academy, Book 1: The Seer's Legacy?</u> **<u>Read all about how Sophie's visions send her halfway across the world to Genesis Academy, where she meets the very off-limits Xander.</u>**

<u>Check out the Barbara Hartzler Author Page for all the books in the Sacred Stones Universe.</u>

BOOKS BY BARBARA HARTZLER

THE MONTROSE PARANORMAL ACADEMY SERIES
Reading Order
Montrose Paranormal Academy Book 1:The Nexis Secret
Montrose Paranormal Academy Book 0: The Nexis Awakening
(Exclusive freebie for)
Montrose Paranormal Academy Book 2: Crossing Nexis
Montrose Paranormal Academy Book 3: The European Conspiracy
Montrose Paranormal Academy Book 4: The Seer's Army
Montrose Paranormal Academy Book 5: The Last Ruby
Montrose Paranormal Academy Book 5.5: The Secondborn Seer
Montrose Paranormal Academy: The Complete Series Box Set

THE SHADOWSTONE ACADEMY SERIES
Shadowstone Academy, Book 1: Broken Trinity
Shadowstone Academy, Book 2: Rise of the Watchers
Shadowstone Academy, Book 3: Sacred Stone Squad
Shadowstone Academy, Book 4: The Final Stand

THE GENESIS ACADEMY SERIES
Genesis Academy, Book 1: The Seer's Legacy
Genesis Academy, Book 2: Oracle Unlocked
Genesis Academy, Book 3: Oracle Rising
Genesis Academy, Book 4: The Last Amethyst

To learn more about the world of Shadowstone Academy go to www.barbarahartzler.com

ABOUT THE AUTHOR

BARBARA HARTZLER IS AN Urban Fantasy Academy author writing about Seers, Chosen Ones, sacred stones, and secret societies ... oh my! Her stories are full of snarky heroines, supernatural shenanigans, dreamy guys, and normal teens taking on larger-than-life quests to save the world. Barbara has always wanted to write, not necessarily about angels and sacred stones, but the idea was too good to pass up. As a former barista and graphic designer, she loves all things sparkly and purple and is always jonesing for a good cup of joe. So grab a cup of coffee and peruse her website at www.barbarahartzler.com. You can read her blog, explore all the behind-the-scenes extras in The Seer's Vault, or learn more about her writing journey, fun facts, and The BARBARA awards for best fiction (mostly YA).

Look for the *Montrose Paranormal Academy, Shadowstone Academy,* and *Genesis Academy* series on Amazon. Or join her mailing list for all the latest updates. You can also check out her Facebook Reader Group: Barbara Hartzler's F.A.N.S. - Fantasy Academy Novel Supporters with all kinds of behind-the-scenes extras.

PLEASE CONSIDER LEAVING A REVIEW

Independent authors depend on reviews. If you enjoyed reading this book as much as Barbara enjoyed writing it, please consider reviewing on <u>Amazon</u> or Goodreads.

Thank you!

<u>Click here</u> or go to www.barbarahartzler.com to join my mailing list to download your exclusive free copy of the prequel novella *Montrose Paranormal Academy, Book 0: The Nexis Awakening* today!

ACKNOWLEDGMENTS

I WASN'T SO SURE about this action-packed little sequel, so thanks to Rachel Garber for being a cheerleader of an editor. Your encouragement helped me get this book out!

Another major hero on this journey is my writing mentor Ramy Vance. Your encouragement and direction has helped turn this series into what it is today. Thanks for helping me steer things in the right direction—finally! Additional thanks to my friends at Self Publishing School for propping me up along this new journey.

To my fabulous launch team members and Facebook VIPers who've supported me every time I throw them another curveball: Donna Daigle, Adrian Murphy, Debi Mozingo, Sizi Mann, Linda Force-Messinger, Vincy Stephenson, Kim Lake Benson Bond, Jennifer Jackson, Aoife Wai and so many more. Shh ... don't tell—you guys are the first people I blab to with any new series intel.

As always, thanks to my family and friends who have given me their constant love and support over the many, MANY years I've had this dream. Thank you for all the joy you bring to my life!

To my Lord and Savior, Jesus Christ. During this last year or so of upheaval and turmoil, you found a way to make my dreams come true. Thank you for fulfilling your promises to me in bigger and better ways than I could ever imagine.